The Argentinian Virgin

Also by JIM WILLIAMS

Writing as Richard Hugo
The Hitler Diaries
Last Judgment
Farewell to Russia
Conspiracy of Mirrors published in USA
    as *The Gorbachev Version*

Writing as Alexander Mollin
Lara's Child

Writing as Jim Williams
Scherzo
Recherché
The Strange Death of a Romantic

Non-fiction
A Message to the Children (a guide to writing
    your autobiography)
How to be a Charlatan

The Argentinian Virgin

A NOVEL BY

Jim Williams

QUARTET BOOKS

First published in 2009 by
Quartet Books Limited
A member of the Namara Group
27 Goodge Street, London W1T 2LD

Copyright © Jim Williams 2009

The right of Jim Williams to be identified
as the author of this work has been asserted
by him in accordance with the
Copyright, Designs and Patents Act, 1988

All rights reserved.
No part of this book may be reproduced in
any form or by any means without prior
written permission from the publisher

A catalogue record for this book
is available from the British Library

ISBN   978 0 7043 7180 4

Typeset by Antony Gray
Printed and bound in Great Britain by
T J International Ltd, Padstow, Cornwall

ACKNOWLEDGEMENTS

For various reasons this wasn't the easiest book to write and, with the drafting and re-drafting it has taken a long time. Throughout I have been sustained by the kindness and encouragement of friends, in particular Nick Webb and Rosie Buckman. I can never thank my agent, Andrew Hewson, enough for his generosity in taking a punt on my future as a writer. My wife, in her great wisdom, left me alone to get on with it and thereby spared both of us the tensions that would have arisen if we had allowed writing to spill over into the more important business of ordinary life.

IN MEMORY OF
JAMES HALE
1946–2003

PROLOGUE

> Her lips burn with chillies and she smokes a cigar.
> Her breath is my narcotic.
> Her scent is of cloves, of night fevers and spent seed.
> What man could resist the Argentinian Virgin?
> What woman could bear her horror?

This is a love story. This is a murder story. This is an old movie that went out of fashion years ago along with fedoras and stockings with seams and music that people in love really wanted to dance to. I don't even know if kids feel now how we felt then. I don't know how we felt then. I never understood any of it.

My Uncle Gerald of infamous memory once said no story is ever complete. When I told my wife I wanted to write about the summer I passed in France, now more than fifty years ago, and about Tom and Ben, Maisie and Hetty, she said I shouldn't – no, she *begged* me not to. What's the point of going there? she said. The past is the past, she said. Why rake over it?

The answer is that the past isn't past and the story isn't complete. If it were, there'd be nothing to object to. Unfortunately I remember the past too well, or can imagine those parts I've forgotten, which is the curse of a writer. My wife chooses to forget out of love and I choose to remember for the same reason.

The past is where we buried our innocence like the body of a violated child in a forest no one visits.

CHAPTER ONE

I was sitting by the roadside on the route to Auxerre when a cream-coloured convertible passed me at a crawl. It was the twelfth of June, nineteen forty, Paris was on the point of falling and I was on foot in a crowd of refugees making its way south.

I've heard stories of German aircraft attacking such columns, but, if it ever happened, I never saw. Instead I remember sitting in a froth of ox-eye daisies and the shade of a line of poplars, with wheat fields either side and a skylark singing its heart out.

There weren't many cars or trucks in the column, just plenty of carts and bicycles and sometimes a perambulator with a child, a grandmother or a gramophone on top. The cream-coloured convertible passed me and I thought of a carnival float. It was so bright and gay and the refugees surrounded it like dancers or mummers. Two men were in the front and two women in the back, with piles of baggage strapped to the rear: good leather cases and a steamer trunk with the labels still on. They looked as if they were going on holiday, or maybe finishing one. They had that sparkle of people who are completely relaxed.

The men wore pale tan felts pushed back from the forehead so the sun was on their faces. The women wore white hats with shallow crowns and wide brims, fixed just so. I saw only the hats and heard the laughter, but they were enough to pull me out of my doze among the daisies and I picked up my bag and followed at a trot until I caught them.

'English?' I asked. 'American? Don't tell me you're Irish!'

I was on the passenger side, and Tom Rensselaer – they gave me their names in those first few minutes – turned his head. The blond shank of hair fell forward, and he gave me an open smile that was glad to see me. He said, 'American. You, too?'

'Irish.'

'Boston Irish?'

'No, the real thing.'

Since no one objected, I hopped on the running board and tipped my hat at the ladies. Hetty said, 'Top o' the mornin' to you,' and giggled. Then we all laughed and Tom handed out cigarettes.

Ben Benedict was driving, though without much eye for the road. At first I thought he and Tom might be brothers. They both had those fair, well-set good looks, and perfect teeth. When you saw him, you thought here was a good fellow you could pass the time with, having a drink or a talk about girls. It was a narrow difference. More profound was something else, an indefinable fineness Tom had and Ben didn't: the quality that drew people emotionally to Tom: the one he tried not to notice and hated when he did.

At the time I'd eyes only for the women. We were nudging forward through a herd of pigs with one of them nibbling at my trouser cuffs. Hetty held out a hand that flopped ladylike from the wrist. 'Hester Novaks,' she said. 'Everyone calls me Hetty.'

'Patrick Byrne.'

'I'm pleased to make your acquaintance.'

Hetty was the youngest and I doubt she was twenty-one, which means she was seventeen when she swapped Pittsburgh for Paris. She was pretty though not beautiful. Her blonde hair was bleached, her nose was a little snub and her eyebrows would have been heavy if they weren't plucked. The truth is none of it mattered: I liked her smile, that and her generous eroticism. Her looks appealed to painters, and Tom told me later he'd found her working as an artist's model after some jazz musician brought her to France then dropped her.

Maisie leaned across her friend. 'Margaret Benedict,' she said. 'I'm Ben's wife.' Her voice was low, slightly husky with a Yankee creak in it. She was a brunette, beautiful, narrow and slender hipped. What I noticed most, however, was her neck. Tom called it a 'Bronzino' neck. He meant it had length and elegance, which enabled her to pose her head with an expression that had nothing to do with the face.

It became understood that I'd go along with them a while. This was easy at the walking pace of the refugees. I rode on the running board and, when I got tired of that, strolled alongside.

'Where are you heading for?' Tom asked.

'S. Symphorien la Plage.'

'I don't know it.'

'Along the coast west of Cannes.'

'Is that convenient for Marseilles?'

'It depends what you mean. There's a train.'

'And why are you going there – I mean what do you do?'

'I'm a writer.'

'Really? I'm impressed. Are you any good?'

'I'm world-famous in Ireland.'

'Are you world-famous anywhere else? Would I know your stuff?'

'I don't think so,' I said and went on to answer the other part of his question. I was travelling to S. Symphorien because my publisher wanted to put me out of harm's way at a friend's house while I completed an overdue second novel. When I began my travels there was no war. Paris had distracted me.

Tom asked, 'Will you stay if the Germans get that far?'

'I don't know.'

'Do you think Ireland will join in the war?'

'Not if Hitler doesn't attack us.'

We had some conversation about Cannes. They'd been there over the winter, grown bored and returned to Paris. I asked where they'd go now.

Tom said, 'We thought of Biarritz. I haven't tried painting on the Atlantic coast.'

'Will America declare war?'

They laughed at the idea.

That night we camped by the road. Hetty said it was 'a gas'. They'd left Paris without needing to, and at first thought of the journey as a tour and they'd dine in restaurants in the evening and sleep at hotels. When it didn't happen, things might have turned sour, but Tom brought them round to the idea they were undergoing an adventure.

'I used to go camping on Long Island with my dad,' Tom told me. We were sitting on the bank of a stream that cut through the wheat fields, pitching stones in the water while the swallows skimmed for flies.

He also told me some things about the others.

'Ben's grandfather was T. R. Benedict that you've heard of. His father doesn't do much except clip coupons.'

'How old is he?'

'My age. What about you?'

'Twenty-four.'

'That's young for a writer.'

'I wouldn't know. Writers rarely meet other writers. What about Maisie?'

'She's a Bryan – a relative, not exactly a great niece, of William Jennings Bryan, the Presidential candidate.'

'And you?'

'I?' Tom grinned and shook his head. Later I learned he came from a banking family that had gone down in the Crash, and before that there'd been a *patroon* fortune and an ancestor who'd sold boots to the Army during the Civil war. Ben also implied that Tom had served a while with the volunteers in Spain against Franco.

We were together for five days. On the last couple we made better progress as the refugee column thinned out and people drifted off. Since the weather held, we camped in the open, living out of the cream convertible under a violet sky, and we kept talking as strangers do, not expecting we'd ever meet again.

When I pressed him, Tom told me more of his reasons for being in France.

'Ben's father was over here when he was young – that would be in the 'nineties, I guess, when Europeans and Americans considered each other a marvel. He wanted Ben to have something of the same. He thought two or three years would do no harm.'

'You met him here?'

'God, no. We were at Yale together – college days, *gaudeamus igitur* and all that. I had no money to come to Europe, but Ben wanted a companion and his dad was willing to pay. We came over in thirty-eight and after a while settled with the arty crowd in Paris. I say "arty", but they were mostly regular types.'

I'd have asked more, but the truth is I was in awe of someone who spoke so easy about the world.

That night we laid up in a vineyard. It wasn't harvest time and the vines were straggly because the young men had gone off to war. Hetty was sitting with us, her head on Tom's shoulder as we sat smoking and dreaming. They looked perfectly happy.

We separated the next day and I went south to S. Symphorien while the others pressed on to Biarritz then drifted into Spain and across Vichy into Italy, four glamorous Americans in their glorious youth.

CHAPTER TWO

I was in France because, at the age of twenty-two, I wrote a novel. It had some success, it won a prize and I thought myself a grand fellow, didn't I so. Those in the trade will tell you the second book is the hardest. The passion that delivered the first is spent and the brilliant style that gained so many plaudits turns out to be the chance sparkle a spiteful God grants once in a lifetime even to mediocre talents.

To keep it short: I enjoyed the fame and drank the money. Then my publisher, remembering a cottage owned by a friend, packed me off to the Riviera. War was in the air, but it seemed as fictitious as death, and I didn't let it interfere with my plans, which included going to Paris.

The day after leaving the Americans, I was knocked down by a truck. Or so they tell me. I spent three months in hospital, and, at the end, finding I'd survived the German invasion, I decided it held no terrors. I pressed on to S. Symphorien, and I might have finished writing the book except I was troubled by headaches. They passed off only gradually the following spring.

It was during my convalescence that I got to know S. Symphorien la Plage. My guide was Dr Maillot, who sometimes shared a table with me at the Hôtel de la Gare. He was the same age as Marshal Pétain but had something younger about him. It wasn't his appearance – spry enough but portly. Rather his louche air, the raffishness with which he wore an old beret and a linen jacket. He was a retired widower, who'd lost his savings in one of the *affaires* that rocked France in the thirties. I didn't know exactly how he got by, but thought he peddled quack remedies to old women.

The town had no ancient ruins, no quaint harbour, no spa.

What it had were two beaches of flat sand that creaked and scorched underfoot in the torrid summers, and a warm sea in which I swam. Below the bluff of La Pinède, topped by its villa, the beach was shared by the Hôtel Czar Aléxandre and a few houses built to rent. The hotel and its casino were the largest buildings in S. Symphorien. Standing apart from the town, their domed roofs of fish scale slate glittered white at noonday.

As for the villa, it was stuccoed and in the Italian style with a tower like a campanile. It had been built maybe eighty years before, but who'd built it was a mystery. Legends hang around places like the villa La Pinède: ghostly like the past itself, though more substantial than those of us who haunt the Riviera out of season. For most of the time they rot quietly and the thrush singing on the campanile only reminds us of the silence.

Dr Maillot had a touch of the poet. He said, 'S. Symphorien la Plage – as these structures in their lonely splendour suggest – is an unfulfilled hope of the nineteenth century: like many other small, disregarded resorts, the failed ambition of an impoverished landowner and a railway speculator – in short, my perfect home.'

* * *

The manager of the Hôtel Czar Aléxandre was called Beauclerc. He was slim, dapper and melancholy. As Dr Maillot described him: 'Beauclerc is not a man but a personage.'

I admired Beauclerc for the fidelity with which he executed his duties and filed his reports, though nothing had been heard from the owners since the Germans occupied Paris. Beauclerc spent his life waiting for visitors who never came. Except for a brief influx of White Russians in the twenties, the hotel saw only the remnants of families who'd passed summers there since before the foundation of the Republic and even they were fading away with the war.

Until the arrival of Tom Rensselaer and his party, we formed an unlikely trio. I saw Maillot most often; we usually breakfasted together. Beauclerc I'd meet only on a Sunday when he'd join us after Mass for a walk. I was an indifferent Catholic. Dr Maillot was argumentatively anti-clerical. Our walks took us along the beach and into the pinewoods above La Pinède, and it was on these occasions that we'd look at the old villa and speculate about the Argentinian Virgin and her mother.

Who were the Malipieros? They'd arrived in the autumn after the defeat as a rumour that the villa had been let after standing empty for years. Perhaps if they'd simply booked into an hotel, they'd have been ignored; or if they'd taken one of the smaller places. But they couldn't know of the role of La Pinède in the town's sense of its own significance, because I doubt the town understood it consciously.

Maillot, Beauclerc and I rested on the rising ground in the shadow of some stone pines and looked down on the villa and its campanile. I offered a suggestion.

'Most likely they're the family of a diplomat. Argentina recognises Vichy, doesn't it?'

Normally I avoided politics. Beauclerc was an ardent Pétainist, and Dr Maillot an indeterminate radical, which amounted to opposing whatever anyone else said. There was something romantic in his make-up. It may explain why he said: 'I have heard a story that Señora Malipiero was a mistress of the Duke of Windsor. What do you think, Patrick?'

I said I doubted it.

Beauclerc said, 'She hides her face – the mother. Why does she hide her face?'

'I don't know.'

'Because she is a Negress. Many of the families in South America – even the best ones – are tainted with Negro blood.'

'You're thinking of Brazil, not Argentina. In any case, that isn't true of the daughter.'

'It does not appear in every generation.'

Dr Maillot said, 'The Empress Josephine was a Creole. She held Napoleon in thrall even though she gave him no children – even after he divorced her. It makes one think, eh?' He winked at me. 'The wind is rising,' he said. The air had turned subtly pink, and my right leg, still creaky after the accident, was aching.

On our return, the familiar cream-coloured convertible was parked in the square. Maillot and I were ambling to the Hôtel de la Gare thinking of lunch, when we noticed children scrambling over the vehicle and a gendarme, too bemused to do anything about it.

'Who do you suppose it is?' Dr Maillot asked.

'Friends of mine,' I said. I'd spotted Tom holding court at the Café des Fleurs, with wine and a pile of food in front of him and half the town around. He was at ease and chatting with anyone who spoke to him.

He saw me and called out, 'Patrick!' The effect was to scatter the crowd as if they were wasps round a luscious piece of fruit. They settled on me and I was escorted to the table. Ben Benedict rose to his feet and gave me a sincere American handshake. Maisie and Hetty, who'd picked up the French custom, showered me in *bises*.

'I thought you were in Biarritz?' I said, 'Or Spain.' I was glad to see them but puzzled.

'Oh, we've been to all sorts of places, including Italy. Florence is still wonderful, despite the war.'

'Spain stank,' Ben chipped in.

'Spain wasn't especially pleasant,' Tom agreed. 'Franco seems to have introduced a particularly gloomy and sinister form of Catholicism.'

'You had no problems at the frontiers?'

'The war hasn't made things easy. The officials are difficult and we were followed everywhere. But we got by. And you? Any sign of Ireland entering the war? Still writing your novel?'

I said I was still writing the novel.

Maisie and Hetty had an eye for Dr Maillot. I introduced him and he distributed some bows and elaborate hand kissing for no other reason than that they set the women laughing and amused him.

We all took seats. Tom poured wine and I asked why they'd come to S. Symphorien.

'Good question,' said Tom. 'Uncle Sam discovered that Ben – the *Great* Ben Benedict – was still over in Europe and asked him to involve himself in some committee or other based in Marseilles that's taking care of American property here, now there's a war on. Have I got that right?'

'Right,' said Ben.

'And as for me, well, I wanted to do some painting in Cannes because of the light – which, I may say, didn't suit Ben in the least because of the distance. Then I remembered you'd mentioned S. Symphorien and thought you might still be here. And so we compromised.'

'Are you at the Czar Aléxandre?' I asked.

'Ben's taken a house. What's it called? La Chênaie? Do you know it?'

'On the other side of La Pinède. My place is nearby.'

'La Pinède?'

I pointed out the rock and explained something of the layout of the town, but, as Tom had said, they were tired and paid little attention except to the view.

It was past noon and the sun was high and the sky white. In this light the pines of La Pinède rose in shades of cigarette smoke and the villa was a dim lilac.

Tom asked, 'That isn't La Chênaie is it by any chance?'

Dr Maillot spoke up and I think he picked his words just for effect, to see what they would do. 'No,' he said. 'That is the home of our local celebrity, *la Vierge de l'Argentine.*'

Tom said, 'Really? Do you mean it's some sort of religious shrine?'

'No,' I said. 'A couple of foreign women live there, that's all.'

I was looking across the square at them as I spoke. Katerina Malipiero was fresh and lovely in a printed cotton dress. Teresa Malipiero wore a black tailored suit and a hat with a demi-veil.

CHAPTER THREE

Between the fall of France and Hitler's invasion of the Soviet Union there was a lull in the war. Rationing came in, curfews and regulations, though none of it so bad as it was later. As for Germans, there were one or two, but this was Vichy, not Occupied France, and S. Symphorien was too insignificant to attract a garrison.

I got used to the demands of wartime. I was Irish and, like the Americans, a neutral. When Tom Rensselaer and his friends arrived, I helped them register at the *sous préfecture* and settle into La Chênaie. I saw them every day – I could hardly fail to since my cottage was next door. Most days, too, I'd eat with them. Ben kept open house and, if the space had been there, I don't suppose he'd have minded if I'd moved in with them. But I had a book to write.

The Americans were liked. When they wandered about town people who were more or less strangers would call across the road, 'Bonjour, les Américains!' It was as if, to some degree, everyone shared in their Americanness: seeing, through them, a connection with the world of peace. In S. Symphorien, where the Germans were scarcely noticeable and the Marshal widely admired, you could hold to this illusion of escape from the war. It was part of the town's character, as much as the beaches, the pine brakes and the torpor of that hot summer.

Yet they had something else, too, beyond their surface glamour: something I think of as a sort of radiance. All four shone with it, even Hetty who was the most straightforward and uncomplicated. It was there in the way Tom talked.

Tom talked about everyone.

Of Ben: 'Even though he's here in Europe, he helps run the business. I once asked him how he knows what orders to give and he said, "I don't – but I'm too rich for my mistakes to matter." How d'you like that, Pat?'

Of Maisie: 'She was one of the "Bryan Girls". You haven't heard of them? In New York they were always in the papers for being rich and living wild. Sometimes she has the air of living through a tragedy. But I think the tragedy is that she can't believe she's so beautiful and that anyone could love her.'

Of Hetty: 'We were living in Paris. I was painting. Hetty just blew in – literally seemed to blow in with arms waving and hair awry. She has her own brand of exoticism – like the smell of fried onions and frankfurters that wafts from a stall on the boardwalk when one's tired of meditating on the sea.'

Tom didn't tell me Hetty was his mistress, but I knew she was.

He once said, 'Hetty isn't beautiful, is she? Her hair isn't really blonde and she has snaggle teeth, though they do something for her smile – give it a sort of spontaneity that I like. Her shape isn't chic. And yet … '

'What?'

'I watch how men react to her. She has an eroticism that disturbs those who don't have true erotic awareness: those who think it's a style like this year's automobile. Is it any wonder I want to paint her?'

This was one day in June when we were on the beach, and the sun was high and scarcely anything could be seen for the shimmer. Hetty was coming out of the water. She was wearing a pink bathing costume and, with the sun at her back, there were notes of blue in her skin tones. Her form was very soft: there was nothing sculpted in her lines; and its sensuousness came from small gradations of colour.

'Like an Ingres nude,' Tom said.

Tom's circle in Paris didn't include any names I'd ever heard of. He was desperate to paint well but not sure he could. He had an explanation.

'I was ten years too late. There was something in Paris in the twenties. It helped define a certain type of American. But, whatever it was, the well was dry by the time I arrived. If I fail at painting, I have a notion to go to California and try my hand at writing movie scripts.'

In the event, Tom didn't go to California, but I did and got my name on the credits for some B movies. That was after the war, and I'll come to it in time. When Tom told me of his ambitions, I was still trying to understand who my new friends were.

Behind their liking for fast cars, fast music and the movies, I detected a flow and continuity with the past that made their surface racket somehow poignant. Its origins lay in 'old money' (perhaps only twenty years old, but in New York that's almost ancestral) and the declining years of the last century. It was calm, self-confident and leisured. I think of certain schools, certain houses on Long Island, certain resorts on the eastern seaboard, and a light that's mellow and autumnal or a soft Atlantic grey. Whatever it was, I got nothing more than fugitive impressions because to the others it was so natural that to speak of it was absurd. I can't press the images further. If I did, I'd lose their frail radiance.

Ben was out and about more than the rest of us. I was struggling to write. Tom was on the beach or in the hills with his paints. The girls played a lot of tennis or rode on hired hacks courtesy of the Czar Aléxandre. Ben acted as quartermaster and often came home with stuff you could get only on the black market. It was natural he'd see the Argentinian Virgin or her mother round the town.

Returning one day, he said, 'Señora Malipiero's face is scarred. That's why she wears a veil.'

I asked, 'Who told you? Or did you see her?'

'The butcher. The lady went into his shop and lifted her veil to look at some meat.'

'He actually has meat?' Tom asked.

Maisie put a hand to her beautiful face and murmured, 'How horrible.'

I knew for a fact that the butcher spoke with a Provençal accent so thick no one – least of all Ben – could understand him.

Still he persisted: 'Her face is burned – maybe acid. Have you ever seen a burn? The scar is big like a splash of something – and red – and the skin puckers.'

Maisie repeated 'How horrible', but the feeling was gone because she didn't believe him either.

Ben had another story, which seemed more probable. He said, 'There really is a Señor Malipiero – the husband. He's not a diplomat.'

Tom asked, 'Is he here in town?'

'Nope – but he's coming soon.'

This was interesting in the way the small affairs of others can be. Maisie wanted to know what Señor Malipiero did for a living.

'He sells war materials.'

'Who to?'

'The Nazis, who else? Apparently he's in Portugal or Spain or somewhere, helping them break the blockade.'

My own contribution to these tales about the Malipieros was to repeat the rumour that the mother had been a mistress of the Duke of Windsor, though I didn't claim it was true. Hetty was taken. She liked scandal and one of her regrets was that she couldn't get movie magazines.

'There could be something to it,' she said. 'The Duke was one of the Riviera set, and didn't he move down here at first after the Germans invaded?'

'He had a mistress – he made her his wife.'

'Wallis Simpson looks like a lesbian: all that flat chest and no hips.'

'I don't see what that has to do with anything.'

Nor did I, except that, imperceptibly, the Argentinian Virgin and her mother had moved from the ranks of ordinary people into the category of a mystery to be explained. This was made clear by Maisie who came out with something she didn't even suggest was true. We were dancing at the Czar Aléxandre after one of our regular dinners.

She said, 'I feel sorry for her.'

'For whom?'

'Señora Malipiero.'

'You don't know her.'

'She's lonely. That's obvious. I can imagine the rest.'

'Which is?'

Maisie was wistful. 'She's suffered a loss of some kind. Of course I don't know what it is, but it has to be something bitter that's made her afraid.'

'A death?'

Maisie nodded. She said, 'I don't care what Ben says. I don't think there's a Señor Malipiero – or, if there is, then there must have been a lover.'

'Who?' I asked and gave a smile of encouragement so she'd know I'd take her answer lightly.

'Oh someone … exotic,' she said. 'A gangster? A tango dancer? A gangster who danced the tango in one of those smoky brothels where they play sad music on a piano accordion.'

'What happened to him?'

'He was shot dead in her arms.'

CHAPTER FOUR

Only Hetty was immune to the mystery of the Malipieros. She said, 'Let's face it, we don't know anything about them.'

We were on the beach shared by La Pinède, La Chênaie and the Czar Aléxandre. The bluff rose directly behind us. It hid a collection of martins' nests; I could hear the birds and the voices of boys climbing the bluff to steal eggs. Tom was painting. I was fooling with corrections to my manuscript, working off my knees. The others read or swam.

Without warning Ben said, '*La belle dame sans merci* is looking at me. I can feel her dark eyes boring into my head.'

'Who are you talking about?' Maisie asked.

'The Argentinian Virgin.'

'*La belle dame* ... ?'

'Because she "hath me in thrall".'

Maisie gave a snort.

Tom asked, 'Can you see her?'

'Nope,' said Ben. 'Not from this angle. Those rocks must be two hundred feet high. I can just see the wall.'

The wall was washed pink and partly ruined. It traced the edge of the bluff.

'Then it stands to reason she can't see you,' Tom pointed out.

That closed the subject, but the poetic reference must have stuck with Tom. As we were making our way behind the others up the path to La Chênaie, he said, 'She's the Lady of Shallott, unseen and seeing the world only in a mirror.'

It was the first remark he'd made showing he'd given any thought to Katerina Malipiero beyond what the rest of us had said. Then, as it happened, he ran across the girl herself, the following day.

'This morning,' he said. 'She was coming out of the gendarmerie – I imagine she'd had to sign one of their pieces of paper. I wonder how they're managing for rations?'

'You didn't ask?' With his confidence, I thought Tom might have.

"We didn't speak, just exchanged glances. And I suppose that was it.'

'What was?'

'Her glance. She has a cool, level gaze. I've seen it before in Victorian paintings of bold-eyed Mediterranean girls with red bandannas tied around their black hair. It's a male fantasy, of course, the image in the paintings. And it could just as easily be that she was shortsighted or distracted or … whatever. Character can't be captured in a glance.'

'You seem to have made a good attempt.'

He laughed. 'D'you think so? No … I was too surprised. When I realised who she was, she'd passed me by and I could see only her back. She was wearing flat sandals and glided like an Indian. Her dress was made of cotton and had threads hanging at the hem that made you want to tug them. The dress was gathered in a belt, but not well: the line wasn't regular.'

'You want to paint her,' I said.

'Maybe I do,' he agreed and his eyes went off somewhere.

'You could always ask her,' I said. 'Hey, Tom. Are you still with me?'

'I was remembering something. I saw a small 'v' of sweat between her shoulder blades. And another, like a dart, just where the buttocks divide.'

As I've said, Tom was serious about his painting, but he didn't follow any of the contemporary styles. Like everything else, the skill came easily to him and he treated it as if it weren't important.

I don't know exactly how the thing is done, but I saw him spend hours scraping and preparing his canvas. Then he'd apply various coloured grounds and build up the work in layers. But the real trick lay in the thin glazes, which he used only when, to anyone else's eye, the painting was done and complete.

Tom Rensselaer's pictures were beautiful – perhaps too beautiful – so the images seemed to float. In his landscapes the effect was a sense of things passing. The view wasn't fixed in place, and I was left always with a feeling that, if I were to leave and return in only an hour, a variation of light or humidity would cause a transformation; the clouds and shadows would move; the season change. I stopped looking at the paintings because they made me sad.

Tom concentrated on landscapes. During my time at La Chênaie, he painted only two pictures from life – at least only two that I saw. There was a third, which I think of as the fatal one, but I'll come to it later.

His technique was exacting. He began the first portrait, that of Maisie, months before I saw it. Ben carped that it'd never be finished, but I could see he liked it. Tom had captured her in a style I can only describe as grand simplicity, without jewellery but in a dress of wine-coloured silk. It was understated yet magnificent. The pose was composed, serene, intelligent, emphasising Maisie's elegant neck, giving it a turn so the picture, instead of being static, moved with a slow rhythm.

My problem was that I didn't see in this beautiful woman the Maisie I knew. The portrait gave no hint of her rebarbative manner, her wit, her doubts. Yet those were the aspects of her character that, attractive or not, made her alive for me. Probably out of kindness, Tom had suppressed them in order to present another Maisie, possibly the one she wanted to be. He couldn't help himself.

The second painting wasn't exactly a portrait since Hetty sat with her back to the spectator and face turned away. She was naked except for a white cloth that only partly fell across her lower back, and her hair was piled high. Tom told me he'd got the idea from a nineteenth century Academic painting of ladies at a Roman bath and it was a study of flesh tones and modelling in colour. I don't really know what that means.

I was there when Tom put his suggestion to Hetty and when the painting was done. She'd modelled before and seemed very easy about the whole idea, even excited at the notion. I was busy with my own stuff and saw Tom only now and then, with Hetty sitting in the lounge of La Chênaie, where she looked like a Roman nude with a cigarette to hand on which she took a drag when Tom said it was all right. The business seemed to go through very smoothly and we laughed a lot.

When her own portrait was finished, Maisie said she was 'wild' about it, 'crazy' to have it. Ben was pleased, too, and offered to buy it. In the end Tom gave it to him.

Tom wanted to keep his picture of Hetty and I could see why. Quite apart from any particular feelings towards her, he was always tender towards women. With all Hetty's deviations from the ideal, he took her body and rendered it sensuously so that to look at it was to see a revelation of something that was always there but unformed and undervalued. And, even though I didn't understand the finer points of his art, I recognised his technical brilliance and I was moved.

After Tom completed Hetty's picture we celebrated at the Czar Aléxandre. In front of the hotel a gravelled terrace overlooked the sea. I'd danced a bit and drunk a lot and I went outside to cool off and smoke a cigarette. I stood in the dark at the stone balustrade where the ground falls away. A few stars were out and a few lights rode on the sea and I was musing over the difference when I heard footsteps behind me and Hetty calling, 'Patrick!' in a giddy voice.

I thought she was a little drunk. When she stumbled against me I put my arm around her waist and hazarded a kiss on the cheek.

'You're crying,' I said.

'Jesus!' she said. 'Now I'll have to fix my makeup. D'you know

I haven't been able to buy makeup since we left Florence?'

'Why are you crying? Is there something? I mean something you feel you could tell me?'

She clutched me. Her head lay on my shoulder, and for a minute she shuddered and sobbed while I patted her and played the Irish boyo.

At last she stopped. She sniffled and I tried to act worldly and indifferent until she came round to talking.

'I wanted Tom to paint my face,' she said.

I don't remember how I answered. It doesn't matter.

'I wanted Tom to paint my face. Without that, it isn't really me, is it? It's just a woman's body.'

I said it was a beautiful painting and we all knew it was her.

'I told Tom, but he said that, if he put my face in, the picture wouldn't work the way it's supposed to. D'you understand that?'

'It's a life study – a sort of exercise.'

'Tom said that, or something like it – arty stuff. He was nice about it. He's always nice. He's the nicest person I know.'

'I'm sure he didn't mean to hurt you,' I said.

Then she astonished me by laughing. She pulled away and her eyes shone.

'He hasn't hurt me,' she said. 'He told me he didn't need a picture of my face because he'll always have the original in front of him.'

'What did he mean?' I asked.

'He meant he wants to marry me!'

'Has he said so?'

'Pooh! And there was me, thinking you were a nice boy. Yes he has! In those very words.'

'Congratulations,' I said.

'Is that all you can say? You – the writer?'

I told her, 'I'm truly glad for you. I wish you every happiness.'

I'd no idea that I'd just heard the words that would lead to the disaster.

CHAPTER FIVE

Ben could play the saxophone and write lyrics. They weren't commercial but they had a certain zaniness. He wrote one about the Argentinian Virgin and sang it to us one evening just before Tom finished his painting of Hetty.

> When I find my babe in Rio
> I'll do my stuff con brio,
> For the lovely señoritas
> Are a heartless bunch of cheaters.
> Oh, dinero! dinero! I'm rich as a pharaoh!
> Oh, holler, babe, holler – if you want my dollar,
> For nothing is free–oh in Rio!

It doesn't matter that Rio is in Brazil.

That same evening, speaking about Katerina Malipiero, Ben said, 'I bet she has hairy legs and doesn't shave her underarms. Her lips burn with chillies and she smokes a cigar.'

We all laughed except Tom, and he told me later that the song and the remark were both cruel. He took that thought to bed with him and it woke him early, when the sun wasn't yet up.

Below La Pinède the various paths wind down to the beach. Tom saw a pale glimmer of dawn in the west and a cuticle of magenta edging the thin, high cloud. At his feet the path passed in a ribbon of dusky pinks and creams between a pair of stone pines, then fell sharply to the olive green sand and an inky sea. Or so Tom tells it in his film script, filling in all the colours.

This side of the height, La Pinède was in shadow. The pines rose in dark billows to the crest and a pair of cypresses formed points either side of the tower.

'I imagined – ' Tom said, not sure I'd understand or accept his language ' – that the Argentinian Virgin lived in the tower. And that, spell-bound, she wove the skein of night.'

'What did you do?' I asked.

'Went for a swim – what else?'

It was early. The two German officers, who were convalescing at the Czar Aléxandre and bathed in the first hour of daylight, hadn't arrived. Tom thought he was alone in his strange mood. He wore espadrilles and watched his feet make rope patterns in the white dust. He scanned the sea.

'Someone was already swimming,' he told me.

But for the moment Tom paid no attention.

He stripped to his bathing shorts. The diving raft, anchored a hundred yards away, levitated on a reflection. Tom swam to the raft in a lazy crawl and clambered aboard.

He guessed at first that the swimmer was one of the Germans come early to the beach. He sat still on the raft and watched the shells by the waterline glitter like lost coins in the first sun. He let his thoughts roam.

'Where?' I asked.

'I was thinking of one of Ben's songs. They're crummy but they get under the skin. D'you know the one that goes:

> At Guadalajara I once dreamed my far away dreams
> With tequila and sand and a Mexican band;
> But it seems
> That my head likes its hits from a bottle of Schlitz
> And who cares if it's noisy in Newark or Boise?

'I forget the rest. The Schlitz made me think of beer and, although dawn isn't exactly a time for hitting the bottle, I had a notion that a beer would be just fine – crisp and sharp, you know? So mentally I was looking over the blue sea and hugging a frosted glass. Maybe I'm getting homesick?'

The swimmer was a girl. She was strong. She did six powerful strokes, then coasted and turned on her back. With the sun on her she was a silver fleck between the raft and the beach where the German captains had arrived and were setting out towels. They called Tom and gave a friendly wave. Tom waved back, but the girl, if she saw them, did nothing.

It was Katerina Malipiero.

'How did you feel?' I asked.

'Like I was meeting a pretty girl at a dance,' he said.

I wasn't sure I believed him.

The girl headed straight out again, beating the water as regular as an engine. She came past the raft, shark blue for a moment, then silver with silver beads stringing off each arm raised in its stroke. Tom was beginning to feel lonely, perched on the raft with the quiet sea around him. He dived in the water and swam to the beach.

'So, Mister Rensselaer, you are early bird worm catching?' said Captain Brenner. 'That is Miss Novaks or Mrs Benedict with you so well swimming?'

Both officers, Brenner and his friend Kellermann, were younger than Tom. Both had been wounded and bore scars. Brenner's torso was burned.

'She's not with me,' Tom said. 'I think it's the girl from La Pinède.'

'Oh ho! But not with you, you say?'

Tom dried himself and put on his espadrilles. He didn't care for Nazis, but his prejudice didn't extend to individuals. Brenner and Kellermann were likeable fellows. Tom offered cigarettes.

He asked, 'Do you expect to stay here much longer?'

'Ha ha! You must ask my doctor. And you?'

'We talk about going home.'

Brenner's good humour faltered; 'Oh, but you should stay,' he urged.

'Why?'

'Because everything in the world is then so normal and we know that Germany and America will not go to war.'

'I don't think we'll go to war,' said Tom.

The Germans went about their swimming. They greeted Katerina Malipiero as she came out of the water.

Tom debated whether to return to La Chênaie for breakfast or speak to the girl.

'I don't know why I gave the idea so much thought,' he told me and still seemed to be thinking. 'I'm used to talking to girls and the worst she could do was give me the brush off, which is no big deal. I don't go around thinking every girl is some sort of unapproachable moon goddess. If I did, I could never go to a dance or a movie. It'd be like entering a temple.'

I agreed. It was no big thing to talk to the Argentinian Virgin. Yet Tom had approached the point so cautiously that now it seemed momentous.

What was he going to say?

CHAPTER SIX

Tom said, 'We talked about cheese and ham and coffee. That's the quickest way to a girl's heart these days.'

'I didn't know she interested you that way,' I said.

'No? Well, of course, you're right. But I admit she makes me curious. She's only eighteen and, to hear Ben talk, you'd think she spent her days reading the Koran and guarded by eunuchs.'

I wondered what, in turn, she'd made of Tom.

She passed in front of his eyes, a blue grey shimmer out of blue water into the blue shadow of the rocks where her towel was kept in a crevice, the sun being still very low. Tom, his hair bleached by months of open-air life, stepped towards her. He was still in bathing shorts and he was tall and his body finely made. Since she was at the rocks, he stood with his back to the sun. She was in his shadow.

'What was she like?' I asked.
  'Do you know something?' he said. 'She wasn't my type at all.'
  'What is your type?'
  'Blond.'
  'Like Hetty?'
  'Exactly. But I don't mean she isn't attractive. Still you know how it is – like calls to like. I'm fair, so I prefer fair-haired girls – I'm speaking generally, you understand.'
  'Go on, then. What's she like?'
  'She isn't especially tall, but slender and delicate in everything but her legs which are good and shaped by exercise. I thought she was a dancer or had done a lot of dancing.'
  Although she was partly hidden by a towel draped like a sarong, Tom formed an idea of her poise.
  'It was the pose of a Dégas bronze,' he said. 'And I thought – I know this is going to make you hoot, Pat – I thought it was so distinctive it would be evident in every articulation of her body so that, even in tying a slipper, she'd do it differently from other women – and it would be breathtaking to watch.'
  He was wrong. I didn't laugh.

Tom approached the girl.
  He said, 'Hi there. Am I right and I'm speaking to Señorita Malipiero?' He caught her uncertainty. 'I'm your neighbour, Tom Rensselaer. One of the American crowd at La Chênaie. Excuse me, would you rather I spoke in Spanish?'
  'I speak English,' the girl said. 'I know you Americans. My mother and I sometimes hear your parties.'
  'Really? I didn't know we'd thrown any parties. We play a few

records and dance a little of an evening. I hope we haven't been annoying you.'

The girl shook her head.

The conversation doesn't matter. I wanted to know Tom's first impressions.

'Her face was incomplete,' he said.

I asked, 'What do you mean?'

He said, 'Most girls are beautiful at eighteen, but their softness and freshness fades quickly. By twenty it's gone. They become indifferently pretty and even that prettiness has vanished by thirty.' He paused to see if he'd caught me, then said, 'That won't happen to Katerina Malipiero. She'll age in stages and each "look" will change suddenly like the falling of a fortress. At thirty she'll be magnificently lovely and at forty possess a kind of imperious splendour. When she's fifty men will still want to know her, but in part because they'll wish they'd known her twenty years before. Then at sixty she'll be *magical*, deeply beautiful as if behind a veil.'

'And at seventy?' I asked, a little stunned

'Bony and hideous,' he said. He added, 'Nothing lasts and it doesn't matter – or wouldn't to anyone who was in love with her.'

'But she's not your type?'

'No,' he said. 'I like girls who are gay.'

Katerina Malipiero, apparently, wasn't.

* * *

Tom volunteered to carry her things.

'I have nothing to carry,' she said.

'So you don't. Well, let me walk with you as far as La Pinède.'

'Why?'

'Because we're neighbours in a way, and this is a foreign country where help comes in useful. D'you have a car?'

'No.'

'See what I mean? We have a car. That could be handy.'

'But you have no petrol.'

'Sure we have. We can get as much as we like on the black market. It's only because we don't want to stand out or attract the attention of the police that we don't use the car more.'

She nodded, but whether she understood or agreed wasn't clear. At all events she did nothing to stop his accompanying her up the path to La Pinède. All the while, Tom kept talking of nothing in particular.

He told me, 'She likes cheese. She doesn't eat ham. She'd die for a cup of good coffee – who wouldn't?'

'What kind?'

'Viennese.'

'I don't know it.'

'It's good. They make it with figs. Oh, and she can slide cream off the back of a spoon the way waiters do. I know what you're thinking,' Tom told me. 'You think I was going on like an idiot.'

I didn't think that. My experience of girls was too limited and I envied Tom's assured approach. I said, 'Actually, I was wondering what she made of it.'

'I normally expect at least to tease out a smile.'

'She didn't?'

'Not a flicker. At least, not after the talk about coffee. She fell silent as if she'd said too much.'

'Perhaps you frightened her after all.'

'No, not that,' Tom answered. His tone was serious: even the thought that he might have frightened the girl appalled him. 'I would have known. No, not that. Her reactions were ... different to what I expected. Remote. Absent. D'you know something? If anyone was frightened, it was me.'

'What happened next?' I asked.

On the steepest part of the path, they halted among the pines. Katerina Malipiero remained standing. Tom sat with his back to the hill and looked across to the Hôtel Czar Aléxandre. Though dawn wasn't an hour old, already the shingles of the domed roof shone as if it had been raining and, to the right, the level sea was in parts too bright to look at.

And then? I felt suspended in the silence between Tom and his Argentinian Virgin. I wanted to know. What did she do?

That – said Tom – was it. They went their separate ways.

I caught my breath, as if he'd said she'd rushed into his arms or thrown herself to her death.

CHAPTER SEVEN

Tom finished his painting of Hetty and we agreed to celebrate with dinner at the Czar Aléxandre. I went into town to collect my shabby dinner suit (the one that belonged to my Uncle Gerald, atheist and freemason – a tale in himself). I'd had it repaired. Evening was falling, and Doctor Maillot was sitting outside the Hôtel de la Gare, nursing a drink in the shade of a lime tree and watching a truck. The truck was returning labourers from a construction project the Vichy authorities were organising somewhere out in the hills.

'So, Patrick,' Maillot reproached me, 'you don't talk with your old friend any more? You prefer your glamorous Americans.'

I said that wasn't so, though it was and he knew it. He gave me a sorrowful look. I agreed to an aperitif, which is how it came about that I repeated Tom's story of his brush with the Argentinian Virgin.

'You have told me in the same way Mr Rensselaer told you?' Dr Maillot asked. 'It is so ... *detailed*. So many – ' he searched for the word ' – *adjectives*. Much feeling but little economy. And why?'

The mention of adjectives made me remember something else Tom said. He was comparing Katerina with the girls he declared to be his 'type'.

'She's dark-skinned,' he said.

'Dark-skinned?' I imagined a beautiful octoroon, sensuous and rhythmical, though God knows I'd seen her enough to form my own impressions.

'Mediterranean maybe? Her skin is … tawny? … olive? … dusky?'

He couldn't settle on a word because for him colours were never fixed – least of all the tones of human flesh. It was there, that uncertainty, in his painting: in the grounds and glazes that made each colour no more than a transition between others, a momentary effect of light.

I explained this to Dr Maillot as he dripped water into his *pastis* and watched the liquor cloud. He'd already had a few and was jolly for no reason except drink and loneliness.

'It is clear,' he said, 'your Mr Rensselaer thinks with an intensely visual imagination. The *mise en scène* of his little story is a theatrical set.'

'He talks of going into films,' I said.

'Really? Then he must be dissatisfied with his paintings. He wants to make his figures move. He wishes to add drama!'

I agreed there might be some truth in this and Maillot flicked his hand dismissively as if I'd just conceded that it was all foolishness

We walked that night to the Hôtel Czar Aléxandre, the men in black, the women in long gowns. The sun was gone but the air was still heavy and the cicadas droned. Only a single lamp under the *porte cochère* cast a pale light. Beauclerc was waiting for us.

'Messieurs 'dames, how delightful to see you!' he said.

'Good evening, Philippe. D'you have a table for us?' Ben asked.

'A table? I shall have to check' said Beauclerc though there was no checking to be done, business being what it was. He picked up a book from the reception desk and made a show of going through it, but it was all phoney. The door to his lighted office was open and a radio was playing.

We waited. There was something dismal in the faded air. Maisie was tetchy; she asked, 'Why d'you suppose he always goes through this routine?'

Hetty said, 'I wonder what's on the menu? I guess it'll be fish. It's always fish. Why is it always fish?'

'The Germans buy up the meat,' Tom said.

'I'd like – oh, I don't know – some pork.'

'With cabbage and mushrooms. That's the Polack in you,' said Ben

'I was thinking of the *fee*-lay. Maybe with a cream and mustard sauce.'

Beauclerc returned from the desk. We stood around the book, following his finger down the entries. I tried to look somewhere else, but couldn't. I was out of mood with the night and our pretence that there was no war. Earlier we'd listened secretly to the BBC. Hitler was smashing the Russians.

'We are busier that usual,' Beauclerc said. 'Truly! Don't look surprised. We have some officers from Toulon and there are officials from Vichy and a businessman who has arrived only today.'

We ate the meal, a choice of fish or tripes. We chatted after a fashion, the same subjects and petty obsessions coming round. I felt an undercurrent of Maisie wanting to go home to America but prevented by Ben's business with the American Joint Distribution Committee. And, too, a sense that they were both somehow held here by Tom – at least it was Tom she put her question to.

She asked, 'Why are you hanging on here? Simply to paint?'

Tom had heard this question before and always avoided an answer. But tonight he was drinking and something moved him – perhaps the tension over the announcement he intended to make concerning himself and Hetty. At all events he said, 'I want to be the last American out.'

Which meant precisely what? I didn't know. I wondered if he was talking about patriotism in the strange way Americans do, but if he was, Ben didn't follow and said so.

I think it pained Tom that we didn't understand. He shook his head. He said, speaking to Ben not me, 'You should be grateful. You've got a wife and a career. If you're lucky, you'll have kids soon. You're committed to the world as it is, because it's the world that feeds you.'

'And?'

'Don't you see? The image of a generation – the stamp it puts on history – is set in its youth. That's when we dream concretely.

'For us it all ends with this war. It doesn't matter if America enters or not. Empires will fall, revolutions will happen, kids will come home from the Front and it's the war that'll define how they feel about things.

'We're the night watchmen for our generation, Ben. We're the rearguard of an army that's already beaten. The best of us are already gone. They drank themselves to death or were eaten up by Hollywood or got tired of everything and went to the dogs any old how. We're the last draft of the young, the weak and the cowardly, with nothing to contribute because our age is already over. Our purpose is simply to *be*.'

'You're tight,' said Ben

'You've got it, Buddy Boy,' Tom agreed.

There wasn't much of a band but Maisie wanted to dance. At one end of the room a dais was set up with a dozen music stands but only a pianist and a fellow with a concertina played and the rest of the stands stood like a line of coffins.

I led Maisie out and tried to liven up the atmosphere. I don't have much technique, but I'm a vigorous dancer, and in Ireland that passes for talent.

Tom guided Hetty on to the floor and took her smoothly through the steps. Seeing them there, beautiful and elegant, I also saw the room in its physical and moral enormity, half closed off by darkness and dust sheets and the rest occupied only by scattered parties of people who were as silent as beggars in a soup kitchen.

I couldn't stand it and took a break to smoke on the terrace. A couple of minutes later Hetty joined me. Tom had just proposed to her – there on the dance floor with the glitter-ball sparkling over their heads. I was astonished – not that Tom should want to marry her, which seemed to me a grand idea, but that she didn't connect the proposal with Tom's little speech.

Hetty's eyes were red with crying. She went to fix her make up while I returned to the others to find Tom had broken the news. Masie was going through her 'Oh! – My! – Gosh!' routine and Ben was ordering champagne. Tom was explaining, 'It just came to me – like an inspiration. I thought to myself, "She's absolutely the best girl I know and, damn it, I'm in love with her!"' He looked at me. He knew I'd missed the first flush of his enthusiasm and there was something fierce now in the way he stared as if I was going to pick a fight over the issue. 'Well, what d'you say, Pat?'

'I hope you'll be very happy.'

'Is that all?'

'Of course he'll be happy!' Ben said. 'Both of them will.' He rolled his eyes. 'You know, I'm *almost* tempted to join you in a drink.' Ben didn't drink. Apparently, so Maisie told me, it was a religious prejudice, a very American thing; at all events he didn't have a drink. But Maisie did, and shortly she asked me to dance again.

So we danced, and this time I took the business slowly. Maisie was drunk and sad. She seemed to wrap herself round me but with her head back, all loose and dreamy.

A quarter circle of the floor brought a couple of French families into view. Two fathers, two mothers, an affianced couple, a handful of friends and reluctant children. Earlier there'd been some false gaiety but now the toasts were over and they were brooding, tugging at the remains of bread rolls and smoking.

Another quarter turn saw the Vichy officials in suits with lapel badges like subscribers to a sinister charity, and behind them two naval officers in undress uniform.

The third quarter brought in Captains Brenner and Kellermann, who smiled and raised their glasses and, almost invisible, Beauclerc's visiting stranger, a small man with a large appetite.

Maisie left the floor to Tom and Hetty. She whispered, 'Tom dances like an angel.'

'I know,' I said. Tom had joked that that was where his trust fund went: on lessons and a year as a 'dancing man' at the parties of every Boston débutante.

Maisie buried her face in my shoulder. She murmured a long 'Mmm!' which sounded like an invitation to sleep with her. She scared me half to death.

Then the music stopped. The German captains clapped. The clapping seemed to wake the other diners from their torpor and they joined in. The solitary stranger raised his fork from a heap of mussel shells and waved it.

I was looking at a dead man, but I didn't know it.

CHAPTER EIGHT

Behind our table, Monsieur Alphonse and Monsieur Pierre, two elderly homosexuals who lived permanently at the hotel at the out of season rate, were arguing.

Maisie asked Hetty, 'Have you firmed up your plans as to what you'll do if – God willing – we ever get home?'

Hetty was thoughtful. I think it was because she couldn't believe her good fortune. She said, 'Well, Tommy and I haven't talked about the future. I've considered the movies. I know everyone does and not many succeed, but I'm steady and, if I fail, I think I'll have the nerve to give up and try something else. If you're not to be miserable, you have to have to have the nerve to accept failure and move on. I think it's the same with love. As to the movies, I was hoping Ben'd help, but he says he knows nothing about them.'

Ben said, 'It's a Jewish business, the movies. I had a cousin saw there was money to be made. He tried to get in but they shut him out.'

Hetty sympathised , 'That's a damn shame.' She turned to Tom and said brightly, 'Maybe we could both go to Hollywood. You'll be a scriptwriter and I'll be a famous actress!'

I found myself smiling at the implausibility of this ambition. Then it came to me that they were Americans, for whom no ambition was implausible.

Ben asked Tom, 'How much is left in your trust fund?'

'I don't know. Why d'you ask?'

'You should try defence stocks, or, if you like a risk, take a forward position in metals. With the war they're both set to rise further.'

Hetty reacted as if Ben had proposed Tom risk his money on a poker hand. She asked, 'How long can you last out?'

'I don't know – a few months, maybe? It's no big thing; my uncle says he'll set me up as a bill broker, or I could turn my hand to law again.'

'You could paint.'

'Give me a break.' Tom put his hand on Hetty's. He whispered, 'Don't worry, we'll be okay.'

The waiter came over and spoke to Ben. There was only one and his name was Étienne.

Ben mumbled, 'Who? Where?'

Étienne pointed across the floor beyond the German officers.

Ben said, 'Okay, tell him it's all right if that's what he wants.'

He explained to the rest of us, 'A guy wants to buy us a drink – didn't Philippe mention someone on business? Maybe he's a travelling salesman who's feeling lonesome.'

The stranger came to stand by our table. He said he was a Spaniard and gave his name as Alvírez. He was about fifty years old, stocky and short in the leg. His clothes were good but bore folds from a suitcase. On one stubby finger was a college ring and on another a diamond. He had hairy cuffs and a hairy necklace and needed to shave his cheekbones.

I don't think Alvírez had any particular interest in us. It was just that he was weary and we were the only likely relief. 'I was watching you dance,' he growled at Maisie. He spoke good English, but low and rough with an imperfect American accent. 'You dance well,' he added, but he was just making noise. I don't think he thought enough of people to compliment them.

'I don't need you to tell me that,' Maisie answered. She needn't have bothered because it was clear Alvírez's motive wasn't sex. He revealed it once he'd ordered cognacs.

'I'm a gambling man; I admit it. I heard there's a casino here.'

'It's closed,' I said.

'I know. On account of the war, or staff, or no customers, or something. But it could be opened.'

'Really?'

'I spoke to the *patron*. He says if there's a demand, he'll open up. He wasn't specific but I think six or eight people should do it.'

'You mean tonight – now?' asked Tom. He was cool. He tried to charm Alvírez out of the notion. He said he was interested and maybe tomorrow. But Alvírez was an addict and a bully and Ben, who'd been strange and distracted since Tom's announcement, said the party tonight was for Hetty and we should make a splash, though he didn't ask Hetty for her opinion. So it was agreed. And before we knew where we were, there were other volunteers, enough for a quorum.

Tom said afterwards that we reminded him of some paintings:

of blind beggars stumbling towards a ditch, by Breughel; and *The Ship of Fools* by an artist he couldn't recall but maybe it was Breughel too. The crowd of us in all our motley spilled out into the night: women in long gowns flashing by moonlight, men in tuxedos, suits, uniforms, all laughing and led by a white duck-tailed waiter and a guy with a concertina in a shuffle over the gravel as if dancing the conga. It wasn't a visit to the casino but a raid by people who'd gone mad.

I knew the exterior of the building: two stories of a baroque stonework and a mansard with round windows. Dr Maillot said he'd gambled there in the last season before the war and it looked like an Edwardian brothel whose whores had fallen into old age. On the ground floor were two large salons, a gaming room and an English tearoom. The furniture lay under dust-sheets, the carpets under druggets. Most of the lights had failed, and those that worked were draped in cobweb.

'Messieurs – messieurs! A thousand apologies. If I had received notice … If in the future … future … inestimable pleasure.'

I was sorry for Beauclerc and happy for his brief happiness. He saw a revival in his hotel's fortunes. He saw good news to inscribe in the reports he still dutifully wrote to the absent Compagnie des Grands Loisirs. It was too much and too incredible. God bless Marshal Pétain!

But he was a practical man. He, Monsieur Beauclerc, must return to the restaurant. Étienne would be sole croupier and therefore only one table could be opened – for tonight. Tomorrow? Who knew about tomorrow? In an excess of emotion he gripped Étienne by the arms and stared at him tearfully as a general might when handing a medal to a wounded *poilu*.

I'd kept my sanity – or maybe I was melancholy mad. Certainly I was drunk. But I wasn't merry: too aware of the falsity of it all. I could only watch as Alvírez, with his greed and animal energy, drove the proceedings forward. Perhaps the war had inured us to recklessness. Perhaps in this gimcrack, dusty splendour we caught a note of satire at what had gone before. Perhaps, sensing it had once been beautiful, we wanted to destroy it because we weren't beautiful any longer. I don't know – only that the affair was sad and frantic.

Alvírez was the type who lets others know he's enjoying himself by making a lot of noise. He moved like an ape with his arms and legs swinging wide. When he collected his chips he gave a loud 'Hah!' – not exactly pleasure but as if he'd hurt someone he wanted to hurt. It was nasty, yet some of the others picked up the manner because this was his night. And meantime Étienne spun the wheel and there was, for a moment, silence elsewhere as the clatter of the ball reverberated in the coffered ceiling. Then we fell to placing bets, winning, losing, laughing and shouting – all sorts of mad stuff.

Hetty, however, had no money. I saw her sidle up to Tom and croon, 'What's up, Tommy?'

Tom said, 'Nothing. I just don't like it – none of this.' It seemed he felt as I did, and that made me wonder if we all did and we were faking it for the sake of the others.

Hetty chuckled. 'We have gone kind of nuts, haven't we? I don't suppose it'll do any harm.'

'I don't like Señor Alvírez. Who is he anyway?'

'You mean he isn't one of the Park Avenue Alvírezes? What a snob you are! As it happens, I heard him say he trades in mercury and chrome. Sells 'em to the Germans, I think.'

'Then what's he doing in S. Symphorien?'

'What are *you* doing in S. Symphorien?'

Tom stared at her and murmured, 'I'm a jerk and you're a good, sensible girl.'

'I don't know about "good", but at least I know why I'm here. I'm broke and have to follow the money – or, at least, I did until I met you. Now I do everything for love.'

'But you do *like* the rest of us?' Tom said, which struck me as strange question to put to the girl he intended to marry.

'Sure.'

Tom fell silent for a while and watched the game with Hetty beside him. Then he asked, 'Do you have a philosophy, Hetty?'

She looked at him thoughtfully. 'Sure,' she said. 'Be nice to people. Suck it and see. Don't wear pink if you have red hair. Would you like to dance?'

'What? Here among the crazy people?'

'Sure, why not? I used to dance in cabaret. If you like you can dance in your head. That's a big place.'

So Tom called the concertina man over, and I watched as he drew Hetty to a spot in the dark between the baccarat tables. Their feet caught in the drugget, but they just pulled it, warm, slow and heavy like sand until they lost connection with the thin, jolly music – lost themselves in tenderness. Then they kissed: small, silly kisses with frills and bells on; ice-cube kisses that thrilled up the spine; party dress kisses that were pink and lacy – all as light as air.

I was only twenty-four years old, and images of love were still fresh for me. Watching Tom and Hetty, I thought I'd never see love better, never truer or more poignant. Yet, if I could have caught the moment and somehow stopped it happening so that the world carried on in the same drab way, I would have because, as they danced, I could sense the horror swirling about them: the meanness that would never leave them be. Alvírez was snarling over his losses, throwing his weight around and spoiling for a fight. Some of the men were for squaring up to him. Others were conciliatory the way drunks are when they get maudlin.

Finally, in the detail about who was going to hit whom and when, everyone got bored and, sensing that things would be spoiled if the words weren't said, agreed it had been a great evening.

We all walked out – murderers and victims alike.

CHAPTER NINE

Next morning Tom broke off from painting and came to my place. So far I'd avoided visitors. I'd been living on my own for months and made a mess with papers all over, ashtrays filled with butts, dirty dishes, general garbage and the sour stink of my laundry.

He began talking about Hetty, 'Of course people are going to talk. They'll say Miss Hetty Novaks of Pittsburgh has no business marrying Mr Thomas Jefferson Rensselaer of Long Island. They'll point out that she doesn't come from the same social background and hasn't known money or pure thoughtless leisure. Oh, she's smart and she'll pass once she's been trained what to expect – that's what they'll say. But they'll mean like some half-breeds pass.'

Jokingly he sketched their future.

'Maybe we'll go to California. None of it'll matter there and all I'll need to say is "Oh, we met in Europe – Paris, France, to be exact." Hollywood is full of cheap people with lots of money; and self-invention is a moral imperative, not a deceit. And if we fail? Who knows? I have that American faith you'll never grasp, Pat. Hetty'll grow fat and raise hogs and babies; and I'll take up law, become a judge in Alabama and hang coloureds for spitting on the sidewalk. But we'll be happy!'

I laughed because laughter seemed to be called for. But the truth is that, if the words meant something, the sentiment escaped me.

Tom asked, 'Have you ever been in love?'

I said, 'I was engaged once. It didn't last.' I offered a drink and made a few remarks about the progress of the war, which I was following on the radio.

He took a sip from the glass, put it down, and brushed away the shank of blond hair that was forever falling across his forehead. He said, 'People are going to say Hetty has made a good catch.' He grimaced. 'I don't see it that way at all. Quite the opposite. You know her. Don't you see that I'll be getting the better part of the deal? What frightens me, Pat, is that I could be cheating, reserving part of myself where Hetty'll never see it. I don't want to do that. I want ... '

'What?'

'To go headlong into love like a berserker.'

The next day he met the Argentinian Virgin again.

He said he'd no intention of seeing her. He was feeling crapulous after drinking and wasn't thinking of anything much when he went early to the beach. That's where I see him. Perhaps he collects shells and tosses them in a dark pool.

As Tom tells it, she came at dawn with the sun low and the beach in bronze shadow. Her feet picked precise, careful steps, each one arched with the toes testing the way before she rested her weight on her firm legs. She wore a short, blue shift over her costume and carried a towel and a swimming cap. Her head was bowed in concentration – *la Vierge d'Argentine*.

Tom chuckled and looked sideways at me. He said, 'I hid. I didn't want to frighten her. I thought how lonely she must be.'

I asked, 'How would you know?'

'She has no friends in town. She's made no attempt to get in touch with us even after she heard we were at La Chênaie.'

'Perhaps she likes it that way.'

'She's eighteen, Pat – *eighteen!*'

He was right. She was eighteen and beautiful.

Tom had learned his technique with girls like Maisie, who at eighteen wanted simple fun and responded to good looks and uncomplicated sunniness. While his mind went over this, Katerina Malipiero removed her shift, standing flatfooted on the sand, weight forward, arms upright, hands gripping the garment, her chest and abdomen taut. Over her head it went, to be dropped on the sand. Then she smiled to herself, put on her cap, and made a dash for the water.

Tom sat in shadow and watched. He lit a cigarette and caught, with the scent of smoke, a whiff of his own perversity, as if he were an old man hunkered in the darkness of cheap cinema to view a movie.

Who was she?

Who was she?

Katerina was strong and self-absorbed. She swam out to sea until Tom lost her in the glitter. A notion came to him that she was mad. He meant clinically mad. Before the war insane rich people and their guardians had filled the rented villas along this coast. Yes, maybe that was it. Her family, in the way of Latins, would be strict in sexual morals if not in every other kind. Suppose, in her youth and beauty, her budding sensual awakening had been stifled into erotomania?

Or maybe she had tuberculosis?

Or maybe Tom was mad?

She came out of the sea, already taking off her cap and shaking out her hair as she walked through the shadows. The two friendly Nazis were coming down the path. They waved at Tom and at Katerina Malipiero. Tom gave her time to towel herself. Then, stubbing his cigarette, he approached her.

'We spoke a few days ago,' he said. 'Tom Rensselaer? The American?'

'Katerina Malipiero,' she said.

'I remember. Your name's Italian, but I was told you're from Argentina.'

'There are many Italians in Argentina. Your name is Dutch, I think.'

'New York Dutch.'

It seemed she didn't understand, so that Tom found himself working at his own identity like a confidence trickster who is about to be blown.

She was gathering her things.

'Have you been here long?' he asked, repeating things he was sure they'd talked about before. 'In S. Symphorien?'

'No. And you?'

'Not long. We left Paris just as the Germans arrived. Afterwards we fooled around in Spain and Italy for a while. Have you ever been to Spain or Italy?'

'No.' She paused, then asked, 'Why didn't you go back to America?'

'Oh, there was some good reason. I forget what it was.' As soon as he said it, Tom regretted the answer. It was flippant. For other girls – his 'type' – it would have been fine, but for this one it wouldn't do.

She took a step from the beach toward the path and Tom matched her. He made small talk, but couldn't remember later what it was.

He told me, 'I don't know what came over me. It isn't like I wasn't used to handling girls – all kinds of girls. Women too.'

Tom didn't elaborate but Ben had given me some history. Girls and women both, they'd chased him in droves. Ben had known Tom at Yale, where he'd been kept by a woman of thirty-five. Yet no one had thought of him as a gigolo, Ben said. Tom's ease and intelligence had made the affair seem perfectly natural and, even though he couldn't have been more than twenty, he never crowed about his conquest.

Ten years later, all he could say was, 'With Katerina Malipiero I keep finding myself wrong-footed. All the stuff one normally says just sounds wrong. I don't know – the words have a sleazy feel.'

I heard him; yet, as he described it, the situation didn't sound out of the ordinary for two strangers meeting. Then again, I didn't have Tom's sense of decency, his respect for women, his desire always to do the right thing in his own eyes.

They reached the place where the path divided: right to the hotel, straight on to La Chênaie and left to the height of La Pinède. Tom saw Alvírez labouring ahead of them up the left-hand path. The Spaniard halted, struck by the heat, or maybe he saw a lizard or a basking snake. Katerina also stopped.

She said, 'You needn't come any further.'

Tom was looking at Alvírez and thinking there were one or two small places on La Pinède; so the Spaniard mightn't be going to the villa.

'I don't mind,' he told her. 'I'll tell you what. Call on us. We'll go riding or play tennis or … well, whatever you like.' He confessed, 'It doesn't seem right for me to sit there watching you swim.'

'You were watching me swim?'

'See what I mean? It doesn't seem right.'

'Why were you watching me?'

'We could go riding or play tennis … I was just walking when you came to the beach, and I figured you'd like to be alone; so I hid out of your way.'

Alvírez had resumed puffing his way up the hill. Tom let his glance follow so he shouldn't seem so intently interested in the girl. And yet, he told me, even when he wasn't looking at her his senses quivered with her physical presence.

He laughed when he explained this to me.

'You see, I hate it. It seems so … so *nasty* to like a girl only for her looks, especially if she isn't asking you to. And Katerina Mailiero doesn't show any sign of caring whether I look at her or not.'

'Then there's Hetty to consider,' I said, which shocked him.

'Good God!' he exclaimed. 'That isn't it at all!'

CHAPTER TEN

Katerina and Tom parted on the path. What happened next I learned only years later, after Tom had been destroyed and one way or another the rest of us had gone to hell.

She didn't go home straight away but sat a while among the vanilla-scented broom and tried to make sense of what was happening.

She asked herself why the American was so persistent. She understood that he might be attracted to her, but she was used only to the attentions of boys she knew: boys of her own age – boys who weren't strangers. Tom's easy manners and sophistication intimidated her even as they seduced her. She didn't know what to make of him.

She waited until she saw Alvírez leaving the Villa la Pinède by the path that led to town. He walked in his bustling style, a man in a hurry and angry about something or other.

She went to the house. She called out, 'Mother!' and went inside by the french window.

Tom had a version of how the scene looked. Like a desert tomb the Villa la Pinède is composed of dust and its lifeless chambers are piled with the wreck of former splendours: broken furniture, torn tapestries and portraits of dead people. It lies about in heaps devoid of life or order, much of it cleared from its original setting and dumped like plunder in secretive closets and abandoned mansards among old toys, chests of clothes and strongboxes containing nothing more than bundles of old letters from dead lovers.

Or so Tom described it. You don't have to care for his language. I'll have more to say about it when I get round to telling you about the crazy film script he wrote; the one that came years later out of the blue, when my wife and I were living in Dublin. The same script that got me thinking about these things and, I suppose, made me finally realise what had happened.

But I'm getting ahead of myself.

Teresa Malipiero was a beautiful woman. But she had twenty years more experience than her daughter, and those twenty years had given her an inflexible single-mindedness. Katerina trusted her. Who else could she trust?

'Alvírez has been here,' Señora Malipiero murmured.

'I know,' said Katerina. 'I saw him. I waited until he left.'

Her mother nodded. On the table in front of her was small box of black lacquer inlaid with abalone and mother of pearl. Beside it were several empty trays lined in black velvet. In the bottom of the box was a diamond collar in the style of forty years before. Several stones had been removed from it.

Teresa closed the box and smiled at her daughter. She asked, 'What have you been doing? Swimming?'

'Yes.' Katerina hesitated. 'I saw Mr. Rensselaer again.'

'Really? Would you – ' Señora Malipiero's eyes, vague and distracted, fell on two used glasses and a bottle which stood on the table by the jewellery case ' – like some wine?'

'So early?'

'Alvírez insisted.' The mother poured a glass for herself and left the other untouched like something filthy. 'He had no news,' she said. 'No, that's untrue. He had stories designed to lift our hopes. Stories and promises – always promises. If only we are patient and make one more effort … And provide money, of course.' She drank the wine quickly but calmly, then poured another glass.

'Can we give him more money?' Katerina asked.

'He wants the entire necklace – not a stone at a time. He says that, as a matching set, the diamonds are worth more than their individual values. And, naturally, he is right.'

'Then surely we should give it to him?'

'And then what? We shall have nothing.'

'Alvírez won't know that.'

'He will when he returns with more stories, more promises – and more demands.' The second glass of wine was finished. Teresa Malipiero smiled at the emptiness, sighed and replaced the cork. She said, 'You should get to know Mr. Rensselaer better. He is ... a gentleman? He and his friends are ... '

'I don't want to speak about him,' said Katerina.

'I should like to meet him.'

'No.'

Teresa extended a hand, took her daughter's and stroked it. She pulled Katerina towards her, kissed her cheek and embraced her.

'You or I,' she whispered, 'one of us must make a sacrifice.'

The Czar Aléxandre hired out horses. Tom took one next day before breakfast. He rode as well as he did everything else and broke off into the pines and went higher and further into the oak and chestnut woods.

There, in the mountains in the first hour after dawn, the air was limpid. Tom rode for five miles or so over rock and leaf fall, pausing only now and again to glance through a break in the trees. Below him S. Symphorien lay in its morning doze, and beyond the town the tepid sea was still and ribboned.

Or so he said, and I believe him

He turned the hired hack back along the path. It took him down a slope of cork oaks. He heard a voice singing and Dr Maillot stepped out of the undergrowth.

The old man called out, 'Monsieur Rensselaer! I heard the horse and knew it would be you. Who else would be idling in the mountains except mad Americans and disreputable doctors *en retraite*? These days Patrick doesn't come with me and I must take my walks alone.'

Maillot was unsteady on his feet and clutched a bottle of spirits.

He held Tom's horse by the head while Tom dismounted. 'Drink?' he offered.

Tom asked, 'Isn't this a little early?'

Maillot shrugged. 'Consider it emergency medicine.' He took another mouthful of brandy.

'Why?'

'One of my patients has died – someone I was treating informally, you understand. She had a miscarriage and I was unable to stop the bleeding. She was seventeen years and foolish, and it is all too *triste*. And so I am drinking as you see, Monsieur Rensselaer.'

Tom knew Dr Maillot only slightly and pretended not to understand him. He'd already told me he saw something nasty and furtive in the old fellow.

Now Maillot made things worse by blubbering, 'The girls! Even the ugly ones are pretty! They make me think of all the mistakes I made when I was young and, God forgive me, I have to help them! So pretty and so helpless, you understand, Monsieur Rensselaer?'

Then he remembered himself. He had a sense of his own foolishness, which made him shake his head and smile. He was still thinking tenderly of the girls he helped, and it was probably this which made him ask, 'Do you know this path Monsieur Rensselaer? Be careful because it falls very dangerously here and there. I have warned Mademoiselle Malipiero. If you continue down this way, you will find her.'

Tom turned his horse away. He'd no intention of searching for Katerina, but his route took him inevitably downhill. Because the ground was treacherous he dismounted and led the horse. Either side were landslips that fell abruptly fifty or a hundred feet, sometimes with a shallow step where grass and saplings grew: secret places that could hardly be seen from above.

Now, as he looked down from the height onto a strip of green hanging midway down the face of a bluff thinly covered in bramble and young oaks with spurge and cranesbill growing among them, he saw a dark-haired girl in a white dress dappled blue by leaf shadow.

Tom tied the horse and found a narrow path that snaked down the almost vertical slope, and Katerina was so absorbed she didn't hear him. So he took her by surprise when he called, 'Señorita Malipiero.'

She was standing in a white dress against a white sky at the edge where the ground plummeted. After that first little shock, she smiled.

'Mr. Rensselaer,' she said.

Tom had no idea why she was there, but he knew he'd intruded and he tried to look harmless.

'I was out taking a ride,' he said to the girl. 'And you?'

'I was thinking.'

'A penny for them – that's what they say.' He followed her gaze toward the distant sea. 'Don't you get lonesome, sitting here with only your own thoughts?' When she didn't answer, he took a risk most of us wouldn't take with a stranger and said, 'You're in trouble, I can tell.'

'How?'

'No one chooses to be alone if there's someone they can confide in. Oh, I don't mean you should confide in me, but Hetty and Maisie are much of your age. We're nice people. You'd like us. You know that – and yet you stay away. Is it your mother wouldn't approve? What'll it take? D'you want me to march up to the house with a bunch of flowers, tip my hat and ask politely? Say the word and I'll do it. I ... '

Tom was wondering how far to push his blind sense of what was appropriate. He could tell he was carrying her with him, but who was she and where were they going?

'I want to help,' he said, making the offer sound nonchalant.

So there it was, Tom's offer. Everything turned on Katerina's reaction. She only had to reject him and Tom would have given up. He liked her, she interested him, and he felt sorry for her. But it wasn't as if she was a tragic figure or a dying child.

No, *nothing* was inevitable – not at that time anyway – and I can imagine any answer on Katerina's part. Tom's life hung on that answer, but nobody could have predicted it, so that sometimes I go back in my mind and hear the alternatives and they sound all right – I mean they sound the sort of thing Katerina *could* have said.

In which case Tom might have survived.

Instead she said, 'I'll talk to my mother. I'm sure she'd like to see you.'

CHAPTER ELEVEN

'I swear to God, she was thinking of killing herself,' Tom said.

We'd turned up at the hotel full of innocent swagger and ordered two bottles of cool muscadet and *de l'eau gaseuse, s'il vous plait* while we looked at the lunch menu.

Tom told us about his morning ride and his brush with Dr Maillot. He said, 'He's an abortionist, would you believe it? He killed a girl and now has the gall to cry over her. I can't stand cheap sentiment that passes for morality.'

His thoughts about the dead girl may have affected how he spoke about Katerina. He described the bower she haunted in her white dress like a figure in a gothic novel or a ghost. Then, while I was trying to hold that image, the lonely hideous beauty of it, he said she was thinking of killing herself. It shook me – I mean: how could he know?

'Girls are always killing themselves or threatening to,' he said as if repeating something everyone knows.

'Not in Ireland,' I said. 'Their mammies wouldn't let them.'

I was trying to be urbane, but Tom took me seriously. He said, 'I can't speak about Ireland. I was forgetting you're different from us, Pat. You'll have to take my word for it. Girls try to kill themselves – after parties or at the end of summer when the boys go back to college. I've seen it.'

Hetty was as puzzled as I was, but Maisie nodded. 'I made a couple of attempts,' she said, making it sound like the annoying stuff kids do. 'Once over the De Witt boy and once when Chester Miller got engaged.' She placed her left hand on the table with the wrist turned up and a scar ran across it. 'More fool me,' she added evenly.

I was taken aback by this cool talk of a world where beautiful girls slew themselves on a whim. We all have a vision of Arcadia, tranquil places where the wind blows only music. I had a picture of a trim lawn leading to an Atlantic shore: the sun is shining, a record is playing on a gramophone, and the boys and girls express their eternal joy by discussing things that are perfectly trivial.

But, of course, it isn't like that. *Et in Arcadia ego* – as my Uncle Gerald used to say when whiskey and the Spirit moved him. Death is everywhere.

Tom went on, 'I don't attach much importance when a girl flies into a temper because a boy throws her over. It's a damn nuisance if she takes an overdose of veronal, but at bottom it's all a piece of theatre and she's sure there's someone who knows what's going on and will help her out. No, the ones who're really at risk are those who give the world a cold-hearted stare and decide the game isn't worth the candle.'

'And you'd know?' I said.

'My sister Alice killed herself,' he said. 'It was unfathomable. But some things are.'

We went to the beach. Monsieur Alphonse and Monsieur Pierre, hot in their old-fashioned summer suits, were sitting at the water's edge. The German captains were performing exercises.

Talk about affairs in Marseilles and the business of sequestrated American property led to Ben going on about money in the unembarrassed way that disconcerts those who aren't Americans.

He said, 'There comes a time when you have so much it isn't like ordinary money. It can't be spent and in can't be entirely lost. There aren't enough things to want or mistakes to make. My dad dropped a bundle on steel in twenty-nine, but by thirty-four we were back where we started and then some. We didn't do anything smart. The money went out and came back on the tide. The sea is always there.'

I had an image of his fortune as a monument of empire. It would survive the vicissitudes of any single life and weather slowly over generations.

As we set out our towels and umbrellas we heard a cry. I looked up and maybe eighty feet up the rocky face of La Pinède, two boys were clambering. It was an adventurous climb but there were plenty of handholds. The lads were from the town. Their cries were simple enjoyment.

Watching them, Ben said, 'That's me as I was fifteen years ago.' He paused then added, 'Now I've lost the taste for danger – no, not the taste, the talent for it. If I fell, it'd be on to a bed of bank notes.'

Tom said, 'Become a mountaineer. Hunt sharks.'

'That isn't living dangerously. Heroes don't die from holiday accidents no matter how colourful. Fall off a mountain and everyone would call me a damned fool with more money than sense and they'd be right. I need – ' he searched the sky for ideas, then looked at the boys again before saying ' – to be saved by a good woman or a good book, or burned for heresy, or … Say, is my sax in the bag?'

'It's here,' snapped Maisie. 'I hope you're not going to get gloomy on us.'

Ben didn't drink. When he felt low, he took his saxophone to the beach, where he sat apart from us, by the water, and played snappy numbers while the girls danced on the sand and the German captains clapped in time.

Today, however, Ben didn't take out the sax.

Tom lay on a towel for a while and read. He said he'd paint when the sun was nearer the horizon. The girls played ball and did nothing in particular. For the moment I was stuck with my writing. An Italian aircraft droned overhead from the direction of Nice.

And there was a scream.

Afterwards Tom said he didn't know what caused him to look at the rock face again. The strangest thing was he couldn't have seen what he said he saw. It just wasn't possible because of the speed of everything, the lack of warning, the angle of vision. Yet the whole image was so sharp.

One of the boys fell off the cliff and was killed.

The facts were that the two boys had almost reached the top of La Pinède. One – the survivor – was higher than the other when, so he swore, a rock tumbled from somewhere still higher. What caused the rock to become dislodged was never established. The wall surrounding the villa came right to the cliff edge and was partly ruined. Maybe someone – Katerina or her mother – had been in the garden where they sometimes sat by the wall to look at the sea. An action as slight as this might have started a movement of soil or small stones and finally caused the larger rock to fall. Who could say? From the beach it was always difficult to tell if anyone was in the garden of La Pinède, and the two women couldn't say where they were at the precise moment of the accident, though they agreed they'd been near the ruined wall during the course of the afternoon.

In any case the detail didn't matter. There was no indication that anyone intended to kill the boy.

He fell from the cliff and lay in the spoil at the base. Tom, who'd seen the fall – or said he had – was there first with Ben on his heels. Ben shouted to the rest of us, 'He's all smashed up. Don't look,' and ushered the women away. The two Frenchmen and the German captains also came over.

Captain Brenner tested for a pulse, then covered the body with a towel. He said, 'We must inform the authorities,' which we all agreed was a sound idea. In the meantime we tried to coax the other boy down.

In due course a gendarme arrived, then two more men with a stretcher, a doctor, the fire brigade and usual hangers-on. The air was very still, the beach flat, the sea calm. On this motionless stage, people formed and re-formed in little groups and voices carried a long way until the body was borne off and, in ones and twos, the rest of us also left.

That night we didn't bother with dinner. We ate cold cuts and sat outside playing gin by the light of an oil lamp despite the curfew. With a sudden burst of noise, the cicadas struck up and, a few hours later, with equal abruptness stopped.

'Are you serious about going to Nice?' Maisie asked.

Ben had mentioned the subject as relief from the tedium of S. Symphorien and his business trips to Marseilles.

'I don't see why not. There are probably still some Americans there, so we could have company. If you want to shop, you can shop. I know there are shortages, but that's just a question of money.'

'I'm going to stay here,' Tom said.

Hetty asked, 'Do you want me to stay with you?'

'No, it'll be all right.'

'I don't have money for Nice.'

'I'll lend you some money,' said Ben.

'You're always lending me money,' Hetty said. Sometimes she was tired of being grateful. She looked to Tom again. He gave a good-natured shrug because he had no money either.

Ben asked, 'Why do you want to stay here?'

'I need a rest from your ugly mug.' Tom smiled sunnily. 'Seriously, I need to paint. The bug's gotten to me and I shan't be much fun until I get it out of my system.'

'And you, Pat?'

'I'll tag along,' I said; but the truth was I thought the project would come to nothing without Tom.

The evening was warm and fretful. Organised conversation petered out to be replaced by occasional squibs. This was one from Hetty:

'You know, I've decided we must be nice people. We've been living together for a year and more and we're bored stiff with each other and this country – and yet we never fight.'

Another came from Maisie:

'I feel as if I'm living in a trance in which I can't do anything. No – I feel as if I'm waiting for a thunderstorm to break. The air is stifling and electric, but somehow the rain won't come.'

Hetty again:

'Once I was in love with a boy. He went on vacation for a month, and during that month it was like life was suspended. I was all jumpy with emotion but with no way to get rid of it. I was working at a soda fountain. It was hot and I poured sodas all summer long, but it was like I was thirsty all the time. I didn't dream of the boy, just of long cool sodas.'

Ben:

'For me it's like sailing with the sun in my eyes and only the horizon to look at and no wind blowing.'

Tom:

'My trustee called me in. He said, "Son, we've tried to keep this from you in the hope that something would change for the better. But the fact is, it hasn't and the money your father left you is all but used up." My uncle warned me that my trustees were stealing from me, but all I remember is a feeling of relief that I was free of all that.' Tom grinned. 'I was only a kid. Now I wish I still had the money.'

'And you, Pat?' Hetty asked.

I don't recall what I said that night. Now, in my dreams, I scream, 'Murder!' because I can see everything that was to come: the destruction and wasted lives. But at the time – who knows?

I said something unmemorable.

Beyond the wall two people were walking down the path to the beach by moonlight. They whispered in French, softly as they approached, loudly as they passed, softly again as they were gone.

We got to talking about the accident again. Tom mentioned something that disturbed him.

He said, 'I think the rock came out of the wall of La Pinède. If you look careful you can see that just there the wall is ruined and it wouldn't take much to shake a rock loose.'

In my mind I saw a dribble of earth and felt the sudden shock of the rock moving. Tom said, 'It should have hit the first boy – the one who was higher up the cliff – the one who survived. But he saw it and put out his hand and the rock struck it – it struck his hand on the palm, and he seemed to sweep it aside like a baseball catch, but he didn't try to hold it; so it carried on falling and picking up speed until it struck his friend. By then it was going too fast and he had no warning – so there was nothing to do but fall and die.'

He looked at the rest of us. I was intrigued but at first I didn't pick up the horror.

Tom explained, 'The *wrong* boy was killed. In fact I'm not sure *anyone* need have been killed. The rock hadn't fallen far when the first boy knocked it aside. I don't think it was going to hit his head – his shoulder, maybe, which might have gotten broken, but that wasn't fatal since he had a good hold with his other hand.'

For a while he left us to picture the incident; then he said, 'The boy – the first boy could see his friend when he did what he did. He knew the rock would strike him.'

I asked, 'Do you mean he did it deliberately?'

Tom thought about that. 'Yes – well, no – I guess it depends what you mean by "deliberately". I'm not saying he hated his friend or wanted to hurt him or anything like that. But ... '

I don't know why, but I was annoyed. I snapped, 'But *what*? You said "But ... " '

'Somehow it was worse,' Tom answered.

'Worse? Worse than hating his friend?'

'I know ... It was a cruel accident – no one's fault, I'm not saying otherwise. Yet, you see: it was as if the first boy accepted the cruelty and wasn't going to do anything about it except make sure it happened to *someone else*.'

He still wasn't certain he'd got his point across. For a moment it seemed Hetty understood because she said in a voice tinged with revulsion, 'That's a horrible.' But then she spoiled the effect by going on, 'I don't see how you could have seen what you say you saw. I'm sure you don't know what was going through the boy's mind. It was probably one of them yelling that made you look up, and by that time everything was over.'

'I think we should go to the funeral,' Maisie suggested in order to bring the matter to a close.

CHAPTER TWELVE

The gendarmerie was in the Promenade des Russes, overlooking the public beach. The police hauled in Dr Maillot to explain his patient's death, though he said the girl wasn't his patient and he'd no idea she'd been pregnant. That morning over breakfast at the Hôtel de la Gare he asked me to accompany him.

'Not into the station, Patrick, but ... '

If he didn't emerge after two hours I was to contact Maître Viremont, his lawyer.

I took coffee and brandy. I watched two trucks loading labour for some project of Vichy – there were rumours of remote camps somewhere in the hills. After an hour or so, the old man shambled out of the gendarmerie blinking in the sun and wiping sweat from his face. He saw me, raised a tired hand and fixed a smile where I'd seen fear.

'Patrick – Patrick! What horror! These poor girls one tries to help. They bring nothing but troubles!'

'Are you in the clear?' I asked.

He shrugged. 'Who knows? The mother – the *sale putain* who gave me the money (only for expenses, you follow) – denies all knowledge, but the police may persuade her to remember. 'Still, who cares? Today I am free! Tomorrow the mother may die or I may die or God will raise the girl from the dead and she will give birth. Buy me a cognac, Patrick. Let us celebrate.'

I bought the brandy. Maillot threw it back and ordered another. He was merry but also ashamed. He wasn't without moral feeling. Indeed his morals were as acute as his selfish passions.

'I am right, aren't I, to help the girls?' he asked.

'I can't say. I'm a Catholic, even if a bad one.'

'And I am a rationalist and an atheist.' He rubbed the stubble on his chin. 'Still,' he said, 'one should not allow atheism to interfere with loving God.'

'You love God?'

'Naturally. Atheism is a belief of the intellect, but the love of God is a feeling of the heart. There is no logical inconsistency because the two debates are in different terms, with different tests of truth. And in any case what does consistency matter? Any fool may be consistent in his folly.'

'I don't think that can be right.'

'No? Well God can sort it out – or not, since He doesn't exist. Tell me, Patrick,' the old fellow said warmly, placing his hand on my shoulder, 'would you forgive me if I did something terrible? Out of sin, you understand, not malice?'

'It depends. What do you have in mind? Are you drunk?'

'That is possible. I don't know what I have in mind. I am old, Patrick, *voyez*? Old! I cannot go to prison because of my kindness to the girls – not even on a point of principle. I despise martyrs. One should live!'

I nodded but didn't want him to go on. I'd decided Maillot was drunk and wavering, as drunks do, between profound truth and simple silliness, and I was in no mood to sort the two. Also I'd noticed Alvírez sitting a couple of tables away and he'd noticed us.

That night at the casino, Alvírez had a farouche air, but I didn't know the reason. Now I saw it was part of his normal character. He was reading the newspaper angrily, somehow defying it. When he turned the pages, wafts of patchouli and bay rum blew off him.

At a break in the conversation, the Spaniard folded his newspaper and barked across the intervening tables, 'I know you! You were at the casino, the night I dropped a bundle! You're one of the American kids – hah!'

'I'm an Irish kid,' I said and threw in a 'begorrah' for no reason except to disconcert him, though he wasn't the disconcertable type.

He gave me a sly dog look. 'One of your crowd has been making pals with the Malipiero girl – huh!'

'Tom Rensselaer?'

Alvírez paused, a little astonished, then began dealing names: 'J. P. Rensselaer – Rensselaer Merchant Guaranty Bank – the Rensselaer Shipping Line. Your guy must be connected with that bunch – heh?'

'I've no idea,' I said and considered telling him to go to hell, which I fancied he was used to. Alvírez was a man who knew he was disliked, but didn't know why. The clue was in the small explosions of breath that ended his sentences. They weren't exactly laughter – too much like a snort – but they showed he thought himself a good fellow, and each time he waited warily for a reaction. I disliked him but – God help me – I was sorry for him because he wore the loneliness of his corruption.

'I think I'll join you,' he said. He pulled his chair to our table. Amused, Maillot offered his hand, 'Delighted, Monsieur … ?'
'Alvírez.'
'Doctor Adolphe Maillot.'
'Sure,' Alvírez agreed without interest.

From his turn of phrase, I understood Alvírez had spent time in America. I said, 'You speak English well.'

'What? Oh, yeah. I went to school in the States.' He named a college I'd never heard of, and, when I asked where it was, he ignored the question. I realised then that he was a small man with a small but focussed understanding of the world. He said, 'He must be rich, your friend, Tom – huh? And I hear there's a Ben Benedict with you. Benedict Oil – Theodore Benedict, the old pirate himself – who'd have believed it, heh?'

From his interest in money I thought Alvírez might know of Tom's fall from grace and say that the Rensselaers were all washed up, but it seemed he believed rich people formed a kind of freemasonry from which it was impossible to be ejected.

Just then I noticed a family going into the gendarmerie. I don't know why I should think it was that of the dead boy, but I did and mentioned the accident to Alvírez. He grunted as if it were the story of a dead cat. He asked, 'How come you know the Malipieros?'

'I don't know them,' I said. 'I've seen them, that's all.'
'And your friend, Tom Rensselaer?' He grinned cunningly.
'He's run across the daughter a couple of times. I wouldn't say he knows her.'
'You wouldn't?'
'No.'
'She's a good looking girl.'

'So I believe.'

'A guy could fall for her.'

'Possibly,' I said and asked, 'What's your interest in the Malipieros?'

'I'm a businessman.'

'What kind?'

'This and that. I made my pile in the war – the Spanish one. There's enough money to be made out of war. Plenty of buyers. Not so many sellers. Enough problems in the way to keep the chumps out of the game and allow good profits – hah!'

I remember the rumour that the absent Señor Malipiero was in the business of supplying the Germans with war materials. It made a connection with Alvírez comprehensible. Still I was surprised when he confided, 'The family used to own a department store.'

'Used to?'

'They sold out.'

'Why did they sell out?'

'Circumstances.'

I was going to say more but Dr Maillot wisely changed the subject because it was clear Alvírez, in what I think of as his search for friends, had decided he'd said too much. The old man asked, 'What is he like, Señor Malipiero?'

Alvírez shrugged. His notions of biography didn't extend much beyond money, but he offered, 'Art – he collected art, paintings. He has an eye for them; bought Russian when you could buy Russian for a few dollars – hah!'

'Kandinsky?'

'Kandinsky – Trotsky – Lenin – Russian anyway. He sold those, too. He "liquidated his assets", as we call it.'

'Why?' I asked.

'Why do you think?'

'I don't know.'

'Tough,' said Alvírez with another of his leering smiles, and I understood he was boasting. He was probably trying to boost his credit with me so I'd tell my rich American friends and prepare them for some crude financial proposition he intended to make.

Dr Maillot sniffed the air like a connoisseur of rottenness might. Alvírez picked up that we were laughing at him and said he had to leave. He forced his pasteboard on me, which bore an address in Madrid and the unrevealing title *Commercial Agent*.

He said, 'Rensselaer or the Benedict kid or their folks should give me a call. I know the ropes.' When we didn't rise to this, he snapped, 'I got to go. I'm not a New York swell with a place on Long Island and a crowd of swanky friends. I got to earn my bread.'

He was angry again and I watched him rise and wander off along the Promenade des Russes, dissatisfied and baffled at the fact that no one liked him. Dr Maillot said, 'He is an original, that one. What does he do? Black marketer? Currency speculator? He makes me feel virtuous.'

'You always feel virtuous,' I said.

'Even in my sins?'

'The virtue of recognising your need for forgiveness.'

'Ah, perhaps you are right, Patrick. The God of atheists is a subtle fellow – far more so than the vulgar ruffian worshipped by the religious. Still, *à propos* Monsieur Alvírez, he gives cause to think, no? If he does business with the Malipieros, it seems the feet of our Argentinian Virgin are as firmly planted in the mud as those of lesser mortals.'

'Assuming Alvírez was speaking the truth,' I said without quite knowing what I meant except that a bizarre, probably nonsensical idea had come to me.'

'You mean?'

I shook my head. The idea was too strange. I was thinking that maybe Alvírez himself was the Malipiero's alienated husband/ father/lover, and all the rest was an elaborate deceit. Who was to say he was Spanish, not Argentinian? I knew that sexual jealousy could be devious. Perhaps it suited Alvírez/Malipiero to cloud his wife's reputation as part of a vile power game?

No – there was no evidence of this. But what could anyone know, when no one had ever met Teresa Malipiero?

Now Tom was about to.

CHAPTER THIRTEEN

Katerina slipped a note under the door of La Chênaie inviting Tom to meet her mother, and Tom accepted. He didn't tell the rest of us.

Outwardly he carried on in the same easy style. I knew he was attracted to Katerina Malipiero, but so was Ben and so was I. She was innocent and lovely, and when I looked at her I felt a faint wonderment. Yet I've felt the same when looking at shop girls and typists as they rush through the rain to catch a bus, or bite a lip while looking in their purses, or perform any of a thousand other luminous actions of youth, and it means nothing. In any case Tom was to marry Hetty, and he talked about it as a thing he was set on.

But circumstances alter cases. The distant war rumbled on and a long hot summer of inaction was wearing down our spirits. Tom was changing and, as I came to realise, the changes terrified him.

In a letter he wrote me years afterwards he said that at this point – before the second fatality – he knew he was becoming infatuated with the girl and he hated himself for it. Yet he couldn't hold back. Without her he was starting to view his future as a kind of martyrdom to selling bonds or practising law; and whatever it was he was now experiencing seemed like his final chance at authentic feeling: one that would have to last him for a lifetime. You have to understand this.

I mention Tom's letter – and the package that came with it – because they gave me an insight into what happened next, though I don't swear they represent the truth.

I'm speaking now of a time after the War. For a while I quit writing novels and did a spell in Hollywood working on B movie scripts for Fox. Nothing much came of it and by nineteen fifty I was married and back in Ireland, doing books again and radio plays. I wasn't home long when the studio forwarded Tom's package unopened.

We hadn't spoken or corresponded much since France, but bits and pieces of news reached me, mostly from Ben because he knew Tom's family. It seemed that, after a spell in the Army, Tom stopped painting but turned down his uncle's offer of a job in the bill broking business. Instead he completed law school and got a position with a firm on Wall Street. Why he gave that up and took himself off to Albuquerque, I don't know, but he was living there when he wrote to me, alone and practising law.

I didn't like the letter. It was false – unbalanced. It sounded at one moment like a confession and at another like one of those letters that people who aren't used to writing take a stab at come Christmastime in order to tell the folks at home that all is well. It was cheerful in some parts and sad in others. It reminded me of laughter through tears, the sentimentality of drunks, a song crooned to an empty nightclub and all the other hints of life's indefinable madness.

My wife said, 'Poor Tom – he's finished, isn't he?'

I said, 'I don't know why you think that. He says he's making good at law in a small way.'

'Helping Negroes and Mexicans?'

'Why not? He always was a liberal at heart. So now he's found a purpose he thinks is worthwhile.'

'A purpose like those crazy people have, who do good to others because they're no good to themselves.'

We were going through a patch of having no money, reduced

to eating potatoes and watching the bills, which explains why we were snappy.

I asked, 'Why are you so hard on Tom? What am I doing except working to make ends meet and writing books no one reads?'

'There are purposes and purposes.'

'Right! And isn't Tom's purpose – helping blacks and immigrants – a higher one than mine?'

My wife shook her head and said with quiet obstinacy, 'Don't knock feeding your family and just getting on with life. It's tough and ought to be enough. And, if you do it right, everyone benefits. Don't be fooled: Tom isn't a saint. He's a sick man playing at being a doctor.'

As usual she'd gone to the heart of the matter. Whatever Tom was doing in his law practice, it didn't seem important to him. Instead, most of his letter looked back to our fatal summer, because it was the foundation of his existence. That was why the tone was uneven. On the one hand he was trying to be optimistic about the present, while on the other he was full of bitter reflection – though, being Tom, he tried to disguise his bitterness by pretending he was better and wiser for the experience. As if any of us were.

I imagined Tom crying in self-pity as he wrote. God knows, Lucky Tom Rensselaer had reason to.

Then there was the package.

My wife asked, 'What's in it?'

I opened it and found a movie script. I remembered Tom saying he wanted to break into the business. Dr Maillot and I had talked about it, and the old man had remarked acutely that Tom was trying to transfer the static vision of his paintings into drama. Now here was the result.

I couldn't complain at the care he'd taken – he was always meticulous – but he didn't know what he was doing. The director, the camera and the lighting men wouldn't appreciate the shooting instructions burdened with detail about the sets, costumes, camera angles and lights: all of it old-fashioned and overblown in the way that stuff done by amateurs often is. But for me the whole thing was painfully vivid.

The title was *The Veiled Woman* and it was *film noir*, a genre I'd tried my hand at and failed. Tom couldn't handle it, even at the basic level. The writing was beautiful in an agonised, lyrical way, but it had gone out of style. Tom had been right when he said he was the last of his class and generation. Whatever it was that shone in him was bright precisely because his kind was passing into shadows.

I studied a few pages and murmured, 'Poor devil.' I read further and asked myself, 'Is that how he really saw the thing?'

What he'd written was the story of our summer at S. Symphorien, transposed into a cheap murder mystery. It was no wonder he couldn't get it to work. In his letter he said, 'I want to write cynical trash for money. It's the way the world is going and I want to be in on the racket.'

But the joke was he'd written a crippled thing of passion and haunting loveliness that was of no use for anything.

In nineteen fifty we were living in Dublin, in ground floor rooms of one of the old houses in Amiens Street – Georgian before it became fashionable again. There, within sound of the trains going in and out of Connolly station, my wife pounded washing in a galvanised tub in the yard and I wrote winter and summer with the window open to clear my head and the black smuts blowing in.

Oh, there was romance enough to be had for a pair of fond fools – and dancing too – my wife in Wellington boots and me in my carpet slippers, with the scent of *Sweet Afton* on the breeze and Mantovani on the wireless set. Style is a subtle thing, but there if you have an eye for it.

'Don't stay up too late, reading that stuff,' my wife said, meaning Tom's script.

'I won't,' I said.

She asked, 'Will you write to him?'
'I'll have to.'
'Give him my love. What'll you say?'
'That I've sent his script to the studio.'
'Will you do that?'
'No, of course not.'
'No, I don't think you should.'
'That's settled then.'
'Yes, it is.'

Then she gave me a slow kiss as she did whenever we met or parted – as if life were precarious, love a matter of chance, and any separation in danger of being final. Tonight the kiss was longer and slower because she knew what was going through my mind.

'*Te amo, querido,*' she whispered.

Lately my wife had begun to tease me in Spanish.

CHAPTER FOURTEEN

Tom said we had to go to the dead boy's funeral despite Maisie's second thoughts.

He told her, 'It'll be expected. This is a small town and folks notice these things, and, after all, they've been kind to us. Also we were there when it happened – we're involved.'

We discussed what to wear. Compared with the French, we had good wardrobes and it'd be so easy to get things wrong. When it came to flowers Tom said, 'We shouldn't send any. We need to be there, but we mustn't put ourselves forward. Flowers would look insincere.'

In the event Hetty cried off. She said she was unwell; she'd stay at the house and read a book or maybe sleep. And the fact is she did look miserable.

The cemetery was in an out of the way corner up a dusty lane. The graves mostly bore simple crosses of rusting iron. I was used to the damp, green burying grounds of Ireland and, to my eyes, this stony field was stark with rocks like exposed bones and the sun was unforgiving.

They carried the corpse in a deal coffin on a long, flat handbarrow. Seeing the boy's male relatives and the undertaker's men jolt it over the ruts of the lane I was reminded of a crew manoeuvring an artillery piece. There was something defeated about the cortège, an air of poverty and meanness.

Dr Maillot joined us at the rear behind the family. He said, 'He was a bad boy, that one. His people have something of the *gitane* in the blood, something of the brute. Still, it is a *triste* affair.'

'And your own affair?' I asked.

'*Ça marche.*' He indicated behind us. 'You see that our *Vierge de l'Argentine* has come with her mother? I ask myself: why?'

We'd thought ourselves the last with the stray dogs and the town vagabonds, but back along the road a pair of black figures was walking slowly. 'Even now they attract attention,' said Maillot. 'Like Monsieur Rensselaer, they cannot help it.'

'Tom attracts attention?'

'Everyone knows he is rich. He has the manners of a king.'

'He's hardly got a penny. It's Monsieur Benedict who has the money.'

'Monsieur Benedict? But he seems so – ordinary.'

I glanced at the others, who were slightly ahead. Ben was solemn and uncomfortable and Maisie looked morose and hung over. She was exchanging words with Tom. I knew Maisie when she was in this sour mood and most people wouldn't give her the time of day – except that Tom always had time for everyone, and I guess that's what Maillot meant by the manners of a king.

The town *pompiers* turned out in uniform and brass helmets and flanked the grave. The mourners stood about any old how and a drab priest read through the service. Maillot took sips from a flask of spirits, the gravedigger hawked and spat, and a thrush sang from one of the cypresses. For me it was a shabby business, but people come away with different things from funerals, and some among the crowd were sobbing.

We hung on the outskirts of the mourners and the Malipieros stood a way off by the cemetery wall. The service dragged on a while and I wasn't surprised when Tom expressed concern that the girl and her mother were left out of things.

'You've met the mother, haven't you?' I said.

Tom had told us that Katerina had invited him, but it was just a piece of neighbourliness.

What had they talked about?

'Oh just small talk, the stuff you forget the second it's out of your mouth. Teresa was interested in my future and I mentioned that fool idea of getting into the movies as a scriptwriter. She agreed with Ben that it was a Jewish business, though I don't see that extends to script writing.'

That was all he told me. He went over to speak to the women. Meantime Ben complained of the dust and the heat and sloped off with Dr Maillot to the shelter of one of the monuments. I was left to kick my heels with Maisie, who still looked sour.

'I hope Ben doesn't get drunk,' she growled.

'I thought he didn't drink,' I said.

'He doesn't as a rule,' Maisie answered quickly. 'But he hates funerals. Your friend Dr Maillot is a creep. I wish I'd stayed behind with Hetty.'

'You're not feeling too good?'

'There goes Tom, after the waifs and strays, always the Good Samaritan. No, I feel like hell. What d'you think he's up to? Is there anything between him and the Malipiero girl?'

'I don't think so. He hardly knows her.'

'Tom doesn't care for the girls he knows. Of course,' Maisie added, 'he may have changed. After all, he's going to marry Hetty.'

'You sound doubtful.'

'Do I? I don't mean to. Tom is too decent to let Hetty down. No, there's absolutely no way that could happen. I was just meaning that girls lose their magic. That's what Tom wants, magic in a girl. It's too absurd. Did I ever tell you we had a fling?'

I was curious. I didn't know girls who had 'flings'.

'It was when I first arrived in Paris. I was feeling low after coming from Switzerland – I'd had some problems and given my chaperone, my Aunt Victoria, the slip. I was staying at the George Cinq and dining on my own and Tom was dancing – simply the most gorgeous man I ever saw. He knew – he has an instinct – that I was alone and in a mess, and he came over and one thing led to another. For a while.'

'You were magical?'

'Don't be ridiculous,' she said. Then she gave a sharp laugh. 'Oh, I suppose so – I mean, God knows I tried to be. It's very wearing.' She eyed me slyly. 'The problem with magic is it lies in qualities you don't know you have – if it exists at all, which I doubt. And what sensible woman wants to be magical all the time? It'd be like never being able to take your girdle off. I mean it's a pose – that's all it can be, isn't it? '

'And Ben?'

'Oh, Ben,' she drawled. 'He's so solid, good-natured, dependable. I can't tell you how much fun we've had together! Really, in any company except Tom's he'd shine. We have our problems, but … well, people have their problems, don't they? We'll work them out or … why, I'll become a dashing divorcée! Don't give me that Irish Catholic look.'

She was trying to be droll, and so I laughed and kissed her on the cheek. Yet I was sad, though I wasn't sure whether it was on Maisie's account or for Hetty who had nothing to rely on except her own bravery and Tom's commitment. And how strong was that? Masie's comments contained an element of malice – if only the kind we all have towards our friends – but she was no fool and I began to look at Tom differently.

For the moment he was still talking to the Malipieros. Both the women were wearing black and both were veiled, and it was a mistake that was bound to attract attention.

Maisie sniffed. 'Those dresses are Chanel. Who do they think they're impressing?'

I didn't think they were out to impress anyone. I suspected the dresses, like the renting of a house as prominent as La Pinède, were part of a series of subtle misjudgments. I said so and Maisie threw me a look that said I knew nothing about women, then changed the subject.

'I'd have married Tom if he'd asked,' she said. 'Everyone loves him, even Ben. But no one understands him – least of all Tom himself, I suspect. What a waste of a good man, to spend his life chasing dreams. D'you think we're coming to the end? I hope so, I need a drink.'

The knot of mourners was breaking up. Ben and Dr Maillot reappeared. The doctor steadied himself by grabbing my shoulder. His eyes were dazed and weepy. He pointed out Tom and the Malipieros.

The old man said, 'They make a pair, Monsieur Rensselaer and the girl, *n'est-ce pas?* One sees these things, even with strangers.'

I knew what he meant. Katerina had lifted her veil, the better to speak to Tom. And both their faces shone.

After the funeral we returned to La Chênaie. Hetty was in bed and we had to rouse her. She wasn't running a fever but she looked terrible, and burst into tears for no reason. Tom hugged her like she was a child and she agreed there was nothing really wrong with her.

The sun was at its height, the heat smashing down and the day dying of drought. There was no talk of going to the beach. Instead we sat inside with windows open and the air turgid and stiff as syrup. Tom started on a story about playing cards with blacks and Italians in smoky rooms above grocery stores. This was in the days after the Crash took his family's fortune with it. No one took up his offer of a game, but he opened the cards anyway and began to shuffle and fan them while Hetty groaned in the next room and the radio played.

There was news on the BBC and that led to talk of whether America would enter the war and who would come in with her. Argentina, maybe? Ben said there were reasons – trade and politics – why she might. And now I remember, she did in the end. We exchanged our knowledge of Argentina, which amounted to nothing very much, and arrived inevitably at the subject of the Virgin. Maisie repeated her comment about the dress.

'You know her best,' she said to Tom. 'What's she like?'

Tom hesitated. 'That's a hard one. I've spoken to her … what? … three times? She reminds me of those girls one meets for the first time at a tennis party, a girl who hasn't "come out" and can only remember her mother has told her not to be too forward. Or perhaps I mean a governess in an English novel, who isn't allowed to speak. There are hints of a passionate inner life. Yet is it real?'

'You sound soft on her.'

'I should hope not! No. But I do admit I'm intrigued. Who wouldn't be?'

'Passionate, huh?' Ben said. '*Her lips burn with chilies and she smokes a cigar …* ' He winked at Maisie.

'So you said before.'

'*Her breath is my narcotic.*
Her scent is of cloves,
Of night fevers and spent seed.
What man could resist the Argentinian Virgin – huh, buddy boy?
What woman could bear her horror?'

Tom sighed. 'OK, maybe you have a point, though I wouldn't put it your way.'

'And the mother?' Maisie asked.

'Oh, she's ... a mother, I guess. She isn't The Spider Woman.'

With that Tom riffled the cards half a dozen ways. He smiled and changed the subject to talk about Hetty and the things he'd like to do for her, once they were married. She must have heard him because she came creeping out of the bedroom and nestled at his feet where he could stroke her hair. We talked and drank and stayed like this until dark. Tom laid out a set of card tricks.

In the Villa la Pinède two women worked furiously by candlelight since the electricity had failed. They set the fallen furniture upright and swept the broken glass. They went to and from the kitchen to bring pails of water and mopped the floor furiously. They took the candles and on their knees examined each tile and the spaces between tiles, looking for the least trace of blood.

Only when, at the close of evening, the cicadas ceased their racket did they look at each other and realise in the sudden silence that neither had spoken for an hour.

Then, with horror around them and inside them, they began to cry.

CHAPTER FIFTEEN

I left the others and returned to my cottage. I poured a nightcap, fooled a while with my manuscript, and went to bed. In the morning I was still in no mood to write; so I strolled to La Chênaie where Ben and Maisie were eating breakfast in the garden and Tom and Hetty were asleep.

Ben said, 'Now here's a story for you, Pat. You can make of it what you want.' He glanced at Maisie as if it was something they'd rehearsed.

'Tell me.'

'Okay. Get ready for it. Katerina Malipiero came here last

night after you'd gone. The Virgin herself! How d'you like that?'

'She came for Tom?'

'Who else?'

'What did she want?'

Ben shrugged. 'They spoke out here in the garden; then Tom went with her. I waited for him until – two, three o'clock was it, honey? Finally I fell asleep.'

'Were you drinking?' Maisie asked.

'As if I would!' Ben grinned and kissed her.

'So you don't know what it was about?' I said.

Maisie said with a certain satisfaction, 'I can tell you she looked terrible. She'd been crying, there's no mistake about that.'

I poured some coffee. I decided to wait for Tom to explain. For the moment I said something about what were we going to do today. But without Tom we had no ideas.

He came out about a quarter of an hour later. He was wearing an English outfit: soft shirt and cravat, drill trousers and brogues. A good tweed jacket hung on one shoulder. I'd expected him to look seedy because, except for Ben, we'd put away a load the night before; but he was fresh and glowing and we looked stale and used in contrast. He beamed at us and kissed Maisie on her pale cheek. He took a seat and began to attack the rolls and *confiture*.

I asked, 'How's Hetty?'

'Fine,' he said. 'A little tired, but fine. I think she's had too much sun.'

'And you?'

'Fine. Say, Ben, do you mind if I borrow the car for the day?'

'That's a little tough. I told you I planned on going to Marseilles. There's a meeting of my committee and a chance to stock up from the black market. In any case, why do you need it? Where are we going?'

'Nowhere. I thought I'd take Katerina and her mother for a

spin. They've been cooped up in that house for too long. They need a change of scene.'

'And the rest of us?' Maisie asked.

'Oh, you don't need me, do you?'

I saw then that Ben was angry. He didn't care about the car or object to doing the Malipieros a favour. What got to him was the sense we were being excluded from something – not the trip, about which he didn't give a damn, but whatever was causing Tom to shine this morning.

Ben said, 'Take the damned car. I'll take the train. By the way, what was that business with the girl last night.'

Tom said, 'Katerina? Oh, it was nothing. Her mother had eaten something that disagreed with her, but all she needed was some seltzer and a rest.'

'She was upset about that?'

'Her mother is all she has.' Tom wiped his lips with his napkin. 'They're lonely, Ben. You can understand that, can't you?'

Hetty came out of the house. Tom got up and hugged her and helped her to a chair. That sort of small, tender gesture came to him naturally, and you could feel guilty just watching it, wondering if there was something missing inside you. Hetty was wearing a white terry robe, her skin was waxy, her hair lank and uncombed. I was shocked because she reminded me of the women at home, tired of child bearing and husbands who stink of drink and ignorance. We asked how she was and she said she wouldn't die.

'Tom's going to borrow the car and take the Malipieros for a spin,' Maisie said.

'Is that so?' Hetty murmured. She fumbled the pack of cigarettes that lay on the table, but didn't take one.

Maisie raised an eyebrow. She said, 'The car will take a fourth.'

'Then go, if you like,' Hetty said. She turned her lacklustre eyes on Tom and asked, 'If you get to town, Tommy, can you check the pharmacy? I'd like something … a tonic, I guess. I'm feeling very low. Can you think of any reason I should be this way, Tommy?'

'None at all,' said Tom, 'You're my best girl, aren't you?'

And so she was. But was it enough?

I found myself asking what had happened the night before when Katerina had come for Tom.

The Argentinian Virgin came in the night, and Tom followed her without hesitation. Together they climbed the hill to La Pinède with the sky black above them and the stars glittering.

The girl was frail, cold and terrified. She urged Tom that he *must* come, but she gave no reasons. Yet the night was warm and fragrant with resin and marjoram, so that Tom, caught on the point of going to bed, felt he was dreaming. Except that *this* dream was concrete. *This* was the dream when all that is best in us seems somehow possible, and love and excitement and the stuff for which we have feelings but no words can be found, and the senses are sharp, and the heart is full.

Or so the rest of us have to suppose, as we look on from our failed, muddy lives, heartsick that some, like Tom, can live so vividly and with a sincerity so ardent it seems almost a parody of itself.

Unprompted Katerina placed her hand in Tom's, knowing there was comfort there. Maisie had known this moment too, because she'd sat in loneliness at a table in the George Cinq, watching Tom and longing for him to dance with her. Hetty knew it because she'd been booed off the stage of cheesy nightclubs and abused by artists until the day he spoke, saying nothing in particular but everything that was necessary. God alone knew how many other girls there were: at society balls and weekend parties; pale girls and dark girls, and girls with red hair and pert noses; girls who seemed to have everything yet needed Tom's steady confidence. And in return he asked only that they should be magical.

I have only Tom's film script to tell me what happened next – the script with its flat dialogue and painterly sets and lighting. Was it as Tom describes it? Was it all so ... fantastic?

Moonlight filled the room and Teresa Malipiero sat composed and calm in her fading beauty. She rose from her chair. She extended a hand.

She said, 'I can't tell you how glad I am you've come, Tom. But I knew I could rely on you. I knew you would be our friend.'

Her voice with its hint of indefinable accent was careful as if she'd been often hurt and would allow her feelings to show only once she understood her situation. A glass of wine stood on a small table. She offered it.

'I'm sorry to call on you so late. We have had ... a crisis.'

'A crisis?' Tom asked.

'A disaster.'

'I see ... ' Tom took the glass. He caught the odour of ammonia from the new washed floor. 'I mean, I understand you want my help. Well, that's all right.' He stared at the woman with his frank eyes. 'So?'

'Please ... come with me,' said Teresa Malipiero.

I was never inside the Villa La Pinède and Tom never truly described it. For him it wasn't a simple house where the stuff of ordinary life goes on: rather a theatre of dreams or nightmares, where disasters begin and people are murdered.

I think of it as from another age. The rooms have names like "drawing room" and "boudoir" that no one uses any more, and, though we think we know what goes on there, really we don't

Tom was drawn by the Malipiero women into a dark room with heavy drapes and arsenic green wallpaper. There, on a chaise longue with its head resting on a newspaper, was a corpse.

Tom hadn't expected it.

He followed Teresa's candle. She held it over the dead man's mouth and the flame didn't flicker.

'I know him,' Tom said. 'His name's Alvírez. We met ... d'you mind if I smoke? Like I say, we met one night at the Czar Aléxandre. I didn't like him. He wasn't the sort of person people like.'

He lit a cigarette and put the lighter flame where he could examine Alvírez more closely.

Teresa said, 'We didn't kill him, Tom. I'm speaking the truth.'

Tom studied her a moment. He said, 'No ... I'm sure you're right.'

'We found him here when we returned from the boy's funeral.'

'Here? Like this?'

'In the next room.'

'And you moved him? But of course you did. How did he die?'

Teresa raised and turned the head. Dried blood circled a depressed fracture. She said, 'Someone hit him with an oil lamp.' She let the head fall.

They returned to Katerina and each took a chair. It registered with Tom that Alvírez was really dead – murdered it seemed. He accepted without question that neither Katerina nor her mother had killed the Spaniard.

'Who was he?' he asked. "A friend?'

'No, a business acquaintance of my husband.'

'What sort of business?'

'I don't know the details.'

'Where is your husband?'

'In Germany.'

'When do you expect to see him?'

'I don't know. He should be here already, but Señor Alvírez came with a message that he was delayed.'

Tom detected that he was interrogating a woman he hardly knew. He felt a flicker of the shameful pleasure men feel when they bully women, and knew it for what it was.

'I'm sorry,' he said. 'I'm trying to figure who Alvírez was; what he wanted; who else might have been here.'

'I can't help. He wasn't expected. No one was expected. The house was empty.'

'Locked?'

'Do you lock your cottage?'

'No.'

Tom looked around.

'We cleaned,' said Teresa.

'There was a lot of ... mess?'

A nod.

'Blood?'

'Some.'

'You realise you've got rid of the evidence – the evidence that might point at someone else? Except the body, of course.'

'Yes. Katerina, will you make some tea? Tom, you'll have tea – we have only *tilleul* – or perhaps a cognac?'

'Tea.'

Katerina rose and left the room. Teresa lit a cigarette. She offered one to Tom.

'I understand if you have some difficult questions,' she said.

'You haven't asked if I believe you.'

She shrugged. 'I can't control your belief, Tom, only ask for your trust.'

'I'm puzzled by the timing. You were at the funeral – yet Alvírez came here.'

'There is no telephone. Señor Alvírez was staying nearby. If he wished to see me, he had only to come here.'

'What would he want to see you about?'

'My husband, I suppose. Perhaps he had news?'

'But you don't know?'

'No.'

'Can you guess?'

'No – I can only think his reasons were perfectly innocent.'

'And yet he's dead,' said Tom.

A candle guttered and went out. Teresa made no effort to

replace it and the room went dark. It was late and Tom found himself tired. He wondered what mystery was holding him here. Was it the killing of Alvírez or the beauty of the women? Both were unfathomable.

Katerina brought the tea. She lit another candle.

Tom asked, 'So, do you have any idea who killed him?'

'A burglar, I imagine,' said Teresa.

'Is that speculation, or d'you have evidence?'

'A diamond necklace has been stolen.'

'Show me.'

Teresa nodded. While Katerina poured the tea she left the room and returned with a lacquer box. She opened it to show a black velvet lining speckled with lint. The jeweller's label said it came from Amsterdam.

Katerina hadn't spoken much. Now she said, 'You're tired, Tom. Mother, he's tired.'

Her concern touched Tom. He wanted to do something for her, it really didn't matter what. He said, 'D'you know something? I'd like to paint your portrait.'

"You paint?'

'A little.'

"Really?'

She was so surprised, Tom wasn't sure how she'd take it: maybe think he was the sort who always claimed to be able to do things, the way men did.

'But that's wonderful!' she said.

Tom was moved by the way Katerina said 'Wonderful!' with her voice rising in joy and her whatever-it-was accent from a country he'd never been to. Stupid. Really it was stupid to be so taken by a voice.

He asked Teresa, 'It's valuable – the necklace?'

'About fifty thousand American dollars, I'm told,' said Teresa.

'Insured?'

'No,'

'Then you'll want it back.'

She shook her head. 'I'm realistic, Tom. The thief will never be discovered, or the police will steal it or … who knows what will happen in a war? It doesn't matter, because I can't allow it to matter. Am I becoming philosophical?'

'I understand.'

'This is a terrible day and all I want to do is sleep.'

'You should have called me earlier.'

'We were frightened. We are strangers and there is no one to defend us.'

'You must know you can't go to the police,' Tom told her. 'Alvírez died when? At noon or earlier, before you got back from the funeral. It's now well past midnight, the room has been cleaned and Alvírez has been laid out next door. How could you explain all that not to me but to them?'

'I couldn't.' said Teresa.

'No,' Tom agreed. He waited for her to ask something – to reveal herself. Instead she looked away as if he'd disappointed her; but she was a woman who expected men to disappoint because that's how men were.

He placed his hand on hers and said in his confident way, 'Of course I'll help you.'

CHAPTER SIXTEEN

He arrived from the town side. Teresa met him by the gate. She wore pale green *matelot* slacks and an ivory blouse. Her hair was gathered in a turban.

He asked, 'How's Katerina?'

'She slept well. Tom, she isn't coming with us. I can't ask it of her. It's too horrible.'

Tom nodded. Of course.

They walked through the garden. The air was soft and out of mood and it came to him that Life really *was* the thing, and, despite the murder, he felt full of callous joy and mildly crazed with adventure.

As he was about to step into the house, Teresa stopped him.

She said, 'I've asked Katerina to stay in her room. The body has begun to smell – the heat I suppose. Oh, Tom, I hadn't expected that! Not so quickly!'

Tom tried not to care that she was upset. He'd armoured himself against what they had to do, and she needed his composure. But it was hard. He murmured something, a few words of encouragement, and she said thanks. Then their eyes met and at that moment she saw into him: saw his compassion, his terrifying desire to do the right thing. The shock made her stumble and he held her. Both stiffened at the contact, but neither drew back. They embraced, but he didn't kiss her and she didn't ask him to.

Alvírez lay in the shuttered room with its foul green wallpaper. His corpse was bloated and sighed with escaping gas. Tom gagged on the stench. He raised the torso and found it heavy and uneasily comic as if the Spaniard were a slapstick artist, a gross vaudeville type whose job was to be humiliated.

'I don't know how we'll move him,' he said. He felt like striking Alvírez's face and telling him to wake up.

'We must try,' said Teresa.

'Yes. You take the legs and I'll take the top half and … we'll see how we get on, I guess.'

They heaved and a fly rose from the body and buzzed at the shutter. Tom smiled to encourage Teresa and they heaved again.

No, Tom thought, not so horrible after all. He didn't have to think about Alvírez as a person. After all, he didn't like him or know much about him. No, it wasn't so bad, and Teresa Malipiero was a practical woman as well as lovely. They could do this.

So they got out of one room and into the next. There, to take a breath, they set the corpse in a chair.

'I couldn't manage without your help,' Teresa said. She managed a grim smile. In a touch of vanity she brushed aside a hair that had escaped her turban. 'Again?'

At the french window they had a problem. They had to balance the dead man so Tom could free a hand to work the lock. Teresa giggled. Just nerves, but it made Tom realise there was little that couldn't be faced with the support of another. A substantial part of murder's horror must be its loneliness. Not that he thought Teresa was a murderess.

They stopped again in the garden. Tom glanced at the sun and thought of southern mornings: how they fooled him in their cool, clear beginnings. Plans made in their optimism were so often defeated by the brutal heat of noon.

'Once more!' he said.

This time they succeeded in dumping the corpse in the trunk of the car, where its limpness was an asset in fitting the space.

Teresa looked at her hands. She said, 'I must wash.'

Tom asked, 'D'you have any tools. I couldn't bring any from La Chênaie – it would have looked odd.'

'I don't know. I … '

'Oh, don't worry, an old place like this is bound to have some. You go wash while I look for them.' Tom chivvied her gently through the gate. He didn't want any time for second thoughts.

He found a spade in a disused laundry. When he returned to the car, Teresa was sitting in the passenger seat. She'd unfastened her turban and shaken out her black hair.

'You look nice,' he said.

'Thank you, Tom.'

'I was thinking that, once we've done … what we have to do, we should push on. Maybe go as far as Grasse, what do you think? We could get some lunch there and, who knows, maybe take a tour of one of the perfume factories? I'm guessing they still do tours with the war and all. Seriously, I know the idea sounds crazy, but the story is that we're spending the day having fun. What d'you say?'

'I … yes … that is a good idea.'

'It's just a pity Katerina can't come. She'd like it.'

'A pity,' Teresa agreed.

Tom drove them into the high oak woods. Teresa sat quietly beside him. The afflatus that had carried him through the morning wore off, but its passing didn't leave him with doubts about the woman or the body in the trunk. It simply didn't trouble him that Teresa Malipiero might have killed Alvírez. He was concerned only that she was desperately unhappy.

He pulled the car to the side where the trees thinned to a few hornbeams.

He said, 'I was looking for a loggers' road to take us off the highway, but it's too much to hope for, I guess.'

The highway followed the contours of a wooded ravine. It was noon but the day seemed timeless and silent.

Tom said, 'We're going to have to carry the body a way into the trees. I'd do it alone, but I don't think I can.' He glanced at Teresa. 'What d'you say? Are you up to it?'

Alvírez had filled up again with gas and let out a hideous belch. Tom was angry with him for his vulgar life and shabby death. He hated him for dragging his soiled carcass through the lives of the Malipiero women.

Teresa stared at the body. She said, 'I don't know how much more I can do.'

'You're doing fine,' Tom said and meant it. He didn't think most women could manage half so well. He didn't consider his own part.

He heaved Alvírez onto his shoulder. Teresa held the dead man's head so the juices wouldn't spill. They manoeuvred through the brush a couple of hundred yards until they were out of sight of the road.

'This is as good a place as any,' Tom said. He dropped the body in a spot that was more or less clear. He asked Teresa to fetch the spade. He didn't want to leave her with Alvírez.

Tom hadn't considered the ground. Thin soil covered roots and bedrock: too shallow and hard to dig much of a grave.

'What will you do?' Teresa asked.

'Cover him with rocks and a little dirt. We don't have a lot of choices.'

'He'll be found.'

'I don't think so. These hills are pretty empty.'

'People will search for him.'

'Let them. They'll grow old trying.' He grinned. But she was right, of course. He said, 'I have something to do – and it's best done alone.'

'What is it? I don't mind, Tom. If you can face it, so can I.'

'It really doesn't take two. Why don't you go for a walk or back to the car, if you prefer?'

'How long will you be?'

'A quarter of an hour, maybe.' He added, 'I really would rather do this on my own,' making it sound like one of those slightly embarrassing things like shaving, that fellows did.

Once Teresa was gone, Tom stripped the body. He collected rocks and built a long low cairn over the remains and covered it with soil. He used the edge of the spade to hack pieces of scrub and scattered them over his handiwork.

When he was finished it looked like a place where a body was buried.

It looked like a place where a body was buried, but the passage of a year would cover it in leaf fall and seedlings, and maybe that would be enough. It came to Tom that successful murder depended as much on probabilities as certainties. People could suspect what they liked, but the chances were Alvírez's grave would never be discovered – or, if it was, that nothing could be proven.

Teresa came running through the trees.

She said, 'There's someone else here. I've heard noises!'

At first all Tom could think was how lithe she was – how lovely. He held her and said, 'Quiet now. Most likely it's squirrels,' he told her. 'They make a racket when they're scratching after acorns. Yes, most likely squirrels.'

'You've taken off his clothes!' She was aghast, no longer bothered by noises or squirrels.

'We don't want him identified,' Tom said. He watched the flicker of horror vanish and went on, 'By the way, he seems to be carrying some sort of packet. Didn't you search him?'

'No!'

'Well, we'd better check. It occurs to me Alvírez might have taken the diamonds. No? Let's see.' He pulled a thick manila envelope from the jacket pocket and patted down the rest of the clothes. 'No diamonds. I guess it was unlikely he'd have them, not if the burglar theory is true. Any ideas about the papers?'

'Give them to me!' Teresa demanded. Her hand darted to grab them, but Tom instinctively recoiled. For a second she was angry – terrified. Then, catching herself, she apologised. 'I'm sorry, Tom. I'm acting as if I don't trust you.'

'That's all right.' Tom said. He weighed the papers in his hands. He held them out. 'You want them?'

'Please. They may concern my husband.'

'That worries you?'

'Everything worries me – as long as this war continues.'

'I understand,' Tom said, though, if he'd thought about it, he'd have realised he understood nothing beyond a vague sympathy. As if to make the point, Teresa's expression became remote and unfocussed.

'I have to trust you and it's hard. Only believe that – whatever I do – it's for Katerina's sake.'

'Take the papers,' Tom offered. He picked up her hand and folded her fingers round the envelope. 'I don't need them and they're none of my business. I guess you have as much right to them as anyone. The only thing I'd say is you should be careful with them – in fact destroy them unless it turns out they're valuable. You do understand? Somebody – the police most likely – will come to speak to you about Alvírez.'

'Do you think so?'

'I don't see how it can be otherwise. He's bound to be missed.'

'But … '

Tom raised a finger to her lips and smiled. He said, 'It's problem for another day and I'll figure out something.'

They returned to the car. Tom threw the clothes into the trunk. As agreed, they drove on to Grasse and saw no one on the road except a gendarme on a bicycle.

Teresa said, 'He must have noticed the car when we were parked.'

She glanced at Tom. His calmness left her so she no longer knew how she was supposed to feel about things.

'So he must,' Tom agreed. He checked the mirror and said, 'Did you notice he waved to us? I've spoken to him now and again in town. I don't suppose he'll remember us.'

But Tom knew he would.

CHAPTER SEVENTEEN

At a village near Grasse they sat on a terrace. Below them fell slopes of lavender, and swallows circled in a vivid sky. Tom wore his fine English clothes and Teresa her fine French ones. And the waiter thought they were in love because money and good taste have that effect. They suggest the world is nothing less than perfect.

Tom said, 'Don't you think it's time to tell me something about yourself? As I recall, when we first met, you pumped me for my history. Now it's your turn.'

'What do you want to know?' Teresa asked.

'Tell me about Argentina.'

'About what? The pampas? Rainy Patagonia? I've never been outside the cities. In fact most of my life has been spent in Europe.'

'Where? Here?'

'Germany.'

'Because of your husband's business?'

'Yes.'

'And Katerina?'

'She's never been to Argentina.'

'So … ' Tom was on the point of telling her the name of Katerina's *alter ego*, the Argentinian Virgin, but now it sounded like a joke dreamed up by college kids. Instead he said, 'I heard Señor Malipiero used to own a department store.'

'Who told you that?' Teresa asked sharply. She corrected herself. 'Forgive me, Tom, I'm still … '

'That's all right,' Tom said. 'I understand. I really do. Who told me? I think it was Pat, and he got it from Alvírez. So, is it true? You don't have to tell me.'

'It's true. It seems a long time ago. I don't like to talk about the past.'

'Now there we're different. I do. Sometimes I wonder if the past isn't all I care for. I have a theory … No, I won't tell it. That's how men become boring: explaining theories to women who don't want to hear them. My Uncle Jonathan has one about the Gold Standard. It's his party piece. He tells it at Thanksgiving and Christmas and, when I get married, he'll tell it at my wedding. D'you want to hear? I can't swear to get it right, but I can do the funny voice. What's this? You're laughing at me?'

She was laughing, and enjoying it. Tom saw then that, at other times and places, she was a woman at ease with herself: briskly and assuredly feminine. Her identity as the woman masked by a demi-veil had been forced on her.

And so it went on for a couple of hours, with the murder of Alvírez forgotten and the day slipping into its afternoon doze. They talked of painting, of poetry, of history and philosophy, of wine and cheese and French regional cookery, of fast motorcars and tastes in soft furnishings. In short they acted like people do who really don't mind what they talk about.

When strangers delight each other – as they sometimes do – they believe they're getting to understand each other. But, of course, it's no more than a subtle lie compounded out of the moment.

Still, it isn't surprising the waiter thought Tom and Teresa were lovers.

It was one of the nights we ate at the Czar Aléxandre. There was a celebration going on. The Germans had won a battle – I forget which – and the Nazi flags were out. The Vichy officials were treating Brenner and Kellerman and a band had been brought in to knock out some songs

Tom was gone all day and we were kicking our heels. Hetty had cleaned herself up after her crying fit but was flat and aimless.

I was stuck with my writing and Ben had taken himself off to Marseilles on committee business.

Ben's absence brought out something in Maisie. She collared me about their stay in Europe, asking: was it never going to end? She finished by calling him 'a spineless jerk' and appealed to me.

'Tell him, Pat! Tell him we've got our own lives to lead! He can't wait for Tom to decide. Tom's too tied up with his Argentinian floozy.'

I said I thought Ben was kept here by the American Joint Distribution Committee.

The next minute she was telling me how crazy she was about her husband. The way Maisie put it, it was Ben who needed to go home, and maybe that was so. But I'd noticed on a previous occasion that when he came round to agreeing and asked her to name a date, she became vague as if she wanted to but something held her back. Now it came to me that Maisie was still in thrall to Tom and that her 'fling' had been nothing of the sort. She'd come from Switzerland feeling sordid and wasted – the mad rich girl who wasn't to be trusted – and Tom had picked her up, made her come alive, and brought out a flicker of magic that was really there. Who, having once been magical, would give it up?

The Vichy officials had brought some girls, so with them and the band and the dancing the restaurant was gay except for our table. To lighten the atmosphere I pulled Hetty on to the floor, but it was a mistake. She laid her head on my shoulder and we didn't get far before she was sobbing, so there was nothing for it but to take her back to the table.

The question of Tom came up – where was he? And that led naturally to talk of the Malipieros.

Maisie said, 'You remember those dresses?'

I remembered. 'At the funeral? You said they were Chanel.'

'Uh huh. But have you noticed what the girl wears every day?'

'Not especially.'

'Cheap stuff you wouldn't be seen dead in.'

'I couldn't say.'

'I could. Now why d'you suppose that it?'

'The war?'

'You can still get decent outfits. The couturiers are still in business, and rationing is baloney if you have the cash.'

'What are you driving at?'

'Money!' Maisie said brutally. '*Money* – the Malipieros used to have it, but they don't any more. They're broke!'

What she said sounded reasonable, though not so terrible in my eyes. My Uncle Gerald was so insolvent, everyone thought he was a gentleman. But, for Maisie, to be broke was to suffer a moral affliction.

'That's what this business is about! They're after Tom's money – at least the mother is – I can't speak for the girl, who could be witless as far as I can tell.'

I reminded her that Tom didn't have any money. Maisie snorted.

'Open your eyes, Pat! *Look* at Tom! Wouldn't you think he had money?'

'Tom would never say it. He wouldn't lie.'

'He wouldn't have to. They'd never ask – not outright. They'd come at it sideways and get all that history about the great J P Rensselaer, summers on Long Island and the place in Park Avenue. What conclusions are they going to draw except that Tom's loaded?'

It was a dirty thought and – true or not – I didn't like her for it.

Maisie had been drinking and now she was reckless. When Beauclerc came past she grabbed his sleeve. She growled, 'Say, Philippe, is there any chance of opening the casino?' Just as unpredictably she asked, 'Where is Alvírez? Has anybody laid eyes on him?'

'Not for a couple of days,' I said

'I don't see him missing the chance of a free drink and a woman courtesy of Hitler.'

'As I say, I haven't seen him'
'I'll ask Philippe.'

Maisie was truculent and I was afraid I couldn't hold her and she'd say or do something. I didn't know what except I had a notion it would be appalling – as if she knew some terrible truth and was going to blurt it out, and, knowing it, we'd never be able to live with ourselves again.

Instead Tom walked in. It would be about nine o'clock.

Tom had changed into a lounge suit. He was smiling and smoking. He came to our table, kissed the women and sat down.

'I'm sorry I'm late,' he said. 'Have you folks eaten? I guess you have. It doesn't matter. I ate lunch. Ben not back? He's late.'

He called Étienne over and ordered a cognac.

Maisie asked, 'How was your day?'

'It was okay. Hetty, how are you feeling?'

'I'm fine, Tom,' she said, and suddenly she did look fine in a fevered way.

'Only "okay"?' Maisie said. 'What did you get up to? Do tell.'

'Katerina wasn't feeling too good. I took Señora Malipiero for a run to Grasse.'

'That must have been a disappointment – Katerina being ill.'

'It happens.'

'But you still enjoyed yourself?'

'Sure.'

'Uh huh?'

'That's right.'

Tom took a sip of his brandy. It was a moment made for a row, but he grinned instead and said, 'What d'you want to hear? That we found an *auberge*, rented a room and spent the day making passionate love? All right, you got me. I confess. I'm a louse.'

Hetty laughed. It was a good laugh that picked up some of Tom's sparkle. Maisie looked ashamed. She mumbled, 'If you're going to be like that.'

I think only I guessed there was a lie in the heart of what Tom said, but I'd no idea what it was. I didn't think he'd made love to Teresa Malipiero – at least not in the way we usually mean when we say the words. Had it been anyone else, well … But Tom was pledged to Hetty and that was that. A cheap affair would go too close to the core of his integrity. He just couldn't do it – not and remain Tom Rensselaer.

Meantime he went on about his day, though he omitted the stuff about burying corpses. We got a description of Teresa: her hair, her clothes, her opinions. We heard about the journey, the lie of the land, the colours of the sky. Tom didn't see this as deceit.

All that evening we basked in his charm. He lifted Maisie and Hetty out of their gloom. He talked to me about my book and let me run on about language and technique, as though I knew anything about either. He seduced us without thinking about it – without thinking about *us* and how we'd all feel when he took himself away. And we loved him for it.

One way and another Maisie came round again to the subject of Alvírez – where was he?

'I saw him this morning,' Tom said. 'He was taking a stroll in the woods a couple of miles out of town.'

I said, 'Walking doesn't sound like his style.'

'No, it doesn't,' Tom agreed. 'But the fellow could've had a hangover. Whenever I tie one on, I find a raw egg and a long stroll set me up again. Or maybe he collects flowers? There's no telling what people will do. My uncle used to put in an evening a week working at a soup kitchen – or he'd pay his butler to go there, which in his eyes amounted to much the same thing.'

'He should be back now,' I said.

'So he should. Though he may have got lost,' Tom added.

That was how he planted a notion to explain Alvírez's disappearance. It came to him from something Dr Maillot had said: his warning about the treacherous ground up in the mountains:

the landslips and hidden cliffs, where someone might fall and his body be lost in the brushwood.

That night Teresa Malipiero returned to the Villa la Pinède. For the moment she felt raised from her fears and loneliness into a brief happiness. She found Katerina sitting in the darkness of the garden, listening to the pulse of the cicadas.

'Is it done?' Katerina asked.
'Yes – we'll hear no more of Señor Alvírez.'
'Was it horrible?'
'Not so horrible.'
'Because of Tom?'
'Yes.'

It was because of Tom. Teresa Malipiero was a courageous woman, but courage can be crushed by loneliness. Now she wasn't alone. Miraculously, Tom had accepted her without judging. More than that: he'd shocked her into a feeling of being alive and quickened her sense of her own sexual existence. It was difficult to explain even to herself. She didn't want an *affaire* with Tom Rensselaer. She didn't suppose he wanted one with her. Rather she'd been overcome by Tom's emotional generosity. But as for what Tom wanted, that was simply a mystery.

'He's a good man,' Teresa said. 'I wish you liked him more.'
'I do like him.'
'Then what's wrong?'
'He frightens me.'

Teresa found the answer incomprehensible but she had the wisdom to be quiet. She gave her daughter a kiss and proposed a nightcap, leaving the subject of Alvírez as firmly buried as his body.

That night Teresa sat at her dressing table and brushed her hair. The mirror was spotted and, in its reflection, her face looked stark and old. Seeing it, she felt Tom's attentions as a faint memory to which a younger woman had responded. How strange it was that Katerina thought he was frightening. The reaction was unexpected and unwelcome because it showed how impossible it was to know even one's own children entirely.

She remembered then the package removed from Alvírez's body. She opened the manila envelope and emptied it out. Letters and telegrams.

In them she learned that her husband was dead. Alvírez had already known it when he was demanding her diamonds under the pretence he was still alive.

The Spaniard had deserved to be killed and she had no regrets at his death.

CHAPTER EIGHTEEN

Next morning I stayed away from La Chênaie because I knew it would mean another wasted day. Instead I strolled into town to collect my mail. The censors had let through a letter from my publisher pressing for my book. I read it, threw it away, then went to take coffee at the Hôtel de la Gare. Tom found me there.

He came straight to the point. 'Could I ask you a favour?' he said. 'Will you come to Marseilles with me? Ben didn't come home last night.'

'Maybe that committee of his had more business than usual.'

'No. I've just come from calling one of the other members. They had no special business and wrapped up around three o'clock. Ben was talking of returning here. So, you see, he should have made it.'

'Have you spoken to the consul?'

'Yes, but he says that, if anything *has* happened, he wouldn't hear right away – not for maybe twenty-four or forty-eight hours.'

'You think Ben may have been arrested?'
'Or an accident.'
'What do you intend to do? Go round all the hospitals?'
'Will you come to Marseilles with me?' Tom repeated.

We took the car and drove to the city by the empty wartime roads. We arrived at about one. I was concerned at the vagueness of Tom's plans and the curfew if we didn't quickly sort whatever had to be sorted. I didn't know how much of a risk Ben had been running with his committee and Tom's replies were vague.

'They call it 'Le Joint',' he said. 'Because the United States still recognises Vichy, there's a whole bunch of stuff that has to be arranged. Taking care of American property over here is only one part.'

So far it sounded innocent; then Tom added, 'I've heard talk of buying arms. I don't say there's anything to it, only that at some point the French people will begin to fight back against Vichy and the Germans both.'

'Is that what Ben's involved in?' I asked.
'I shouldn't think so.'
'But he could be?'
'I doubt it.'

We parked in the Vieux Port but stayed away from the quayside and the ships in case some fool thought we were spies.

'D'you know this town?' Tom asked.

I shook my head. 'Do you?'

'We passed through last winter on our way from Spain to Italy. Know it? I wouldn't say I know it.'

'Where are we going?'

'I thought we'd check out some places. If Ben stayed here overnight, he had to sleep somewhere – a *pension* or hotel.'

'Unless he was arrested or had an accident,' I said.

'I can't do anything about that. We'll hear sooner or later through the consul.'

'You don't seem to think that likely,' I said, though no other explanation seemed to account for the facts. Still, now we were here, Tom had become cool as if getting ready for something distasteful.

We took a right up a hill into narrow streets crisp with shadow. I remember seamen's hostels, a smell of fish, oregano and faulty sewers, and a view of a harbour fort with its stones scoured pink by sunlight. Tom left me while he dropped into bars and the kind of hotel entered by a single door squeezed between shop fronts. He made his enquiries and each time came out with a sad smile, and sometimes he lit a cigarette.

If he was lucky he said, 'Ben was here.' Once or twice he elaborated. 'The bartender says Ben was with a sailor and a couple of girls.' The sailor was sometimes a soldier and the number of girls varied. Apparently there'd been quite a party until midnight or so when the numbers had fallen off. There was talk of a fight, but Tom didn't have the details. He couldn't always follow the local *argot*.

Over lunch in a workman's café, I asked. 'Do you think he's picked up a tart?'

'No,' said Tom. He was definite. 'Maisie's the only girl for him. She understands him. Still,' he added – and I didn't know what he meant – 'his wife isn't easy.'

Thinking about all the partying, I said, 'I understood Ben was nearly tee-total.'

'Once in a while he'll take a drink. There's nothing so wrong in that, is there?'

I didn't know. My Uncle Gerald had a fondness for whiskey, which others considered reprehensible or heroic according to whether they were drinking whiskey at the time.

Tom said, 'His father is a drinking man. Sometimes these things run in families.'

By the time we paid our bill a man had turned up. He was a swarthy type in a beret and a leather jacket belted in the middle.

Tom said he was a policeman and that was to be expected. He didn't care.

We tried a few more bars and hotels. Then Tom turned on his heels and went back to our follower. I didn't hear the conversation, but, on his return, Tom said, 'I've told him we're looking for a friend. He doesn't know anything. I've promised we'll let him keep us in view.'

'How does he feel about that?'

'It's just a job. He likes anything that makes it easy.'

It was four o'clock, the white sky became blue and the narrow streets filled with shadow except for a bright strip below each roof. We tried an hotel that looked like the rest, with a small lobby of tans and browns. The concierge was sitting behind the desk, reading a newspaper and swatting flies. We didn't ask, but he said, 'Your friend is in his room.' He gave us the key.

We went to the first floor and a windowless corridor with two rooms either side. The doors had been badly painted green over cream and the numbers were on enamel plaques. I listened but heard nothing. Tom said, 'I'm used to this. It isn't so bad.'

'It's happened before?'

'I'll tell you some time. If we're lucky, we'll get him home without the need for a doctor.'

We let ourselves in. The room had an overpowering stench of sweat and urine. Ben was in his underwear, asleep on an iron-framed bed. I counted four bottles: three wine and one spirits: not as many as my Uncle Gerald could get through in his prime but enough. In any case, Ben had only had a day to settle in.

Tom said, 'Check for damage.'

'How would I recognise it?' I asked but Tom only looked at me sternly.

'Here's my wallet. Go pay the concierge something – anything within reason. We don't need an excuse to involve the police.'

I did as he asked. When I returned Tom had got Ben on his feet, his face set in a solemn daze and his eyes large and moist like poached eggs. He seemed to recognise me because he muttered, 'Hi'.

I felt someone at my shoulder. It was the concierge goggling at the drunken American. He said, in English, 'This is a terrible thing. The damages are *énorme*.'

Tom asked me, 'Have you paid him?'

I said I had and told him how much.

Tom said to the concierge. 'You've been paid. Now buzz off.' His tone was very quiet and flat, and the more sinister for that. Still the man protested. 'There are laws! I shall call the police!'

Again Tom spoke low and flat. 'I said buzz off. Now do it or I'll bust your nose.'

The concierge scurried away. A moment later I heard him speaking with the policeman in the belted coat.

I wasn't used to Tom's farouche air and didn't know how much of it was assumed. He was gentle with Ben, coaxing him into his clothes. Ben wasn't taking in much, only repeating, 'I need a drink.' He did this several times, the last time very carefully and earnestly as though asking Tom if he were saved.

He said, 'You don't understand, Tommy. I really *need* a drink.'

When Tom refused him, he didn't become angry – rather, sorrowful as if Tom had done something unforgivable, yet he, Ben, would forgive him. It was odd to see and almost convinced me that we'd got the morality of the thing wrong: that Ben was a kind of martyr. But Tom wouldn't have it.

So we got Ben dressed and we bustled him downstairs. The policeman was in the lobby. The concierge was hanging around like someone intent on making trouble but without a clue except to look ugly. Tom stunned me by taking his hand, shaking it and announcing that the man had done a fine job and he, Tom, was grateful. Then he took the policeman aside. He confided that he didn't want to get the hotel in trouble for harbouring a foreigner who was drunk. You understand? It was the hotel would be in trouble. There was no suggestion of irregularity on Ben's part, still less Tom's. On the contrary Tom was everyone's friend who would help if only you accepted his assessment of the situation.

And, if a little *douceur* would assist …

'I don't like bribing people,' Tom said. He caught my amusement. 'Ben says I've a talent for it,' he explained.

We were in the convertible, driving back to S. Symphorien. The day was fading.

After a while Ben said, 'You got it, pal.' I glanced at him and saw his face glowing orange as a pumpkin in the low sun. His few remarks all had this same character. They were relevant but mistimed like badly dubbed dialogue.

Tom said to me. 'I suppose you're entitled to know what's going on.'

'This has happened before?' I asked.

'Not for a few months.'

'I had no idea. Ben and Maisie seem so happy with each other.'

Tom didn't comment. Instead he said, 'It goes back years – ten or more. Ben was thrown out of Yale because of his drinking. Of course his family laughed it off as high spirits and, at worst, it seemed for a while as if he'd go down the same road as his father, who always carried a load but bore up under it. Then four years ago it got serious. Ben started disappearing, taking himself off until there'd be a call from the cops or, once or twice, a hospital. D'you follow?'

I followed. But I was used only to drinking from poverty and frustration, which isn't the same thing. This was somehow worse – a flaw in the vision of Paradise, like the suicides of young girls Tom had talked about.

Tom was still telling his story. 'Ben's family asked me to take him to Europe, away from his hard-drinking buddies. They offered to pay the expenses.' He glanced at me to see how I took the suggestion that he was the hired help. 'Frankly, I wasn't in a position to refuse unless I wanted to take up bill broking. So now you know. Ben drinks. And I'm his nurse.'

'You seem to have managed,' I said. 'I never guessed.'

'No … ' Tom said. 'You wouldn't. Ben's a sweet fellow when he's sober. And he can stay sober months at a time – almost a year once. But there's no curing him. I took a chance once and left him in Paris to go to Spain. I didn't care for Franco and wanted to help.' He paused. 'I had to come back.'

When I heard this I felt ashamed. I knew Tom had been to Spain and thought he'd no stomach for war. I didn't realise until then that Tom had the stomach for anything.

That and his ideals were the fatal problem. He had no moderation. Nothing would stop him doing what he thought was right.

Next day he took another step to disaster.

CHAPTER NINETEEN

Tom announced, 'I'm going to paint Katerina's portrait.'

I said, 'Were you asked, or did you volunteer?'

'Does it matter?'

'I'm curious.'

'Well, I can't rightly say. The subject sort of emerged from my conversation with Teresa.'

'You call her Teresa?'

'Why not?'

It was morning. We were walking in the woods, three of us because Dr Maillot had tagged along after checking on Ben.

I asked, 'Do you have any thoughts on how you're going to do it?'

'I've been studying Sargent's style.'

'I thought he was out of favour these days?'

'That's true. They say he's all surface – nothing more than high class kitsch.'

'But?'

'There's something to be said for painting beauty in and for itself without trying to get behind it. In any case I've got my doubts about the 'psychological' school of portrait painting. Unless you believe that physiognomy is a science, all the artist paints is an accident of nature. Sure, we attribute character to facial features. But that may be no more than a set of conventions. I'm told that Socrates was hideous.'

'So portraits don't have psychological meaning?'

'I didn't say that. Though if I paint an ugly soul, am I ugly? Maybe I'm just interested in ugliness – though one might wonder, why?'

'*Et la Vierge?*' Dr Maillot mused. 'Ah – who knows what that one is like? It is dangerous to imagine virgins. Me, I see them everywhere, even – no, *especially* when they come to me to relieve them of their troubles.'

Tom didn't like the allusion to Maillot's dirty little practice as an abortionist. He ignored him and said, 'At all events, there you have my reasons for trying my hand at Sargent. Not that I paint half so well.'

In the rue de la République was a cinema. It was a converted theatre with a haze of *tabac brun* hanging in layers in the projected light. We paid a visit from time to time when heat and boredom weighed us down and Hetty and I went there that afternoon, after Tom had gone to the Villa la Pinède to make his first sketches while Ben nursed his hangover and his shame and Maisie watched over him. We saw a film with Madeleine Sologne, but I forget which.

'I don't think Tom's going to marry me,' Hetty said. We were walking back to La Chênaie.

I was so astonished all I could say was, 'Has something happened? Are you angry with him?'

'With Tom? Don't be silly. Nobody ever gets angry with

Tom. In any case he's always been straight with me. No, a girl's only got herself to blame if she loses her head and acts like a fool, that's what I say. Tom promised to marry me only because he thinks it's the right thing to do.'

'I'm sure he'll keep his promise.'

'Thanks, Pat. You're a nice person. But I'm not complaining. A girl's got to make the best of things, right? Problem is I sell myself cheap – I always do that. I guess that means I am cheap and it can't be helped. Shame, huh?'

She squeezed my arm and fixed me with her glittering eye and trembling mouth.

'You mustn't call yourself cheap,' I said. 'It isn't true.' I meant every word. There was something about her that shone in my eyes: a mix of courage and humility, a feeling that this was a true woman who would make a man true.

We reached the house as a thunderstorm broke, the first for a while. In our relief we pulled chairs to the window and watched it roll over the sea where it stopped at the mirror bright horizon.

There was no sign of Tom. Ben was swaddled and looking sick. He said, 'He'll be stuck at La Pinède till this blows itself out.' He fell gloomy for a spell, then added, 'To hell with him. I don't know about you, but I've got to get out of here.'

'Where to?' I asked. I thought he and Maisie had finally decided on returning to the States.

'Somewhere. Monte? Nice? We've talked about going there often enough. Maybe now's the time. Tom can do what he likes. What d'you say?'

'I don't have the money.'

'I'll pay. For you, too, Hetty.'

'If that's what you want to do.'

'I've got to do something,' Ben said.

So that's how the thing was decided. Without involving Tom. Perhaps to spite him.

Tom took his painter's kit and went to La Pinède. Teresa was waiting in the garden with the sun shining through her pale dress. She kissed him on the cheek.

'Where's Katerina?' he asked.

'In the house.'

'How is she taking things?'

'Well enough. Of course, I haven't spoken to her about the details,' she went on, perhaps to convince him of her courage – their mutual commitment, 'I enjoyed our lunch, Tom. I know I shouldn't say that, but it's true.'

'I understand.'

'And I'm glad you've come to paint Katerina. She needs something to distract her – human contact.'

'I'll do my best.'

He would have gone into the house, eager to summon the girl, but Teresa held him back.

'Has there been any news?'

'About? Oh, about Alvírez. People have noticed he isn't around. I don't know how long they'll let it ride – a day or two, maybe; I can't see its being more. I've spread the story that we saw him in the hills two days ago, a couple of miles out of town.'

'Why?'

'Because we need to distract attention from the day before. Someone may have seen him come to the house. Everyone knows you have business with him – don't fool yourself. You don't want to be placed alone as the last person to see him alive. I've got no connection with him, so the last sighting looks perfectly innocent.'

'But the hills, Tom!'

'He has to be somewhere. Where better than a spot where no one can reasonably expect to find a body? The hills are an enormous area to search, and, by saying we saw him, we can direct where they look – if they ever do. There are ravines everywhere where a man might fall and kill himself and never be discovered. Plant that idea and people will accept it. Trust me, Teresa.'

'I do.'

'Good,' Tom said. Then, while he was at it, he decided to get something else off his mind. He asked, 'Is it possible there's something in Alvírez's room?'

'What sort of thing?'

'I don't know. Something that links you. Something … ' He meant evidence that would give Teresa a motive for the murder. 'I've been breaking my head on how to get in there but can't come up with anything. Well? Is there?'

There couldn't be. It followed from the fact that neither Teresa nor Katerina had killed the Spaniard, and Tom waited for an indignant denial. But what she said was a quiet 'I don't know' – and repeated, 'I don't know,' with her eyes losing their focus in pain.

Tom pretended it was enough. He said, 'Fine – good. Well, we'll meet that hurdle when we come to it. Now, how about I do some painting?'

'Please.'

They went into the house. Teresa called for her daughter. Katerina appeared in the blue cotton dress that didn't suit her and gave Tom an uncertain smile.

'I haven't changed,' she said. 'I didn't know what you would want me to wear. I have other dresses – would you like to see them. And my hair? How do you want my hair?'

How? Tom didn't know. It was impossible for him to prescribe for the Argentinian Virgin, for that would be to fix the unknowable – to solve the mystery by saying there was no mystery at all.

Still he went with her to a room with a large oak garderobe. It held a rack of dresses from workaday cotton to the black Chanel number. Also a white one which for a moment reminded him of the gowns worn at *bals blancs* by wealthy Boston virgins in his grandfather's day.

He put aside his notions of John Singer Sargent and realised he'd got no idea how to paint her. Not even the basics: whether to try inside the house or in the garden.

The garden had attractions despite the technical difficulties. Bright, diffuse light might drain flesh colours and eliminate shadow so the effect would be insipid. On the other hand, there was in Katerina a luminosity: that same quality which attracted eyes to her as she walked in town or on the beach in the very sunlight that now challenged him.

The alternative was a studio portrait. If he could find a spot in the house where the light was steady, it'd be easier. The manipulation of shadow would allow him to add drama and mystery, which, like luminosity, were also a part of her.

The question was: what *did* he see? And the answer was: whatever he chose to see.

'You're smiling, Tom,' said Katerina. 'Is there a joke I do not understand?'

'The problems of an artist.' He laughed. 'I don't know that I understand either.'

Tom returned in the evening with some drawings to transfer to canvass.

We were sitting with Philippe Beauclerc from the Czar Aléxandre. He'd arrived about ten minutes before, more agitated than his usual stiff manner

Tom said hello and acknowledged Beauclerc. If he was surprised, he didn't show it. Instead he asked about our day and would have gone on about his own if Ben hadn't interrupted.

'You should listen to this,' Ben said. 'Philippe here is Pat's friend and he's come to ask his advice on something you know about.'

Tom lit a cigarette and poured himself a drink. He took a seat on the arm of the chair where Hetty was sitting and I thought he looked at her wistfully as he said, 'Do go on. Is it something I can help with? What is it I'm supposed to know?'

'Monsieur Alvírez,' Beauclerc blurted out. 'He is completely disappeared!'

CHAPTER TWENTY

I said, 'Apparently Alvírez has been missing for a few days. He hasn't checked out and his bill isn't paid, and Philippe is worried because he's a foreigner. Ordinarily he'd go to the police – and I don't see he has any choice – but he doesn't want to cause a stink over what may amount to nothing. What do you think?'

'Going to the police is probably the wise thing,' Tom agreed. He asked, 'Have you checked his room?'

Beauclerc said, 'The maid cleans. The bed wasn't slept in.'

'She mightn't have bothered to take a peek at the bathroom. He could be there – heart attack or something. It happens.'

'My cousin Henry died of a heart attack in the john,' Maisie said, and, to make the story seem true, added, 'He was only twenty-six, but he was a drinker and liked Italian food.'

I asked Tom, 'Didn't you say you saw Alvírez two days ago?'

'Two days ago?' repeated Beauclerc.

Tom stubbed his cigarette and helped himself to another drink. 'That's right. It was morning – around eleven or so. At least I think it was Alvírez.'

'You are not certain?'

'Fairly certain. It wasn't important.'

'And where?'

'Oh ... let me see ... four or five kilometres out of town on the road to Grasse. I don't suppose the place has a name – just hills, trees and stuff. I guess I could find it again if I needed to. Drink, anybody? No?'

'You don't normally drink hard liquor at this time of day,' said Hetty.

'I don't?' Tom smiled at her. 'You know me better than I know myself. Philippe, if you like we could take a look at Alvírez's room together.'

Beauclerc accepted this suggestion eagerly.

At this stage we didn't really believe anything had happened to Alvírez. Yet, in an odd way we wanted him dead – preferably with an oriental dagger in his chest and blood all over the Turkish carpet on the study floor – for the entertainment value. Which is why all of us went to the Czar Aléxandre.

However, only Tom and Beauclerc went up to the Spaniard's room. The rest of us stayed in the bar where Étienne served cocktails.

The suites at the Czar Aléxandre were full of the gimcrack Louis Seize reproduction furniture good hotels buy. Sunlight had faded it but it still had the charm of cheap perfume and costume jewellery.

Beauclerc opened up with his bunch of house-keys. Tom went inside and caught the stale odour of cigars and the dead man's scent of patchouli and bay rum. The light was dim with evening and rationed electricity. The main room had the lonely feeling railway terminals get at night when only people with strange purposes haunt the empty concourse.

'Why don't you give the bathroom the once over while I check the bedroom?' Tom proposed. In the bedroom he found a painted garderobe on bowlegs.

'There is no-one in the bathroom,' Beauclerc called.

Alvírez travelled light with a single case in alligator skin, three suits, six shirts, two pairs of shoes, all of good make. The suits yielded a few pesetas, a few Reichsmarks and a toothpick. His socks and underwear were silk.

'*Il n'y a personne,*' Beauclerc said as he came through the door. 'What are you doing, Monsieur Rensselaer?'

'Looking for a diary. It might tell us if he had some appointments.' Tom had found nothing except a rosary with ivory beads and a nasal inhaler. 'I guess there isn't anything,' he said.

'*Alors?*' enquired Beauclerc.

'We call the police, I suppose. I don't see what else we can do.'

It was Maillot who mentioned that Beauclerc had filed a report at the gendarmerie. But we didn't know what happened to it since we didn't eat at the Czar Aléxandre for a couple of days.

In the meantime Ben raised again the subject of a trip to Nice.

'I think it's a good idea,' Tom said.

'Are you going to come?'

'I'll pass, if you don't mind. You know what I'm like when I get into a portrait.'

As to that, he'd decided on his approach and explained it to me.

'I'm going to paint her *en plein air* in the blue dress. Did you ever see it?'

'The one you said didn't suit her?'

'That's it.'

'Why?'

'Because I want her face to float free in the light. D'you understand – *float?* The composition will be perfectly centred – still – linear – Katerina looking straight ahead and her arms hanging down but folded at the hands. It's dangerous as hell, but that's what I want to do.'

I didn't understand. I asked what had happened to Sargent.

'Oh, that. It doesn't suit. I'm not painting the "Duchess of Dollars", Pat. This is the "Argentinian Virgin".'

La Vierge de l'Argentine. I recalled Maillot's words and a plaster statue my mother kept in her bedroom. I said, 'The Blessed Virgin is always pictured in blue – the colour of purity. Did you know that?'

'I'd forgotten. My family are Episcopalian.'

'Protestant bastard.'

'If you like.'

Still, Tom was open to new ideas. 'You know, maybe you're right. This painting – ' it was in his eyes: he could see it ' – is an icon. Tell me: have you ever seen any Byzantine icons?'

'They talk of little else in Tipperary.'

'You're making fun of me. That's okay. But, about Byzantine painting, it isn't in the slightest naturalistic. The gestures are stylised and the faces often viewed straight on. The costumes are very stiff and – probably because they're painted separately – the faces seem detached. Of course, if it's realism you want, the result is hopeless. But, on the theory that spirit and matter are separate, this detachment of face from body makes the effect all the more intense. Are you with me?'

I said I was, and we talked about other things.

Tom went off to paint. He was no sooner gone than Ben and Maisie fell to one of the quarrels that were becoming frequent. Hetty pretended to be cheerful but she wanted to be alone and went to the beach. For the moment I was sick of them all.

I spent the afternoon in my cottage and emerged at evening. It had rained and, when I stretched my legs and strolled to town, the Place Victor Hugo was cool and free of dust. Maillot was sitting at one of the pavement tables, three sheets to the wind.

'Have the police been to see you again?' I asked.

'Yes, but so far the woman keeps her nerve in what concerns her daughter and says nothing – not, you understand, out of regard for me but because she fears her own skin.'

I took a seat. I suggested Maillot take some food. I suspected he didn't eat much and might go the way of my Uncle Gerald who died drunk enough to sing in his coffin. He was able to manage a bowl of onion soup, and I joined him.

He became silently companionable, taking me back to the days before the Americans had arrived, when we enjoyed ourselves doing nothing in particular. Now I still did nothing in particular, wishing Tom and the others would go home to leave me in peace.

When Maillot spoke again, the conversation took a curious turn.

He asked, 'What are Monsieur Rensselaer's relations with Monsieur Alvírez?'

'Why do you suppose they have any relations at all?'

'I only ask. May I put another question: what do you know of your friend?'

When I thought of it, there wasn't a lot. 'He comes from a rich family that's gone down in the world. Surprisingly, it doesn't seem to bother him. He's sociable, charming, talented. Where is this leading?'

'Monsieur Alvírez holds an American passport.'

'You're joking. Who told you – Beauclerc?'

Maillot nodded. I believed him. It would explain Alvírez's college ring and excellent Americanised English.

'I am thinking,' the old man said, 'that they have business together, those two.'

I laughed. 'You're completely mistaken. Tom doesn't have "business" with anyone. He doesn't work for a living. He lives off a small trust fund and the little he earns from painting.'

'So he tells you.'

'No, not just Tom. Ben Benedict knows him from the States. He confirms that Tom's broke. You don't know him. Money and business don't interest him in the slightest.'

Maillot shrugged, unconvinced.

What was odd about this exchange was that the topic of a supposed connection between Tom and Alvírez should have come up at all. I couldn't see any reason for Maillot's suspicions and he wouldn't admit to any. Yet, clearly something had happened.

When the old man began to doze, I packed him off to bed and decided to return to La Chênaie for a nightcap. It was still cool and the cicadas were chattering.

I walked by the road behind La Pinède on the landward side. There was no moon and the light from the Czar Aléxandre was faint in wartime; but I came across Tom carrying a torch as he came down from the height. I stopped him and we walked the remaining distance.

'How was your day?' I asked. 'I thought you'd be back earlier, when the light faded.'

'Oh, I stopped painting hours ago,' he said, 'but Teresa made a little supper and we talked, you know how it goes.'

'You're drunk?'

'I swear I had only a single glass of wine. But – I'll admit it, Pat – it's flattering to be the centre of attention of two beautiful women.'

'I should think you were used to that.'

'You make me sound like a gigolo.' He paused and buttoned me. 'Seriously, Pat, that's the last thing I am. I'd hate it if people thought I just played with women's feelings.' He let me go and was bright again. 'Ah, you're pulling my leg, aren't you?'

A bicycle was parked against the wall of La Chênaie – we almost fell over it in the dark.

'I wonder whose it is?' Tom said and called out to say we were back.

We went inside, where we found the others sitting and a gendarme at his ease drinking cognac. I guessed straight away that he'd come to follow up enquiries concerning Alvírez. Evidently Tom did, too, because he allowed himself a smile, extended a hand and said in French, as easy as could be, 'Hi there, Monsieur Tisserand; I imagine it's me you're looking for.' And, to the rest of us, 'Is anyone going to offer me a drink?'

As I say, he was as easy as could be, and it shows his icy nerves. Because Tom knew this particular policeman. He'd been on the road to Grasse and had passed the empty car as it stood, parked, near the spot where Tom had buried Alvírez.

CHAPTER TWENTY-ONE

The policeman was one of the half dozen who manned the post in the Promenade des Russes. He was a genial type and we knew him from the times when we dropped by to report those things foreigners had to report.

Ben said, 'He's come about the Alvírez business.'

'I take it, then, that he hasn't showed up,' said Tom. 'In which case I can see why you want to have a word with me.'

As I say, Tisserand was a nice fellow, ruddy-faced and easygoing. It was clear he liked us and regretted any inconvenience. 'It seems you are the last person to see Monsieur Alvírez,' he said to Tom.

'Am I? Well, I guess that can't be helped. I'll tell you whatever I can, though, frankly, it's not very much. I can't even be certain it was Monsieur Alvírez I saw.'

'No?'

'I just glanced into the woods and noticed someone walking. It was a man and I supposed it was him.'

'What day was this?'

'The day after the boy's funeral – Tuesday was it? I went for a drive to Grasse – almost to Grasse: we didn't quite make it.'

'In Monsieur Benedict's marvellous car,' Tisserand said with an enthusiasm that made us smile.

'Yes.'

'I saw you.'

'So you did. You waved to us, as I recall.'

'You were stopped.'

'That's right. We were in no hurry. We decided to take a stroll. It's very beautiful in the hills.'

'And that is where you saw Monsieur Alvírez?'

Tom was fixing drinks as he spoke. He gave me one and offered to refresh Tisserand's glass.

'No, it wasn't there,' he said. 'We'd only just started. I don't think we could have gone more than four or five kilometres out of town. We were on the move – which is why I can't be absolutely certain the person I saw was Monsieur Alvírez. I caught little more than a glimpse, you understand?'

'And this place?'

'It was … just a place. I don't know if it has a name. I can't describe it, but I might be able to find it again if you like.'

'And Madame Malipiero – you were with her?'

'That's right.'

'She saw Monsieur Alvírez?'

'I really can't say. At the time I said something like 'There's Alvírez'.'

'There's Alvírez?'

'Something like that. Maybe I said, 'Is that Alvírez?''

'And she said?'

'I don't know she said anything. She probably said something. I don't see it matters.'

Tisserand nodded. I think he was scratching for things to ask. His eyes were everywhere, especially on Maisie and I suspect he was excited about *les Americains*.

He asked, 'How well do you know Monsieur Alvírez?'

'Not at all. We've spoken only once.'

'But Madame Malipiero knows him?'

'I believe so.'

'A friend?'

'Business – that's what she tells me.'

'What sort of business?'

Tom shrugged. 'I've never asked. I'm not certain Madame Malipiero knows either. It involves her husband, who's expected here any day. It's my impression he's in the import-export line, but I can't tell you more than that.'

For the time being Tisserand seemed satisfied.

The following day Tisserand sent one of his men round to La Chênaie to bring Tom in. It was early and I wasn't there, but I got the story from Ben and then from Tom when he returned at about noon.

The gendarmerie owned a truck. Tisserand loaded it with his men and some sticks so they could beat about the undergrowth. Tom was allowed to ride up front.

'They were very jolly,' he told me. 'I think they want Alvírez to be dead. What d'you think of that, Pat? They want him dead so they can have something interesting to do.'

They drove out of town by the route Tom had taken and he told them to go slowly if he was to identify the spot where he'd seen the Spaniard. The police, he said, were more nervous than he was.

The roads out of S. Symphorien rise sharply. Here and there a lonely *mas* presides over a few dry terraces, but most of the land is pines, or oak. The subtle configurations may have meaning, but city people don't know what it is.

'Here,' said Tom as they came out of a bend.

'Here? Are you sure?' Tisserand asked.

'I think so, though all places look pretty much the same.'

They pulled to the roadside and dismounted from the truck.

'Where was Monsieur Alvírez when you saw him?'

'Just a little way in. He was heading downwards.'

'So you saw his face?'

'I suppose I must have – for a second or so.'

Tisserand gave directions to his men to spread out five yards apart. Tom wasn't asked to, but he advanced with them and, although it was crazy, he found himself scanning the ground intently as if he really would come across traces of Alvírez – as if the death, now that it had passed from immediate experience, was a debatable event, and things might turn out differently.

It struck Tom then how unlikely his story was. No one who'd seen Alvírez would take him for a walking man. And this wasn't walking country. A man might stray and stumble in these thickets, but he wouldn't continue, not with the road hard by. And Alvírez had known – *would have known* – of the road. He'd have heard the noise of automobiles.

Yet, it seemed, none of these points occurred to Tisserand, who directed his men to swing at right angles so they could follow the probable line of Alvírez's descent.

'This is hot work, Monsieur Rensselaer,' he said.

'I hope the poor fellow isn't hurt.'

Tisserand said, 'He is dead, Monsieur Rensselaer! Don't look so shocked. It is the only reasonable explanation.'

'He may have quit town – been called away.'

'And leave his valuable possessions – including his only suitcase?'

'No, I guess not.'

'No,' said Tisserand. 'He is dead. But I am not hopeful that we shall find him with so many hills and so few men, and we begin, perhaps, in the wrong place.'

'I'm as sure as I can be that this is where I saw him,' Tom said. In a corner of his mind he sincerely wanted to help.

'Let us hope you are right.'

Nailed to a tree was a painted sign: *Chasse Privée*.

'I am thinking,' Tisserand mused, 'that Monsieur Alvírez has met a hunting accident. That happens sometimes.'

The thought hadn't occurred to Tom. He imagined the situation. Alvírez hears a noise among the leaf fall. He stops. The woods are dense but not dark. Everywhere splinters of sunlight shatter any coherent shapes. To the hunter's eye he's what the hunter needs to see. He's prey.

'I suppose that could be so,' Tom admitted.

'A hunting accident, and the hunter panics.' Tisserand seemed pleased with his explanation. 'In which case we shall find the grave.'

'The grave?'

'Of course. The hunters in these hills do not have motor cars, Monsieur Rensselaer.'

Suspicion quivered over the circumstances of Alvírez's vanishing but I consoled myself that the Spaniard was one of those characters, like the fraudsters and gamblers who frequent the coast, whose disappearance is somehow expected and goes largely unquestioned. As for Tom, he had the armour of his calm, steady purpose.

When he returned from his morning in the hills he had an appetite and said over lunch, 'You know, Tisserand is a nice fellow. He was quite apologetic about dragging me off.'

'But you didn't find Alvírez?' I asked.

'With only half a dozen men in all those hills, it's hardly to be expected. I shouldn't be surprised if some old lady turns up to say Alvírez has run off with her life savings.'

'Does Tisserand have a theory?'

'He thinks Alvírez may have been shot by a hunter – happens all the time, he says.'

'I still can't see Alvírez walking in the hills.'

'No, neither can I. But there's no accounting for people.' Tom looked up, his eyes a smiling, unfocussed sapphire. He was feeling good. He quipped. 'Who truly knows anyone? Maybe I'm a murderer? Maybe you are, Pat – or any of us.'

'I don't think I could murder someone,' I said.

'Don't sell yourself short,' Tom said, as though my lack of murderous instinct was only modesty.

'I could commit murder,' remarked Maisie. 'You, Hetty?'

'If I loved someone enough, I suppose – and he treated me bad.'

'Watch your step, Tom,' I said.

'I don't mean *that!*' Hetty was upset. 'I'll never forget how good you are to me, Tom. That's a promise.' She crossed her heart. I hadn't realised people actually did that.

'Then I'm safe,' said Tom.

He did believe he was safe. At one level he did believe in Lucky Tom Rensselaer.

So far as concerned Tisserand's enquiries that was that. For a little while we heard no more. We went through an interlude in which we pursued other interests. Tom applied himself to his portrait of Katerina Malipiero. The rest of us went to Nice.

Nearly thirty years later, in a conversation with Ben, I remembered Tom's remarks about murderers. Absolutely anyone can be a murderer. All it takes is circumstances. And some of us fool ourselves that what we're doing isn't murder at all.

CHAPTER TWENTY-TWO

Now I remember, it was in nineteen sixty-three that Ben Benedict and I met in a Dublin pub. Kennedy hadn't yet been shot.

Tom's movie script lay around in a drawer for a dozen or more years after I wrote to him and told him the studio rejected it. Now I showed it to Ben because I thought it'd give us something to talk about. Otherwise for years I'd chosen not to think about Tom or wonder about his affairs.

The fact is it rankled me that Ben dismissed Tom's work. Don't mistake me: the script was beyond saving. In addition to its technical flaws, it was hopelessly out of date. Also – though some people will say differently – an audience wants to suspend its disbelief only so far. *True* passion – *true* agony never sold seats to a film. They're too unsettling. The audience needs to know that, in the end, the author isn't in the film but safely in the seats as a spectator. If it were otherwise, a trip to the movies would be like a visit to the Coliseum and we'd be shocked at our own sadism. Tom's script was written from the soul. It was beautiful – and appalling.

Ben surprised me with his parting words – surprised me because he was looking plump and comfortable with a good meal and a few drinks inside him – Ben in his tailored suit and me in my ready-to-wear.

He said in a low, middle-aged growl, 'Listen, Pat. It's been nice talking to you – chewing the fat over old times and all. But the fact is, I don't want to see you again.'

I asked why? What had I done? And Ben chuckled to soothe me.

'It's not you, Pat. Believe me, I like you. But what do we have in common? What do we have to talk about except that summer in France more than twenty years ago?'

'It's Tom, isn't it?' I said.

'If you like – yes, it's Tom. I don't want to hear his name – ever. So, if you don't mind we'll shake hands now and I'll go. Give my love to your wife – and kids? You have kids?'

'Two boys.'

'That's nice. What are their names?'

'The eldest is called Tom.'

'Really? Well, that figures. Tom! Hah!' He looked at me strangely. I suppose he was saying farewell to youth. 'So long, Pat.'

It was this meeting that revived my interest in Tom, though it wasn't until a few years later that I did something about it. Meantime I had my own problems. My latest novel had been rejected and I was scraping a living with book reviews and a few plays for Irish radio that were well received but earned no money.

As for Tom, it seemed he was doing all right. He appeared on NBC in a broadcast transmitted in Ireland because of interest in the American civil rights movement.

The last time I'd heard of him, he was in Albuquerque. Now he was in Montgomery defending some blacks on a murder charge. It came from the civil rights agitation. A gang of whites had burned down a church and the blacks had killed one of them. There were no arson charges.

I don't know how Tom came to be in Alabama. I saw him only in a five-second clip on Irish television coming down the courtroom steps and talking to the reporters. The years had attenuated him but he was still handsome. He was a drinking man – I picked up the signals – but this gave him a hard glamour and I could hear one of the female reporters stumbling over her questions, recoiling from his sexual force.

Tom won the case, and I heard he won a few more. My wife knew I'd been concerned about him lately and said with relief, 'See, *querido*, there's nothing to worry about.' She meant that, finally, the effects of our fatal summer had worked themselves out. Tom was recovered. The scars might be visible, but the wounds were no longer sore and the rest of Tom's life would be explained by other incidents, other causes. She meant that in Montgomery, Alabama our story stopped.

In the event, Tom's story wasn't over. A year after the item on NBC I learned he stood for election to the State bench on a liberal ticket and was crushed by the voters. Then I heard he was disbarred and scratching a living no one knew where.

There are two versions of this. My American agent, Phil Alpert, for some reason knew Tom slightly in the sixties and said he was the victim of a conspiracy by the good ol' boys of the Alabama bar who hated the nigger-loving Yankee. On the other hand, I suspected the drinking had finally got on top of Tom's work and his practice had just faded away.

If the first version was true, then Tom's fate had nothing to do with me. It might be a tragedy, but it was a different one.

Recently Ben Benedict died. He left a billion dollars and no will. He never had children and the heirs are disputing the carve-up. The business will be in the courts for years. I don't know exactly who else is still alive or what my attitude should be. Do I want them living so I can learn more? Or dead so I can't hurt them? The case can be made both ways.

It was Ben's death that made me get round to writing this memoir. I considered doing it near thirty years ago, just after I was told of Tom's drinking problem. It cut me to the heart that there seemed to be no end to the catastrophe. That was the occasion when my wife and I had one of those arguments that almost broke us up.

There was still a lot I didn't know – crucial evidence of events once we all left France. I wanted to investigate and speak to people.

My wife pleaded with me. 'Let it go, Pat. Don't you see? Whatever happened to Tom happened because he was weak or because he *wanted* it to happen.'

I told her, 'I don't see how anyone could want it to happen.'

'That only shows how little you knew Tom,' she said.

I brushed her concern aside. 'I don't see it matters either way – not to finding out the truth. In fact I'd like to know if you're right. Was Tom weak? Did he *want* it? – for God's sake. Or was he just a victim – and, if so, *whose?*'

My wife cried. I softened and she might have had her way if she hadn't overplayed her hand with female relentlessness.

'Call yourself an observer,' she said. 'This isn't about observation. It isn't curiosity that drives you. It's cruelty.'

I told her I didn't know what she meant.

So I went and did my researches, and I came home.

My son, Tom, was fifteen years old. Gerald was only nine. Whatever my wife may have thought, I wasn't entirely heartless, and I didn't set down what I learned.

Now Ben Benedict is dead.

He died in the spring, though here on the west coast of Ireland there isn't much in the passing of the seasons. According to the press he went to his place in Maine last summer and was too ill to move by the time winter came. I hear there was late snow in that area. If it was still around, he was buried in frozen earth with no one there except his impersonal staff and greedy heirs, all dressed in black with the trees black and the ground white. But the snow might have gone and the trees been in blossom, in which case the impression would have been quite different.

I don't know why I'm going on about this, except that I need to observe and then describe what I observe; and I become uncomfortable it I can't, which is why I have problems with the truth of Tom's script for *The Veiled Woman*. I wasn't a witness.

However I was a witness to what happened in Nice and I'd better write about it. Previously I've never thought it relevant, but lately I've decided it tells you all you need to know about who we were. And, if you know that, you understand why Tom was murdered.

CHAPTER TWENTY-THREE

'His name is Colonel Glue Eye,' said Maisie, 'or, if not exactly that, something like it. He's Hungarian. We've seen him at the Negresco, but today he spoke to me in the shop – one of those in the Rue Masséna where you can still buy stuff the jewellers have hidden from the Italians because of the value of the Lira. He's very Middle-European – beautiful manners – kisses hands – clicks heels. He makes me think of one of those characters in light opera – one of those soldiers in tight pantaloons. *Very* sinister.'

He wore a good lounge suit, a high collar and an Ascot pinned with a large amethyst. His hair was thick, black and well cut and his moustache was trimmed narrowly like Gable's. I'd noticed him and his table, all loud and seductively vulgar – people you wanted to know, if only to despise them.

That was Nice. That was the war – at least that portion occupied by profiteers, fraudsters and a certain type of sadist. Later we thought of the war's immorality but for some of us at the time – those of us who were privileged and detached – what interested us was the look of the thing. In the summer of forty-one when many of us were still fresh with excitement, it could glitter with infectious tawdriness.

'He swims, he dances, he turns his hand at baccarat and doesn't mind playing the trumpet with a lousy band,' said Ben. 'Behold the new Renaissance Man!'

'You do much the same thing,' Maisie remarked.

'Everyone can. This is the age of mass production. We've simplified the model and its colour is – *black!*'

We'd garaged the car to save petrol and hired a landau. Maisie and Hetty took to dressing nicely in white frocks with straw hats and parasols. I took my colour from Ben and, if an Irish boy can be said to be *soigné*, I was he in my white flannels, open shirt, linen jacket and jaunty Panama.

From our carriage on the Promenade des Anglais we looked down on the strip of pebbles Colonel Glue Eye occupied with an Italian beauty and an honour guard of two soldiers to hold off the riff raff.

'Her name is Anna Pitti,' Hetty said. 'She's an actress. I saw her name in a movie magazine. Her husband is the Marchese da … oh, it'll come to me. Don't you think she's lovely?' The actress and her escort had set out a little theatre on the shore with a crisp white cloth and a basket of rare meats and wine. For backdrop they had a turquoise sea and a blue sky with a pink horizon.

We were facing the direction of the château, following a line of palms and oleanders to a hill covered in cypress and stone pines. That way lay the old town. We left the landau and set off on foot. I found myself walking with Maisie.

Nice must have done something for her. She was more carefree – more like her old gay self. In the narrow alleys we jostled each other and I couldn't escape her perfume in the close air.

She asked me, 'Do they ever call you Paddy?'

'Sometimes. I prefer Pat.'

'Okay, Pat it is.'

'They call you Maisie, but wouldn't you rather they used Margaret?'

'No,' she said. 'Margaret's the girl my parents made – the safe, respectable girl. Maisie's the girl I made myself. I haven't quite got the hang of her yet – for most of the time she's been too young and inexperienced. But I'm getting there. And when she's as hard and bright as I want her to be, then the world had better look out. You won't recognise her. I'll probably give her a different name.'

I wondered if she was almost 'there' because she was laughing. She went on, 'Now it's my turn again. What's your fiancée like? Why didn't you get married?'

'I never knew her well enough. She said I was a hard man.'

In a shocked voice: 'You beat her?'

'No.'

'Uh huh? I was beaten once. By Henry Sturgiss that I was engaged to. Afterwards he swore to me in tears that he'd never beaten any other girl. But he was a drunkard and a dope fiend, and that sort are awful liars. So, what happened?'

'Small things – important, corrosive little things that you have to think long and carefully about before you can understand them.'

'Oh?' She was suddenly uninterested. 'Well, that just sounds like the everyday story of marriage. People can carry on for a lifetime like that and it doesn't lead to anything.' She looked at me curiously. Then she laughed as though she'd uncovered my secret. 'No, there's got to be more. You *did* something. You can tell me. It can't be all that terrible. Let me guess. If you didn't beat her – you two-timed her. Is that it?'

I shook my head.

'I put my fiancée into a book,' I said.

'Oh, my God!' Maisie caught her breath. 'That's the most callous – the most cold-hearted thing I ever heard.'

At dinner Maisie said, 'The first time one visits a nice place one thinks how heavenly it would be to rent an apartment so one could go there any time, just on a whim. But the best places amount to no more than a view and a couple of quaint churches; and the apartment that seemed so-*so* charming turns out to be inconvenient and the landlord is a louse.'

I remembered they'd been to Nice before.

'We passed through last year on our way to Italy. But two years ago we stayed. Of course it was different then – Ben had his yacht.'

'You have a yacht?'

'S'right,' Ben grunted. He was drinking but that was safe as long as he didn't drink alone.

'Two,' said Maisie. 'One in Europe and one back home. When war broke out we sent it from here to England where the British have commandeered it for laying mines or something. The point is that Nice is quite different when you have a yacht. For one thing, you know who people *are* because you invited them on board. And – believe me Pat – there is nothing so dreamy as being on a yacht at night, watching the lights of the town from a distance and listening to music drift over the water. I've done it and every time I want to hug myself and say, "This is perfect and it's mine and I can do the same again whenever I want to." Everyone should have a yacht – but I'm not stupid: I know they can't. Still, they should be grateful to those who can.'

'Grateful?'

'Yes. If no one owned a yacht, the experience I've described wouldn't be possible. If it wasn't possible, no one could even dream about it because it simply wouldn't be conceivable. Poor people need to dream. They can't own a yacht, but they can enjoy something of it in books and movies. Yet how could writers give them what they want if it never existed anywhere?'

Tonight Maisie looked lovely, with a fervent glow to her skin and her elegant neck turning every which way as she scanned the restaurant to collect admiration. She looked like a woman for whom you would throw away your marriage knowing all the time that the affair would be emotionally brutal and the gain a fierce, sordid joy.

Across the room were Colonel Glue Eye, Signora Pitti, an elderly type I took to be the Marchese, and a decaying beauty. The Colonel came gliding towards us with a suave step.

'Messieurs, 'dames, my party were wondering if you would care to join us? Perhaps by pooling our *ennui* we shall find some mutual interest?'

Ben, who'd heard everything his wife had to say, looked up and murmured, 'Okay, buster. We'd be delighted.' Then he glared at each of us in turn. There was no protest. Glue Eye clapped his hands and, to the annoyance of the rest of the diners, tables and chairs were arranged together.

We exchanged some personal details, neither accurately nor sincerely. I wondered where we'd find our common ground. Colonel Glue Eye claimed to be a diplomat of some kind. As if to remind us that Hungary was a player in the great game of war, he said with the confidence of those things that are naturally understood by sophisticated people, 'I think I speak for my Italian friends when I say how grateful we are to those Americans who have stayed in Europe and can see with their own eyes what is going on.'

'Europe' was a restaurant where no bloody horrors were presently in progress.

'Things aren't as bad as they make out, that's for sure.' Maisie volunteered gamely. 'People get the wrong idea.'

'Jews,' said Colonel Glue Eye.

'Really?'

'Oh, I don't blame them,' he offered. 'Each race defends its own.'

'I suppose so. Even back home, Jews can be pushy about getting their own way.'

'Precisely.'

So, it seemed, our common ground was to be civilised fascism, and we were too polite to disagree. I make no other excuse except that at that date, we knew or chose to know little of the reality. It was in any case only a passing subject. Signora Pitti picked up that I was a writer, supposed I was American and thought I wrote for the movies.

She confided in a seductive whisper, marking each sibilant softly, 'I have als–so been to Hollywood, Patrick. I know many film s–stars. Marlene Dietrich? You have s–seen her in her chic gentleman's s–suits, hah hah? She is a less–being. Joan Crawford is a less–being and Talulah Bankhead als–so. It is a conspiracy against real women, that only less–beings have work in movies.'

She exchanged some remarks in Italian with the Marchese and the fading beauty, then addressed me loudly.

'I as–sk Paolo his opinion and he agree. He says men are very attracted to less–beings – *vero?* Hah hah, I don't care! I am glad I am real woman, not less-being!'

I said I was also glad. At which point it came to me that she was speaking for the benefit of the woman sitting next to me, whose name I hadn't caught. The latter put down her napkin and said, 'I have a headache. I am going to bed.' Apparently she was German.

'I go to bed also,' said the Marchese. He rose, bowed to the company and kissed Signora Pitti. His smile had a touch of mischief. As he followed the German woman, I wondered if I was being offered a foretaste of a choice rarity: an encounter between the stout nobleman and a 'less-being'.

At all events six of us were now left, and, since neither Colonel Glue Eye nor Signora Pitti were with their original partners, I was curious what combinations they had in mind.

CHAPTER TWENTY-FOUR

Colonel Glue Eye suggested we pay our bill and go to a club he knew where there was dancing. I was reminded of the night Alvírez drove the diners out of the Hôtel Czar Aléxandre and into the casino. There was the same force of will, the same whiff of moral faintness among those of us who didn't want to go and could have combined against the idea but wouldn't.

'You will like this little *boîte de nuit*,' the Colonel said. 'It is very louche on the one hand and on the other very respectable. I mean that it is civilised and one is not expected to do anything one does not truly wish to do.'

'I know it!' said Ben. 'There can't be two in a town this size. The owner's a White Russian called Seriozha and there's a Latin band with a dago singer. The name'll come to me. Am I right, Glue Eye?'

'There is a Latin band, certainly.'

'Didn't I tell you! Oh, we are in for a time!'

'I am pleased you like my idea,' said the Colonel.

With the war there were no regular taxis but we found two *fiacres* brought out of retirement. The men travelled in the first carriage, the women in the second. I didn't know where we were going in the gloom, but Ben pretended he did. He argued the point with Glue Eye who remained equable.

'We turn left here!'

'I do not think so.'

'Left! Pat, tell the driver to take a left.'

'You are mistaken, Mr Benedict. Perhaps you are thinking of another place? *Continuez tout droit, mon ami.*'

'I thought we were agreed. Oh hell, I wouldn't have come if I hadn't thought … I don't want to go to some sleazy dive.'

'*Soyez tranquil* – do not get upset, Mr Benedict – Ben – I assure you it is not in the least 'sleazy'.'

The assurances didn't convince. I don't think we wanted to be convinced. Ben's protestations were a bolt hole for his conscience at the prospect of a place that was seductive and utterly degrading.

Somewhere beyond the fashionable end of town were a railway station and a Russian Orthodox Church. The *fiacres* dropped us nearby in a street of apartment houses; not sleazy but dreary. Ben was disappointed, saying this wasn't the place at all and he didn't want to go to just any old crummy joint. He told the Colonel that he wasn't the sort that gets pushed around. Then we found Maisie at our side: Maisie in a scarlet georgette gown, with her lips slashed scarlet and her eyes fervid.

'Stop acting like a clown,' she told Ben. 'Sometimes you can be so embarrassing.' She had a sniffle and was shivering so I asked if she had a chill. Immediately she turned to me, radiant as if I'd said the nicest thing in the world.

'You're *so* considerate, Pat,' she cooed. 'Not like some people I could mention. No, I don't have a chill. Anna has given me – you know – a little *something* to pick me up.'

Signora Pitti laughed. 'Darling! You mustn't give away all my little secrets!'

'I don't see why not – we're all friends, aren't we? Pat – Paddy my boy – you'll take me in even if bad old Ben won't, uh huh?'

'I didn't say I wouldn't go in,' Ben snarled. 'Did I say that, Pat? Christ!'

'Of course I'll take you in.'

'And Hetty'll come, won't you Hetty?'

Hetty nodded. She'd been quiet all evening so I'd scarcely noticed her. Tonight, against the svelte Signora Pitti and a highly-coloured Maisie, she looked pale and touchingly insignificant – a nice girl from Pittsburg, which is all she ever was. I thought then that maybe we should go back to the hotel, but Colonel Glue

Eye stepped in deftly, offering his arm and saying, 'I shall escort the beautiful Miss Novaks. Come, I insist. And, Benjamin, have no fear: this club is not unpleasant, it is ... *interesting*.'

There are times when a woman who has previously meant nothing to me will suddenly come alive: a plain woman will be beautiful; a dull woman stimulating; an unsympathetic one reveal a moment of human agony.

Maisie's beauty had always struck me as attractive, but I understood her so little that it never occurred to me to do anything about it. Tonight, however, she was filled with a brilliant fervour: her need no longer selfish but an ardent protest against life's shabbiness – and, God help me, I thought that I could truly see her in herself and that she was a woman worthy of being loved.

I can't account for this sudden compassion, which wasn't just sexual desire. She was lovely tonight, but always was. She was drunk, but neither more nor less than I'd seen before. Livelier? Maybe. But something more. She seemed to burn with a conscious sense of her own femininity – marvel at it – rejoice in it, so that each gesture and movement of her body enthralled me.

That's how I remember her on that one night: a laughing figure in scarlet, spinning across a dance floor. And for the rest I see a seedy club where Italian officers took grim pleasure in fondling French whores; a place that wasn't vicious but only vaguely shameful.

The band was French masquerading as Cuban, the singer a ruined mulatto. They scraped the music with a coarse style as though they could play better if they cared to. The girl sang with a sob in her throat, lamenting her trashy lovers; suggesting the audience were trash, too. My eyes stung with the songs and the smoke and the sight of Maisie smiling and languid as death as she slouched with Ben to a rumba.

Ben had fixed his mood with some shots of grappa and, when the music broke for the next number, he pulled Signora Pitti fiercely to the floor. She squealed and struck his arm lightly. Then she gave in and seemed to collapse in his arms like a beaten girlfriend. Colonel Glue Eye, full of quaint *politesse*, turned to Hetty and asked if she would do him the honour. She said she'd be charmed. They took the floor and, adrift in melancholy, I watched them until Maisie, glittering with vivacity, glided towards me.

'C'mon, Pat,' she crooned. 'Show me how it's done.'

'What is it?'

'A tango.'

'I don't tango.'

'It's easy. You do it as if you're angry and won't be satisfied until you've punched the other fellow and got your girl into bed.'

'That's a dance?'

'The best!'

She led me out and I grabbed her in what I thought was the dance position.

'Tighter,' she said.

'Like this?' My right arm was almost around her for I could feel the silk slide against her skin. The band got into its stride and we took a turn around the floor, as easy as I could make it though my right leg was a little stiff from my accident.

Maisie chuckled, her breath stroking my ear. 'Where's your anger?'

'I'm not angry.'

'No? Ah, well … ' she sighed. 'You know, there is another way of doing the tango.'

'There is?'

'Yes. Forget the drama. You dance it very close and soft – but dirty, that's very important.'

'Dirty?'

'Dirty.'

'So I have a choice – like a madman, or a pimp with a drunken tart?'

'Uh huh.'

'Okay.'

I did my best. We found a rhythm and followed it. I can't say I did well, but Maisie found whatever she was looking for. She moved with boneless sensuality, forcing me to press her body to mine. Her head was now on my shoulder, her lips nuzzling my neck; now lolling back, eyes closed. She was smiling – yet not for me but for the pleasure of the body I was holding, the body that tensed or trembled to its own needs. I felt like someone used, but wanting to be used and, too, the creeping resentment that's the mood of the dance: a fury of sexuality and a faintness of impotence; a longing and a hatred.

As the music stopped, I threw Maisie back abruptly so that she arched over the arm around her waist.

'Whoa there, Mack!' she exclaimed. The band was going straight into a second number.

'I can't do this,' I snapped.

'Don't I know it. It's a killer, isn't it?' She circled her hand around my waist and held me. She coaxed, 'Don't quit, Pat. Not like this – it's just the dance working on you. This time don't think about it. Just push me around the floor a little and I promise I'll be good.'

I hesitated until someone behind jostled me into movement.

'That's it,' Maisie said, 'Am I forgiven?'

'There's nothing to forgive.'

'You're a nice guy, Pat – I think I've told you that already. *Hélas*, I don't seem to attract nice guys.'

'Ben?'

'He's "regular" but not "nice" – they're not the same thing.'

'Tom, then.'

'I couldn't keep Tom,' she said.

Whatever the music was doing, this time I felt cool and detached and Maisie was just dancing the steps without giving into them.

'Tom can tango,' I said.

'Can't he though!' Maisie responded.

'And what's his style – madman or pimp?'

'Tom?' She halted and I had to nudge her on. She repeated 'Tom' gently. 'Oh, he does it his own way.'

'Describe it.'

'Why?'

'You know me. I like to learn things.'

'You do, don't you? Well, let me think. I don't know I've got the words. Tom doesn't dance angry; he dances with ... passion? ... suffering?'

'He suffers?'

'I think so. Crazy, huh?'

'Yes. Go on.'

'I don't know I can... I don't know I want to.'

I waited. I felt her become restless. She looked away, then back again.

'Okay – if you like,' she said. 'When Tom dances it's the most thrilling thing that can happen. It's like being swept up into a tragedy. It's like being loved – but not with the ordinary stuff that passes for love. It's ... I can't put it right ... a sort of unbearable *tenderness* that sees right into the heart of you. Have you ever felt transparent, Pat?'

'No.'

'To be in Tom's arms is to be transparent – bodyless – weightless ... '

'Is it wonderful?'

'No. It's hateful. But at the time that's not how it feels ... the feeling of simply *not being* is too ... Oh, God damn it, Pat!'

She was crying.

A girl got on the stage and took her clothes off. Another girl did the same and they did some moves together while the soldiers hooted and threw money and the band drank at the bar. I suppose this is what Colonel Glue Eye had in mind.

A record was playing and the others were still dancing as we'd last seen them. I took Maisie to one of the booths where we sat in the darkness, her face pale and her scarlet dress glowing.

She said, 'I'm sorry about that, Pat. Do I look a mess?'

'You look lovely,' I told her.

'I can't think straight when I think about Tom.'

'I understand.'

'He's such a *good* man!' she said.

'So everyone says.'

We were silent a while. The record had stopped. Ben and Signora Pitti were standing on the dance floor in conversation. Hetty and Colonel Glue Eye were at a table, heads together, and she looked happy. I felt Maisie's hand on mine.

She said, 'I want you to marry me.'

Her voice was quite even.

'What about Ben?'

'Oh, I love him desperately, of course. But you've seen what he's like. Not exactly the nice, charming man you first thought. We're getting a divorce. I'd get one here, but I'm not sure I can or if it would hold up back home. That's why I want to leave.'

'How does Ben feel about it? I take it he knows?'

'Don't be stupid, of course he knows. He says it's fine by him. In any case, that isn't the issue. Will you marry me?'

I was so astonished all I could say, stupidly was: 'I've got no money.'

'So what? Ben won't be mean, and, in any case, I'm stinking rich. You'd be able to write.'

'Why me?'

'I like you … you're kind … I don't want to be alone. It's so pitiful when a pretty girl is alone. Everyone says there must be something wrong with her and starts feeling sorry.'

'You don't love me,' I told her, trying to make sense of a situation that was beyond me.

'Don't I?' she asked as if this might be a surprise. 'Don't be so sure – I'm not. I've felt the emotions that people call love but they're not reliable. Then again, I'm not a reliable person – everyone says so. They say I'm strange – a little touched, you know? I'm touched only because I want something better but don't see my way clearly.' This was said in one breath so that she sounded urgent when she asked, 'D'you love me?'

'I ... well I ... I don't really understand love.'

Maisie looked at me sceptically then said, 'It's a washout, believe me.'

I was lying on the bed when I heard a rap on the door. The clock said three and I hadn't ordered any room service. While dreaming I'd taken off my shoes and tie and smoked a few cigarettes.

When I opened, I found Maisie there, still wearing her georgette gown though we'd returned to the hotel a half hour ago.

'It's hot and I'm restless,' she said.

'You'd better come in. Can I get you a drink? I won't join you.'

'No thanks, I'm tight already.'

I was used to living in slums. My clothes were dumped here and there on the furniture. Maisie looked around then sat on the bed, Sunday-school upright with her hands folded on her lap. I sat beside her with a space of a foot or so between us and, I fancy, looked pretty much the same.

'This feels odd,' she said.

'Not so odd.'

'No? How's that?'

'I haven't a clue.'

I did know. Strangers confess to strangers: in bars, on trains, in seedy hotels. If there were any oddity that night, it was this: that Maisie and I had thought ourselves friends and discovered we were strangers.

'I find parties sad. What about you, Pat?'

'Every party?'

'What? Oh – I suppose not all of them. Sometimes you go with a boy or you meet a boy, and the party is just a prelude to something wonderful. Other times – these are the ones I mean – the party is over and you find yourself alone, and that is absolutely the saddest thing.'

'What about Ben?'

'I don't know where he is. Downstairs getting rowdy in the bar or maybe with the Italian woman – I don't care. Have you noticed how Ben's changing?'

I didn't answer.

'Used to be a time when he'd take a drink and be the sweetest guy imaginable – I mean unless he was drinking alone. Now – I don't know – he becomes all closed up and nasty and wants to pick fights. Maybe it's my fault. I wanted to marry Tom, but he wouldn't have me and so I married Ben. I guess that makes me a cheat, and of the worst sort where it really counts – I mean love.'

'I'm sorry.'

'It's unfair of Tom,' she complained. 'He's got no business going around making everyone fall in love with him. It wouldn't be so bad if he was a rat. At least, then, you could say to yourself, "I've made a mistake – *it's not my fault!*" and pick yourself up and go on with life. But Tom – Tom – he's so goddamn *decent* and would never deliberately hurt you. That's what so cruel. He leaves you nowhere to go except into yourself – to poke into those dark, horrible places and say, "I'm a terrible person. That's why he doesn't love me". But Tom – he won't say a word against you. Whatever it is that's wrong becomes unspoken – *unforgivable.*'

I decided I'd have a drink. I fixed one and offered a glass to Maisie, who was shuddering.

'Did Tom ever explain?' I asked.

She took a mouthful of spirits and coughed as they do in cowboy movies.

'Oh, sure,' she said, uninterested. 'He apologised – said he blamed himself for giving me the wrong idea. He said he'd be no good for me – as if he'd know, the chump. He couldn't be nicer: telling me I was a fine person and shouldn't think bad of myself and would make someone else happy. It sounds icky, how I tell it; but Tom means what he says.'

'Then believe him.'

'No. He always sees the best in people – but that doesn't mean he's right. I'm worthless, *that's* the truth of the matter. *Worthless*, Pat.'

Maisie dropped the glass. She put her hands to her face and began to heave tears so violently I thought she would vomit. I'd seen girls cry, but never a woman as if she'd give her soul as the price of her grief. It was terrible and – I'll admit it, since this is about truth telling – arousing: though, don't mistake me, I didn't want to take advantage of her. No, I was still at a sentimental age. I let the tears jolt their way out. I murmured some sympathetic stuff, which I honestly meant until, in the end, she was calm again with her eyes red and her face flickering with transient emotion like lightning over the sea. Then she said something I hadn't heard before.

'You know – Tom Rensselaer is the loneliest man I've ever known.'

At the time I didn't take in everything that Maisie said. Not so far as Tom was concerned. That night only Maisie interested me.

Lately – for this book in fact – I've had to go over events again and make what I can of them; though I sometimes wonder how it's possible to recapture a time when I was half man, half boy and full of the pretence of youth. Whatever – I've written what I've written and it'll have to stand for things I've never understood: not about Tom, nor Maisie, nor me. Listening again to her voice with its crisp Yankee drawl softened by emotion (like Katherine Hepburn now I think of it, though never so hard), a thought comes to me and it's this. There was in Tom's goodness something monstrous. If you let him get to you, he became like an incubus attached to your life: an unshakeable ever-presence. Yet it was the last thing he would have wanted.

I stood by the table with my glass while Maisie cried herself out on the bed. When she'd finished I picked her glass off the floor.

'Thanks,' she said.

I was a gentleman. I let her collect herself in her own time, expecting she'd make an excuse for what she thought of as her own foolishness and then go. She didn't. She smiled at me sweetly, then sorrowfully. Her expression wouldn't settle.

'I don't want to leave,' she said.

'All right. Do you want to sleep? You can take the bed and I'll doze in the chair. Or, if you want to be alone, I can doss down in the bathroom – though, in that case, you'd better use it first.'

'What would your mammy say?' she asked.

'Ah, she was a brazen old girl, if my Uncle Gerald's stories are half true.'

'I don't want to drive you out.'

'Okay … I'll go in the bathroom and then make up a bed.'

Which is what I did, spending a quarter of an hour in there, thinking she'd go to sleep. When I came out, she was in the bed with the scarlet frock, and peach silk slip and her stockings thrown on the floor. I cleared a chair of my own stuff and sat myself down.

'Make love to me, Pat,' she whispered.

'That'd probably be a mistake,' I said.

'Probably. But I'm beyond regrets – and one only regrets things because, afterwards, one never remembers the reasons that were good at the time.'

I couldn't answer that, though I don't think it's true.

Was this romantic? Is this what they mean by romance? I took my clothes off clumsily in the dark and slipped under the covers. I'd no idea how it would be: whether Maisie would be fierce or impassive. I wanted to be whatever she wanted. Perhaps, despite her words, it would be nothing: no more than the comfort of another person to fight the still terrors of the night.

She turned towards me, her cheek grazing mine, a hand laid gently on my chest. I hoped she wouldn't speak, because anything said was likely to be false. And she didn't. I turned towards her, embraced her and let my hand stroke the cleft of her buttocks and contented myself with the soft pressure of her breast against mine and the tentative kisses that were scarcely more than breathing.

We made love – inexpertly on my part, I suspect: at least not with the energy I seem to see nowadays – slowly, carefully, tenderly. Just the once, which was all she needed. And I suppose it was okay because I felt her lips smile against mine and the tips of her fingers run over my face as if to make certain I was there. Then, at last, she slept.

I stayed awake a while, wondering what I was doing with or to this broken woman. I didn't know – I *don't* know if I acted wrongly, but it may be I did and, if so, I'm sorry. I thought I was acting for the best, but I don't claim to be a wise man.

If I'd been wise, I'd have realised that our absence from Tom was bringing on the tragedy that was breaking about his head.

CHAPTER TWENTY-FIVE

'So you enjoyed yourselves in Nice,' Tom said. 'I'm really glad. You needed a change of scene. There's nothing like it for making a place fresh again.'

Tom was right. As we came down by the corniche road, S. Symphorien sparkled in the dusty light. This morning even La Chênaie, which had been built by a cold-hearted speculator for the visiting trade, had the warm feel of a house that had grown out of the earth. Which is why we were all stupid with joy to see Tom in white shirt, white pants and espadrilles, vibrant and beaming his head off, grabbing Hetty and nailing her smile with a kiss. He looked as fine and unconcerned as I ever saw him.

'I've made a pitcher of lemonade,' he said. 'If you want a shot of something, I've laid my hands on some gin. How was Nice by the way? What did you do?'

'It was fine,' I told him. 'We went round a few museums and churches. Maisie shopped. We ate a lot, danced a lot, talked to a few people.'

'That so? Anyone interesting? I remember a bunch of White Russians, but I expect they've made a run for it. I don't suppose the English were there, though some of the arty crowd must have hung on. Any of our people?'

'Americans? We didn't meet any. We came across a Hungarian.'

'You don't say? What line was he in?'

'He claimed to be a diplomat but he looked like a gigolo or a confidence trickster.'

Tom laughed. 'That's Nice for you. Monte Carlo is even worse, believe me.'

We left the car to unpack itself. We were hot and took seats in the garden. Tom bounced around, serving us.

Ben said, 'You sound as though you were happy to get rid of us.'

'You're joking. No, I just thought you were getting stale.'

'And you? What have you been doing?'

'Painting.'

'The Malipiero girl? Have you finished?'

'Nearly.'

'Can we see?'

'Soon. I'm keeping the canvass up at La Pinède for convenience.'

'Is it good?'

'Ha, ha. Now, there's a question. You know how I feel about my stuff.'

Tom was talking without saying anything.

Maisie asked, 'How is she, *la belle* Katerina? Does she grow on closer acquaintanceship? Do we know more about her?'

'I'm going to unpack,' Hetty said. 'Pat, will you give me a hand?'

'If you like.' I went with her to the car where she stared at her suitcase with the mute glare of a cat at an empty food bowl. I picked it up and we went inside. Hetty was still determined to hear nothing concerning Katerina though I heard clearly enough.

'They're good people,' Tom was saying, 'both Katerina and her mother. She's just an innocent kid – oh, and she plays the violin.'

'Well?'

'Pretty well. In fact there was talk of her going to the conservatoire, some conservatoire or other. But the war put an end to that, at least for the time-being. Once Señor Malipiero turns up and they go home to Argentina, I expect she'll take up her studies again; that's what she says.'

'And where *is* Señor Malipiero?' Maisie asked.

'Still completing his business in Germany. He should have been here but you know how it is; the war has made everything more complicated.'

'You mean he's vanished,' Maisie said and laughed. 'You want to watch your step, Tommy boy. Alvírez and Pop Malipiero – it seems everybody disappears around those two broads.'

I didn't hear the rest because Hetty gave me a kiss on the cheek. She said, 'Thanks, Pat. You can leave me to see to my stuff.'

'Are you sure you'll be all right?'

She smiled bravely. 'I'll be okay. I meant it when I said Tom won't marry me. Oh, don't look at me as if you don't believe me. I'm not an idiot. I can tell the difference between what I'd like and the way things have to be. I'll be all right – really. Now cut along to the others.'

I returned the kiss and gave her a hug. I went back to the garden where Maisie was still asking questions like a circus knife-thrower wondering how close she dared get.

'Speaking of Alvírez, has he showed his face yet?'

'Not that I've heard,' said Tom.

Maisie gave a little moue. 'Ah, well – who cares? The police, I guess. Has ... whatshisname? ... your friend ... has he been sticking his nose in again?'

'I'm sorry to disappoint you. The police seem to share my view that Alvírez is one of those characters who sail close to the wind and are liable to disappear at any time.'

'Oh, I'm not disappointed. Quite the opposite. I always thought he was a creep.' Maisie put down her glass and, in a switch of expression, treated Tom to a dazzling smile that caused even him to retreat. 'Aw, c'mon Tommy! Aincha gonna give your gal a kiss? I've been away and you haven't welcomed me back.'

The change was sudden, and I glanced at Ben to see how he'd take it. Tom grinned. He clasped Maisie in a firm embrace and let her fall into a backward swoon while he leaned over like Valentino or Ronald Coleman except his kiss must have lasted all of thirty seconds. I saw Hetty, too, hanging about the doorway of the house, a dress or slip folded over her arm. Then I heard a handclap. It was Ben. He was smiling and his applause was ungrudging like the old Ben. Hetty took it up and I did, too, until Tom and Maisie were finished and took a bow, nudging each other and giggling like kids.

This was, I think, the last time we were all together sharing the same mood – all of us happy.

I went to my cottage to freshen up, change and put my dirty clothes to the laundry. I also had in mind to buy my old friend Dr Maillot a drink, so I went into town. When I didn't see him at his usual table at the Hôtel de la Gare and there was no answer to a knock on his door, I collared Antoine at the desk.

'The Doctor has been gone these two days,' he said. He reached behind the counter and produced a letter. 'This was left for you.'

'By Dr Maillot? He wrote it before he went away?'

'No, Monsieur Byrne. He gave it me some time ago. I was instructed to give it to you if the Doctor was … absent.'

I took the letter to one of the pavement tables, ordered a beer and read it.

> Dear Patrick,
> I have left this note with Antoine, not knowing when, if ever, I am likely to be arrested. I cannot predict the circumstances, but, if possible, will inform M. Viremont. You must speak to him.
> Please, Patrick, help me! In doing so, you will also help your friends.
> Felicitations,
> Dr Adolphe Maillot

In itself the plea for help wasn't unexpected, though I couldn't think of much I could do. The puzzle lay in the reference to helping my friends – which meant Tom and the others, I supposed. I was inclined to put it down to one of those vague promises people make when asking a favour.

Viremont's office was in the Rue de la République behind a stout door with a glass pane and a metal grill. The lawyer himself had the whiff of freemasonry and anti-clericalism that used to affect French professional men. But I'm speaking of prejudices. Viremont was perfectly businesslike.

'Dr Maillot was arrested two days ago and is in custody.'

'On what charge?'

'I think you know. The mother of the dead girl has laid a complaint and the matter is before the *juge d'instruction*.'

'I see. And is it serious?'

'Very serious. It is against the spirit of the present régime that unborn children should be done away with.'

'What evidence is there?'

'That an abortion was procured? The corpse itself is evidence.

That Dr Maillot performed the operation? I do not know, but I believe it is only the testimony of the mother.'

This was much as I expected and I still didn't know what the old man wanted. I went to the gendarmerie on the Promenade des Russes, hoping to speak to him.

Tisserand was his affable self. I found him at his desk. He was speaking with a man of forty or so, in a felt hat and a doubtful suit.

'I must talk to that one,' Tisserand said when I asked to see Maillot. The stranger was polishing a shoe on his trouser cuff as he worked at his papers with a pencil stub. He had a moustache and smoked without giving a damn where the ash fell from his cigarette.

'Who is he?' I asked.

'Inspector Joubert.'

'Oh?'

'He has come from Vichy.'

'That explains why I don't recognise him. You don't mean he's come all this way to investigate poor old Maillot?'

'He is looking at the case; but no, that is not why he is here.'

'Now you really have me mystified,' I said in order to jolly Tisserand into giving me his confidence. But, when he answered, I wasn't surprised at all.

He said, 'It concerns the disappearance of Monsieur Alvírez. Information has been received concerning his identity.'

'Can you tell me?'

'I do not know – except that he is a very bad man.'

CHAPTER TWENTY-SIX

Maillot and Tom were alike in one respect. Of all of us they were the only ones following a moral purpose. When he was sober, Maillot was cynical. When he was drunk, he had the subtle integrity of a Jesuit.

Tisserand let me into Maillot's cell. The old fellow was a little nervous, a little tired, a little rumpled, but he rallied to give a smile and grasped my hands.

'Patrick! Oh, my dear boy, I knew you would stand by me. Please take a seat. Alas, I cannot offer you any refreshment. You don't by chance have any … ? No, but of course not. Sit. Sit. Hah! Look at your poor old Maillot.'

'Are you okay? Have you been mistreated?'

'What? Oh, no no, *mon ami*. Tisserand is a good chap who would never harm me. But … there is another.'

'Inspector Joubert?'

'We have so far spoken only briefly, but that one is a dirty swine.'

'I don't know him.'

'Trust me. Also you may believe he will make difficulties in the affair of Monsieur Alvírez.'

'I don't see that need bother us.'

'No?'

'Not that I know of.'

We sat on the prisoner's cot with a bar of sunlight from the cell window dividing us.

'I've been in Nice,' I said.

'I know.'

'I got your note and went to see Viremont.'

'It is black – the situation – *hein?*'

'He seems to think so.'

'He does not want to defend a filthy abortionist. It is "not the done thing", as the English say.'

'Not the Irish.'

'Ha–ha!' Maillot beamed. 'Patrick – Patrick, you are the practical one. I am right to trust you.'

I was warily pleased.

'So, why did you want to see me?'

'I have a favour to ask.'

'Really? Now, why did I think that?'

'Truly, you are more cynical than I am. But, seriously, I need your help.' He leaned forward and whispered. 'It is the old woman – the girl's mother. You must speak to her. It is only her testimony that holds me here.'

So there we had it.

'I understand that, but I don't see how I can help you. Why should she listen to me?'

'Bribe her, *mon ami*. Bribe her!'

I hooted. Even by the old man's standards, this was too much. Maillot waved his hands. 'Hush, now, Patrick. This is not a funny thing.'

'It's the funniest thing since my Uncle Gerald got drunk with a pig. What makes you think she'd accept? And where do you think I'd get the money from?'

'Pouff! Of course she would take the money. She is from the Rue des Oliviers where the peasants live. A few francs – a few dollars – not so very much. Believe me, she will agree. And, if you do not have the money, borrow it from your friends.'

'Tell them I need to bribe a witness?'

'Certainly!'

'They'd never give it me.'

'You think not?' Maillot said. And he fell silent a while.

I told him I'd think it over. Then it seemed he was changing the subject because he became solemn, the same way he did when we were discussing the world and the strange ways of the God he didn't believe in. He grabbed my sleeve as I was about to go.

'Am I really a bad man?' he asked.

'We all fall short of the Glory of God,' I said, remembering something the teaching brothers had told me. The observation wasn't serious, and Maillot ignored it.

'I cannot go to prison, Patrick,' he said. 'Understand that … and forgive me.'

'I don't know what you mean.'

'Get the money!' he urged.

'I'll see what I can do.'

Maillot nodded. I shook his hand off and rapped at the cell door. My back was to the old man and Tisserand was coming to let me out, when I heard him murmur:

'Speak to your friend, Tom. Tell him I saw Monsieur Alvírez on the day he disappeared.'

I went to the beach in the hour when the shadows are long. Monsieur Pierre, laden with mats, umbrella and picnic basket, was trotting up the path behind Monsieur Alphonse. Monsieur Alphonse tipped his hat. I asked him, 'Have you seen my friends?'

'Your beautiful friends? Yes, they are still below.'

My beautiful friends!

Yes, and never more so. They were playing ball on the sand in the twilight, running like fools and squealing like children. So beautiful all of them. And good because beautiful.

I called out, 'Hullo there!' and watched them skitter to a halt.

'Hi there!' cried Tom. He looked around him. 'My God, have you noticed how dark it's getting? C'mon boys and girls, or nanny will be cross. Pat, my boy, how's your day been? You didn't come back from town. Maisie thought you'd been writing. Is that true? Has your muse returned?'

'I'll tell you over dinner. Do you want a hand?'

I noticed then a figure emerging from the sea to join the others. It was so unexpected that I couldn't make a connection with anyone. Then I saw it was Katerina Malipiero and she was looking at Tom and smiling the nervous smile of the ugly girl who is allowed in the company of those she admires.

I said nothing. I picked up some of the stuff while the others towelled off. Tom was chatting to everyone, pretending it was natural Katerina should be there. And they were going along with it though no one spoke to her. When we walked up to the house, she was alongside Tom exchanging words. I couldn't hear but only noted the gestures of head and hands which told me Tom knew no more what to say than I did.

We ate in the garden in the soft night. We drank rough table wine and didn't care. Katerina ate with us.

Tom said, 'So, Pat, you were going to tell us what you've been up to.'

'I've had an odd day,' I said. 'I found a note at my hotel – from Dr Maillot.'

'That's your friend, isn't it?' said Hetty.

'Yes – at least I think so. It seems he's got himself arrested.'

'Ha ha.' Ben laughed over his wine. 'You sure can pick 'em. What's he done?'

'He's an abortionist,' said Tom. 'I told you before.'

''S that right?'

'Yes,' I said. I noticed Maisie. She was ferreting glumly in her salad.

Sometimes I forgot Ben's astuteness. He asked, 'So what does the old guy want? He's got to want something, huh?'

'There's a witness against him, a woman from the town.'

'Who?'

'I don't know the name.' I said. I tried to be casual. 'Did I mention that a girl died?'

Maisie put down her fork. Tom said, 'I don't think this is a subject for dinner.' But Maisie stopped him. 'That's okay, I don't mind. I don't know why you're all looking at me. I really don't mind.'

Ben shrugged. 'So there's a witness. What does he expect you to do about her? Say – you're not a Fenian, are you, Pat? The old guy wants you to bump her off?' He made a gun with his fingers. 'Blam!'

'He wants me to bribe her.'

'Really? Oh well, I guess that'd do the job. Are you going to?'

'I don't have the money.'

'It wouldn't take much. A hundred dollars? A thousand? Not much anyway. You'd be surprised how cheap most people are to buy. Tom's an expert. Would you do it if you had the cash?'

'I don't know.'

'I don't see why you should,' Tom said.

'Neither do I – except that he's a friend.'

'I could lend you the money,' Ben said, 'though I'm not saying I will. Bribing people is a bore. My folks used to do it all the time. Politicians are the worst.'

'I'll bear that in mind.'

Suddenly Maisie snarled, 'Mosquitoes! I hate mosquitoes! I'm going inside.' She scraped back her chair and went into the house. A minute later we heard music.

Tom muttered, 'Poor girl,' to himself then turned to me.

'I was serious,' he said. 'I don't see why you should help Dr Maillot. I don't like what he does.'

'Maisie … ' began Ben.

'I'm not blaming Maisie. The question is what should Pat do; and you, too, Ben if you're thinking about lending money.'

Ben took that as a reminder of a business proposition. He asked, 'Did the old man give any other reasons why you should help him, friendship apart?'

I couldn't think of any, then recalled Maillot's last remark though I didn't know what he meant by it.

'He said something strange – for your benefit, Tom.'

'For me?'

'Yes. He told me he saw Alvírez on the Tuesday he vanished.'

'Good Lord,' Tom said calmly, leaving Ben to pick the subject up.

'That could be important, couldn't it, Tom?'

'I don't see how.'

'Maybe he could support your story to the police. Pat, did he say how this came about? Did he see Alvírez before or after Tom?'

'I don't know. He didn't give details. It's possible he was the last person to see Alvírez. He spends a lot of time walking in the hills. He could have seen him after Tom did. Do you want me to find out?'

Tom shook his head. He looked at his hands and then at the rest of us with a smile full of sorrow for things I didn't understand.

He said, 'Don't bother with Maillot. I don't like him. Let him say what he wants.'

Given what Tom had done and the things Maillot might know, he was a cool customer.

Tom, Katerina, Ben and Maisie went inside to play backgammon and listen to the gramophone. I stayed in the garden at the table smoking. Hetty stood at the wall looking at the stars and the sea.

Her voice was very clear in the night. She called out, 'Isn't this lovely?'

I went and stood beside her. She was leaning with her hands on the stones and her head forward with the neck stretched clean and her eyes shut.

She asked, 'Is there anything between you and Maisie?'

'No,' I said. I didn't elaborate.

'Ben knows.' She looked at me and gave me a peck on the lips. 'He doesn't care. He spent the night with that Italian actress. Funny though – he didn't touch her. They played cards and swapped jokes. She told me … said he was sweet.'

'And you?'

'Oh, nothing. Colonel Glue Eye made a pass at me but I thought of Tom and told him to buzz off. Maybe I should have slept with him if I can't have Tom.'

'You shouldn't say things like that. I'm sure Tom'll marry you.'

'Really? Well, let's see. What do you make of our Argentinian Virgin?'

During the meal Katerina had sat, still and beautiful, answering the few questions put to her but otherwise saying nothing. She waited on Tom for cues and once in a while their eyes would engage.

'Tom shouldn't have brought her along,' I said.

Hetty let out a tinkle of laughter. 'Oh, sometimes you are a honey! Tom knows me better than you do. I'm Hetty, not … Joan of Arc. Knock me down and I bounce right back. If Tom was a stinker or if he was … oh, I don't know … Clark Gable, maybe I'd carry a torch for him forever. But he isn't. He's a good man and if he doesn't marry me I'll just have to get on with life. I need to go home and find myself a millionaire.'

The door of the house opened. Tom came out with Katerina on his arm. I couldn't read his expression, but she was beautiful in her dark loveliness, her poise, her regularity, the tender hurt that played on her lips, the flickering desire for frail, human joy. She called good-night. Tom said that he was taking her to La Pinède and would be back shortly. We smiled and turned away.

'She's lovely,' Hetty said. Seeing I didn't respond she nudged me as if I were a kidder. 'Go on, you can say so.'

'She is.' I agreed. I looked round and they were walking on the path that was white by day and blue by night with broom and thyme to either side. 'But what do you make of her?'

'Do you want me to be honest? Women often aren't.'

'Yes, of course.'

'Well, *entre nous*, she's a bit dull. Oh, I know she's shy and all!

But she's dull because girls of eighteen who've seen nothing *are* dull. Poor Tom,' she sighed, 'I wonder if he'll ever discover that his mystery woman is so ordinary?'

I looked again, wondering if I would now see something different. Tom and Katerina were still walking on the path up the height of La Pinède. They paused and looked back, then vanished among the pine and cypress into darkness.

Teresa Malipiero waited there.

CHAPTER TWENTY-SEVEN

I never reached a conclusion about Joubert. Did he possess a deep, unforgiving intelligence, or did he get there by a slow grind? And what did Tom make of him? He couldn't tell me without disclosing his part in Alvírez's death.

When the Inspector turned up at La Chênaie with Tisserand, Tom welcomed them like a man with a clear conscience

'You don't mind if Monsieur Byrne stays, do you?' he asked. 'I've got nothing to say that he can't hear. Say, do I need the American consul or anything?'

'I don't think so,' said Joubert. And he smiled, 'not unless you are a murderer.'

'Good Lord, you do come to the point, don't you? Can I fix you a drink? Lemonade? Something stronger?'

'You have coffee?'

'We're running low on good coffee.'

'Lemonade. Tisserand?'

'Also for me.'

'Lemonade it is,' said Tom.

Joubert's manner was heavy, lazy. He smacked a fly on his neck. He examined his palm.

'Where are your other friends?'

'At the beach. Pat was about to join them. I've got a headache; a little too much sun I suspect. Pat, will you see to the drinks? I'll have lemonade – no, make it brandy, what d'you think? To hell with it, I'll have brandy.'

The lemonade was tepid and sour. I poured brandy for Tom and had one myself; then returned to the garden where the others sat around the table. Joubert was sweating in his woollen suit and Tisserand in his uniform. Tom was barefoot in slacks and a tennis shirt and looked as cool as could be. The only odd note was that he was wearing one of Maisie's picture hats to keep the sun off. On Tom it looked as if it would be next year's style.

'Thanks, Pat,' he said, and to Joubert, 'Go on – you were saying?'

'You saw Monsieur Alvírez in the hills on the Tuesday.'

'Yes, exactly as I told Tisserand.'

'But you are not certain?'

'I'm as certain as one can be about things that aren't important at the time. I'm pretty sure it was Alvírez, but I don't know I'd like to stake my oath on it.'

'He was making his way uphill?'

'Downhill.'

'Downhill?' Joubert looked at his notes then at Tom as if the point were still doubtful, though I knew what Tom had told Tisserand.

'What was he wearing?'

'Now, that's a difficult one. A suit, I think – a tan suit. I wonder – am I thinking of what he wore at the casino. Pat?'

'He wore a tan suit that night.'

'Ah! Well, there we are, I may be wrong about the suit.'

'A hat?' asked Joubert.

'Uh, huh. A panama.'

'Are you certain?'

'I think you know the answer to that.'

Tom didn't have a mischievous nature, but I could tell he was having fun with the Frenchman. Joubert couldn't tell or didn't care. He was leafing through his notes and grunting.

'Don't you find it strange that Monsieur Alvírez was so far into the hills – and yet wearing a suit?'

'Yes I do,' Tom answered.

'Can you explain?'

'No.'

'No?'

'Do I *have* to explain? Can I be expected to?'

Joubert sidestepped. He said, 'And this was on the Tuesday?'

'Yes.'

'You are definite about *that*.' The statement made Tom's previous answers seem evasive, but he responded blithely.

'Absolutely. It was the day Señora Malipiero and I set out for Grasse; though we didn't get there. That was right after the day of the boy's funeral. Tisserand can confirm the date.'

Joubert stroked his moustache. He sighed 'Ah, yes … Madame Malipiero … You know her well?'

'I can't say I do. But there aren't many foreigners in S. Symphorien and we stick together.'

'She knew Monsieur Alvírez – on business, you say. When was the last time she met him – before the encounter in the hills?'

'Really, you must ask her. I've got no idea.'

'And the nature of the business?'

'Import-export, or so I gather.'

'You have no business with him?'

'Good Lord, no. I didn't even like the fellow.'

'You didn't like him?' Joubert asked slowly and for once Tom realised he'd made a mistake of the most absurd kind: implying a motive that simply didn't exist. But he rallied.

'That's right, I didn't like him. I came across him once, when he bullied Beauclerc at the Czar Aléxandre into opening the casino. I don't like bullies. But I don't murder them.'

Joubert waited. Tom did nothing. I opened a pack of cigarettes and passed them round. Joubert was a chain smoker and accepted greedily. The lemonade stayed untouched.

The Inspector fumbled with his notes again. When he looked at Tom he had the neutral yellow eyes of an old dog.

'Madame Malipiero says that Monsieur Alvírez was proceeding *up* the hill.'

'She does?'

'She says he wore a *brown* suit/'

'Brown – tan.'

'Dark brown.'

'Could be.'

'She does not mention the hat.'

'Is that so?'

'She places the location of your encounter a kilometre away from where you say.'

'Gosh,' said Tom.

'You can explain these differences?' Joubert asked.

'Nope.' The answer was crisp and amused. 'But I can tell you one thing.'

'Now what is that?'

'That it's obvious Señora Malipiero and I haven't put our heads together in order to get our stories straight. And where I come from, that's a sure sign of honesty.'

This isn't a film and the scene doesn't cut on a good exit line. Joubert was too dull or too cunning to be interested in drama. Yet his questions, delivered in an unemphatic voice, were telling.

The Inspector asked, 'Where did Monsieur Alvírez spend Monday night?'

Tom was stumped. All he said was, 'Does it matter?'

'I think so,' Joubert said, checking notes.

'Why?'

'Because Monsieur Beauclerc confirms that the gentleman didn't pass Monday night in his bed.'

'So?'

Joubert spread his palms and looked at them. 'It is strange, that is all. He was last seen – *by you* – on Tuesday. He had an hotel room he did not use on Monday night. So, you understand, Monsieur Rensselaer, the question naturally arises. *Where did he pass that night?* With friends? He had none. In the open air? Ridiculous, *n'est-ce pas?* It is most mysterious.'

'I've got to agree,' Tom said.

'Mysterious,' Joubert repeated.

'Certainly.'

'Mysterious because, except for what you tell me, all the evidence is that Monsieur Alvírez disappeared on Monday, *not* Tuesday.'

'Ah, then I guess I'm mistaken and it wasn't Alvírez I saw.'

'So it seems … '

'But?'

'Madame Malipiero also saw Monsieur Alvírez.'

'Right.'

Joubert scratched his chin. He said, 'For one witness to be mistaken is acceptable. But for two to be wrong about a man they both know … ?'

He shook his head and muttered, 'Problems … problems.' He thanked Tom for his help.

'I think maybe I will go for a swim after all,' Tom said.

'I don't know why you're so cheerful,' I said.

'I don't either. I suppose it's because Joubert has given me his best shot and it doesn't amount to much.'

'Doesn't it? I thought he scored when he pointed out that Alvírez disappeared on Monday – which makes your sighting on Tuesday look damned odd.'

As I've said, Joubert didn't labour his questions. Even so, Tom surprised me when he reacted as though he'd never picked up the difficult position he was in.

'Really?' he said. 'I don't think it's important. There'll be some innocent explanation.'

We went to the beach and swam a while with the others. They were curious about the interview but not especially concerned. Tom was vague and light-hearted as though he hadn't a care in the world.

I told them, 'Joubert seems convinced Alvírez disappeared on the Monday of the funeral. That's what the evidence shows.'

Ben asked, 'What day was it you last saw him, Tom?'

'The Tuesday.'

'Gee, that's odd, isn't it?'

'So Pat says.'

'How strong is the evidence that he vanished Monday?'

I said, 'Beauclerc swears he didn't sleep in his bed.'

'Then where did he sleep?'

'That's Joubert's point.' I looked at Tom to see if he understood at last. He shrugged.

'As I recall, Alvírez liked a drink. Most probably he had a skin full and slept on the floor. That would account for the state of the bed.' He smiled. 'Yes, I guess that's the explanation.'

CHAPTER TWENTY-EIGHT

In nineteen sixty-five I did a book tour of the United States, which is how I came to be in New York in the summer. Phil Alpert chaperoned me.

He had an idea that the Irish drank only in illegal shebeens. I said hotels were fine, but he insisted. He said he knew a bar in a low rent block in the forties where "characters" hung out. And so I found Rooney's.

Rooney himself was a Pole named Czarnecki who thought a touch of Irish was good for the bar-keeping trade. He catered for depressed office workers in bad suits and those natty little hats, common that year, which were good on Sinatra and the FBI but made anyone else look like a horse doper.

Rooney's didn't run to air-conditioning. The decoration was peeling veneered panelling, football pennants, beer signs and the occasional shamrock. A reluctant fan stirred the smoke-filled air, and street-dust and staleness blew in through the open door.

It wasn't a place that looked as if it attracted much Wall Street trade, except that a stranger, perhaps, who knew no better would come in and stay for one beer before moving on. That's what happened that day. Two strangers.

It seemed they'd just closed some deal in municipal bonds. They were at a loose end, feeling pleased with themselves. A couple of martinis made a third and a fourth seem a good idea. Perhaps they felt important among the bad suits and the hats. At all events they stayed, talking in loud voices about commissions and margins, alimony and cottages at Cape Cod.

Behind the bar, above the bottles was a television with the sound turned down. It showed sport. During an interval in a football game there was a news item.

At first I didn't recognise Ben. He'd lost hair and put on weight. I don't know what the story was about, but I mentioned to Phil that Ben and I had been friends more than twenty years before, which meant nothing to him and we let the subject die.

That would have been it if it weren't for the bankers back-slapping each other and getting noisy. Then I heard one of them mention a name that would have grabbed me if I'd been in my grave – Lucky Tom Rensselaer.

'Don't know him,' said the other.

'Rensselaer Merchant and Guaranty?'

'Oh, *those* Rensselaers. Then how come I haven't heard of him?'

'He isn't involved in the bank.'

'No? What's he do then?'

'Dunno. Law, I think.'
'New York?'
'The boondocks.'
'*Lucky* Tom Rensselaer?'
'Thirty years ago he was the most desirable bachelor on the East Coast. Had to beat 'em off with a stick.'
'You don't say. Another drink? Bartender! Rooney or whatever you're called – set 'em up again! Why are we talking about him?'
'No particular reason except that seeing Ben Benedict brought back a story I heard.'
'Uh huh?'
'Yeah.'
'Well?'
'Oh, just a story and probably not true. But they say Ben Benedict helped Tom Rensselaer to murder his wife.'

After our summer, I didn't hear from Tom until the Army let him go in nineteen forty-five and the first of his letters caught up with me in my moves around Los Angeles. I knew then that Tom's marriage hadn't worked out. He didn't say so in terms, but neither at that time nor afterwards did he ever refer to his wife. I would have asked except that I thought that, sooner or later, he'd get round to the subject. He never did.

I know that marriages fail. Even so, divorce was something I couldn't associate with Tom. He'd been so madly in love and cruelty and the affairs that usually lead to a split were so out of character they were incredible. It did cross my mind that his wife might have died – sickness or an accident – but that didn't make a lot of sense. I don't think people keep quiet to their friends about the death of a wife. At least not when the death is innocent.

I spent three weeks in America, and when I returned to Ireland I told my wife.

She didn't want to hear. Any mention of Tom always drew the

same reaction. Tom was just someone I'd once spent a holiday with – a holiday I didn't seem able to get out of my mind. I snapped at her that this time she had to listen; that this time it was different. Then I told her about the supposed murder.

She listened dully and fidgeted with her apron. Part way through, the village priest called with a collecting box for missionaries, and I have a recollection of our both going to the door and finishing the conversation on the step with the sun shining down on a cobbled street still brilliant from the last rain and the sea chopping the harbour walls. We were living in the west, where the Irish die of poverty and beauty.

She asked a few questions, mostly to find out where the story came from and the evidence behind it. She wasn't impressed that it was a rumour picked up from two drunks in a bar.

Finally she said flatly, 'I don't believe a word of it. Tom would never kill anybody.'

'It would explain why Ben doesn't want anything to do with him.'

'Because Ben was an accomplice?' She sighed. 'Listen to yourself. What possible motive could Ben have for getting mixed up in a murder?'

I couldn't think of any. Indeed I didn't believe for a moment that Tom was a wife-slayer. On the other hand I was sure something must have happened to give rise to talk – something sinister and uncertain that allowed people to speculate.

I couldn't let it go, this not knowing. It occurred to me that, at the very least, there must have been a death and probably some police enquiries. The Rensselaer name was well known and the New York papers would have picked up any story. A search of the back numbers ought to turn it up, though it wasn't something I could do from the wilds of County Kerry.

I had a friend who lived in Queens. Ira Berkowitz dated from my Hollywood period. He was a scriptwriter who'd been denounced by McCarthy. He made a living ghosting for writers with less talent.

Tom left France in August forty-one. He was called to the Army in one of the first drafts of forty-two and posted overseas immediately after basic training. He'd been home a month when he wrote to me in December of forty-five. I had these facts from Tom's letters and I set them down when I wrote to Ira.

The timings were important if the task was to be manageable. As I saw it, when whatever it was happened, it had to be in the last few months of forty-one or, just conceivably, in November forty-five before he wrote to me without mentioning any wife. In itself the first and most likely set of dates was odd. Could a marriage fall apart so quickly? Maybe the later date was more probable? Maybe Tom's wife had had an affair while he was in the Army and he'd discovered it on his return.

Maybe she'd died violently.

Maybe … But this is Tom Rensselaer we're talking about: the most decent man who walked the earth.

There was no special urgency and it took Ira three months to reply. He went through the clippings and found no mention either of Tom or his wife. There was no body.

I thought over what I'd written and realised I hadn't told Ira of the Ben Benedict connection. I called him to explain. He almost laughed in my face.

'*The* Ben Benedict? The squillionaire?'

'Yes.'

'I didn't realise you knew him.'

'We don't keep in touch.'

Ben didn't want to speak to me and I didn't know why.

'What you're suggesting is crazy,' said Ira.

'I'm well aware of that. I'm not really suggesting he helped kill anyone. But it occurs to me that, if Tom's wife did have an affair, it may have been with Ben. As I recall, he wangled an exemption from serving in the war. He was available.'

I knew he'd separated from Maisie.

'Maybe there was a divorce.' Ira offered. 'Maybe Benedict married the former Mrs Rensselaer. I could check that.'

But Ben hadn't remarried after he split from Maisie. His name wasn't even linked with anyone. Sure, he escorted actresses to the functions he attended, but it seemed there was nothing in these relationships.

'They call him 'the Benedictine Monk',' Ira told me. 'It's a play on his name. Get it?'

That was all the hard information. However, I'd sparked Ira's interest. He had contacts in the television world, where Ben owned some stock though he'd bought it in the fifties, by which time any involvement he'd had with Tom was old news. I wasn't surprised there were no stories in those circles about an ancient murder. However, there were others that threw an interesting light on Ben's activities.

Ira said, 'The word is Benedict has connections to the Mob.'

'You're joking.'

'Hear me out. It's nothing too heavy. Lots of companies – even household names – have ties they don't speak about. There was a labour dispute that got broken up, and another story, which I don't claim to understand, about a retirement fund. Both situations worked out to Benedict's advantage, and the word is the Mob lent him a helping hand.'

Knowing Ben's cold-eyed view of business, I didn't find this wholly unbelievable.

But was it relevant?

Well, maybe. While Ben wouldn't dirty his own hands to commit a murder, there was a crazy plausibility in the notion that he'd pay an Italian hoodlum to do it for him.

So these were the fantasies I was having. But the truth was I didn't know what had happened to Tom or his wife. Only that there was confusion, unhappiness and mystery.

CHAPTER TWENTY-NINE

The Argentinian Virgin wove a skein of magic round Tom Rensselaer with threads so fine he couldn't see them, yet so strong they couldn't be broken.

I don't think it was done out of wickedness. More likely it was simple human despair. The fact is I can't say for sure how it was done. Tom said nothing, and *The Veiled Woman* is unreliable, because, when he wrote it, Tom was reeling under the cruelty. And it was bitterly cruel.

We saw only what he chose to let us see. Most days, Katerina came to La Chênaie for part of the time. She swam with us. She rode with us. She partnered Maisie at tennis. In her own way she enjoyed herself. But it was an enjoyment tinged with sadness.

She was entrancing. All of us thought so except Hetty. She persisted, when we were alone, with remarks like, 'There's nothing to her' or 'She's smart enough, I suppose. But nothing out of the ordinary. What did she ever say that was witty or interesting?'

As I've said, Hetty was clear-sighted and, in everything except the important thing, truthful. And this is the truth now that I can look back on events: if you forgot her haunting loveliness, there really was nothing exceptional to Katerina Malipiero.

How, then, did she cast her spell on us? There you have me. But you must remember that the audience works with the magician and the trick is pulled off with light, setting and atmosphere. We were living in a world of unreality and we felt used and shabby in the way the whole world does. Katerina's innocence somehow promised to cleanse us.

Or so I suppose. For my part, I saw her like a fool through the eyes of idealism and longing. When I looked at Tom and Katerina, they were immaculate – untouching and untouched.

For the rest, the game was played out at La Pinède, where Tom had gone alone every day while we were in Nice, and I can only imagine how it was.

In his careful manner he was still working on his painting. I think, too, that he might have begun a portrait of Teresa, but I can't be sure. I know he had reason enough to go to the villa.

I place him in the sunlit garden where the shadow of a cypress falls across the dirt. The garden hangs from the sky and looks out onto forever. Katerina trusts Tom. Teresa says nothing. She wears a veil against the sun and sits reading at the spot on the wall from which she may have accidentally killed the boy.

In the evening Tom leaves to return to us to. He smiles a lot and loses at cards. At such times there is another, darker side to La Pinède. The Argentinian Virgin pleads with her mother against what's coming. They quarrel. They rage and cry. They become reconciled and kiss because they only have each other – but the reconciliation is only for the moment since the issue is unresolved. And Teresa is unrelenting.

But there's no wickedness. Katerina fights for Tom's sake just as the mother fights for her daughter's. If Teresa gives the impression of hard-faced evil, it's just an impression. Later, in her room, she cries to herself and prays. If she could save Tom, she would.

Or so I suppose.

Certain subjects were unavoidable and Tom and Teresa had to face them.

Tom said, 'I was wrong to tell the police that we saw Alvírez on the Tuesday. It seemed such a neat idea to distract them from the time and place of death. It just didn't occur to me that they'd have evidence he disappeared on the Monday. Yet I should have guessed if I'd thought the matter through. My fault. I'm sorry.'

'Don't blame yourself, Tom.'

'Oh, don't worry. I'm not that sort of guy,' Tom said sunnily so that Teresa had to smile. Like everyone else, she was a little in love with him.

He asked, 'What d'you make of Joubert?'

'He frightens me,' said Teresa.

'Fear isn't such a bad thing if it makes you cautious. Has he spoken to Katerina?'

'No.'

'See? He isn't so smart after all.'

'He told me my description of seeing Señor Alvírez wasn't the same as yours.'

'What did you say?'

'That people remember different things.'

'I said much the same. It happens to be true and Joubert knows it.'

'He suspects us.'

'Quite likely he does. But he doesn't have anything: no body, no motive – in fact no crime at all. If he tries to touch me, the US Government will raise Cain unless he has me nailed by evidence.'

'I'm not American.'

'I shouldn't let that worry you. Joubert can't arrest one of us without the other.'

'How can you be so confident?' Teresa asked.

'I don't know. I just am. Would you want me any different?'

Tom stopped coming home in the evenings. If the moon was bright, he'd walk along the beach with the Malipiero women.

Tonight, however, Katerina was sick. The sun had given her a headache.

'Why don't you leave?' Teresa asked Tom. 'You could go home. I doubt Inspector Joubert would stop you.'

'I guess I could. Do you want me to?'

'No.'

'Then that's a good reason for staying. And what about you? D'you have plans to return to Argentina?'

'I can't.'

'Your husband? Surely he could make his own way?'

'No.' Teresa halted. They were in the middle of the beach, like castaways afloat on a calm night. 'I'm sorry, Tom. I should have told you. My husband is dead.'

'I see. How long have you known?'

'Since Señor Alvírez was killed. He had papers … I suspect that's why he was at the house. He came to tell me.'

'What did he die of, your husband?'

'I don't know. The papers didn't say.'

'He was sick?'

She shook her head.

Tom took the news quietly, and Teresa was glad.

'What'll you do?' he asked. 'As I see it, there's nothing to hold you here.' A more urgent question occurred to him. 'Has he left you provided for?'

'His affairs are … very difficult. Señor Alvírez was helping us. You understand, the war has stopped people from transferring money as they used to. Now, with both Alvírez and my husband dead … Oh, Tom … Tom! Katerina and I have absolutely nothing!'

Teresa shuddered. Without warning she ran off across the beach. Tom called after her until she disappeared. He followed and found her hiding in a crevice of the rocks, shaking and crying.

'Go away!' She was almost screaming.

'I can't do that,' Tom said. He tried to be practical. 'Look, if it's about money … '

She was appalled. 'I don't want your money!'

'Well that's good, because I don't have any. But be serious, Teresa. If you have no cash, you can't stay. I can probably get Ben to spring for fares for you both to go to Argentina. He's a regular fellow.'

'There is nothing for us in Argentina – nothing for us anywhere!'

She was vehement. And Tom, for whom the world was ordinarily so easy, was overwhelmed by a sense of hopelessness.

He escorted Teresa back to La Pinède in silence. To a degree he'd recovered. In the intensity of his compassion despair had been replaced by a reckless desire to help. He felt his life had reached a defining moment: a chance to cease to be Lucky Tom Rensselaer, the amiable moral nullity: a chance to become something worthwhile.

This night was the most pitiful of all. Yet Tom, stricken with afflatus and possessed by new, fierce certainties was undeniably happy.

They found Katerina reading by candlelight. Teresa offered Tom a drink. He debated whether to accept. Part of him knew he should leave; that he needed time to reflect. But Teresa had told him Katerina didn't know of her father's death and that made all the difference, because her image was now additionally pathetic and her smile unbearably poignant.

They talked about the next day: the usual stuff. Tom smoked a cigarette but pretended to be amusing and careless. He knew what he wanted to do, but still held himself back. He told himself his solution was rational, but he still needed to test its rightness.

He was frightened of behaving shabbily: of cloaking his own longings in a tattered rag of selflessness.

'Sit down, Tom,' Teresa invited him. She detected his nervous energy and had her own fears.

'I'll just finish my drink and go.'

'Yes ... if you want to.'

'What else is there to do?'

'Mother?' asked Katerina.

Teresa looked sharply at Tom and then at her daughter. She asked Tom, 'May I have a cigarette?' She lit one, trembling with indecision.

Tom was determined. 'I really *have* to go.'

Teresa grasped his wrist. 'No – wait. Hear this. Katerina … I have something to tell you.'

'Yes?'

'I'm afraid that your father has died.'

'No!'

Teresa clutched her daughter's hand. 'It's true,' she said. She was on the point of collapse and was restrained only by defiance. Katerina was crying. Tom, appalled as if in the midst of a disaster with fires blazing all round him, struggled to salvage hope from the wreckage.

He said, 'There's nothing for you here. But I can help you. I can get you to the United States. Katerina … oh, hush you now,' he murmured tenderly. ' … hush you now. I … No, not now … I … '

He held out a hand, took Katerina's and stroked it until her tears were reduced to sobbing. Then, abruptly, he fled into the night.

The following day he told Teresa that he was willing to marry her daughter if she'd have him.

CHAPTER THIRTY

Tom couldn't be underhanded. Before he proposed to Katerina he discussed the situation with Hetty. I don't know exactly what was said. By next morning, when he wandered over to La Chênaie, it was all over. The disaster had happened.

I found Tom in the garden. Hetty was in her room. Ben was inside, drinking solidly. I caught a glimpse only of Maisie. She was on her way to go swimming and looked as if she were rejoicing.

Tom tried to explain. 'Katerina and her mother are broke and stranded here. The only realistic way out is for someone to marry Katerina and give her US citizenship. I happen to be available.'

I wasn't sure of this explanation. It seemed to me that a great deal could be cured simply by money, and Ben had plenty of it. Yet I wanted to believe Tom.

I asked, 'What about Hetty? How has she taken it?'

He was distraught. 'I feel like a louse, Pat. Hetty is a wonderful girl – just the greatest. A man would be crazy to let her go. *I'm* crazy to let her go. I just don't know what to do for the best. It's a case of choosing between two evils.'

I wouldn't have let Hetty go if I loved her. But I didn't live in Tom's strange moral world where universal problems impacted on individual choice. At that moment he disgusted me even though I knew he was trying to do what was right and nothing he did was insincere.

He said, 'You know what Hetty told me? She said she'd always known I wouldn't marry her. How could she know that? *I* didn't know. I … I suppose that makes things easier.'

I gave some sort of response. I probably muttered a platitude from the majestic wisdom of my twenty-four years.

Tom wouldn't let himself off lightly. He said, 'No, it doesn't make things easier. The fact that Hetty saw something I didn't see, means I'm not the man I thought I was. And, if I'm not, then who am I?'

For certain I didn't know. So I asked, 'Do you love Katerina?'

He looked at me and answered, 'I'm damned if I know, Pat. But … if I thought that was the reason for everything – if I thought I'd betrayed Hetty out of a fickle sentiment, then I guess I'd kill myself. Because nothing would be worthwhile.'

That was the only explanation I got. I left Tom in the garden with the morning sun on him, and he was dressed in white.

There were things to sort out: calls at the *mairie* and the *sous préfecture* and a visit to the consul when Ben used his influence to ensure that Teresa Malipiero would be able to join her son-in-law in the Land of the Free.

Then Joubert turned up again.

We were having breakfast when he came with Tisserand in a black Citroën saloon.

'Hi there, come on in,' Tom said. 'I've been expecting you. Would you like some coffee – or, at least, what passes for coffee?'

Even so early, Joubert was hot, heavy, breathless. He accepted a chair. Tisserand remained standing.

'So, you were expecting me?' Joubert said.

'Yes. I was telling the others you were the sort of fellow who wouldn't leave the Alvírez business alone until you'd gotten to the bottom of it. And I'm right, aren't I? In fact I thought I'd see you before now and, when you didn't come, I was beginning to wonder if Alvírez had shown up someplace and the case was closed.'

'We have been waiting on information concerning Monsieur Alvírez.'

'You mean he's known to the police? I can't say I'm surprised.'

'The German authorities are interested in him.'

'Now that is news.'

Hetty made coffee and we passed the time in small talk. Tom asked if there were objections to the rest of us. Joubert had no objection. I think he was curious how we all related to each other as well as cautious because we were neutrals.

'So?' said Tom at last. 'What have you discovered that's brought you here?'

'Monsieur Alvírez is a United States citizen.'

'Really? I thought he was Spanish or South American. But if you say so.'

'I must therefore ask again if you know him.'

'I saw him around. That's all.'

'Then it is a coincidence?'

'I guess so.'

'The rest of you?'

We muttered denials, except Ben who said needlessly, 'I run a big conglomerate. Who's to say one of my companies hasn't done business with him? It depends on his line of work. What was he – or should I say 'is' he?'

'A blackmailer – ' said Joubert, adding ' – among other things.'

We were stunned, though Maisie passed the revelation off lightly. She said, 'Well! The people one meets in these places!' Ben snarled at her to be quiet. I don't think anyone other than Tom realised the implications this had for the Malipieros. It was, after all, they who were involved with Alvírez, not Tom.

Joubert said, 'Monsieur Alvírez is an American, a blackmailer, a man you do not like.'

Tom answered, 'I see what you mean.' He was cool. He asked, 'Where do we go from here? Do you arrest me or what?'

'That is not necessary.'

'I'm relieved.'

'But you can help us.'

'In what way?'

Joubert signalled to Tisserand.

'We wish you to return with us to the hills.'

'Oh? Have you found something?'

'No. Our searches at the places indicated by you and Madame Malipiero have been fruitless.'

'I'm sorry about that – I mean about being vague as to where we saw Alvírez. I can try again, if that's what you want.'

'That isn't exactly what we want.'

'No?'

'No. We thought we would search somewhere different – the place where Tisserand saw your parked car.'

They left in the black Citroën, Tisserand up front with the driver; Tom and Joubert in the back; the window down and Joubert smoking.

Later I asked Tom, 'What is Joubert like?'

'He has bad digestion. His stomach rumbles. Listen to me; the man wants to send me to the guillotine and all I can think of is that his guts gurgle like old plumbing. I suppose I noticed because he wouldn't talk.'

Joubert travelled with his eyes closed. Occasionally he sucked on a pastille he took from a tin kept in his smelly suit.

'Should we be thinking of telling the consul or getting you a lawyer?' Ben asked.

'I don't think so.' Tom said, more superbly than we knew. 'It doesn't do to let folks think you're worried.'

'What d'you say to Alvírez being a blackmailer?'

'People will say anything. It doesn't mean it's true or, if it's true, that it's relevant. Maybe he kicks his dog. Who cares?'

Alvírez, however, was buried in the hills not more than a hundred yards from where Tom had parked the tourer. Was he to be confronted with the body? Was Joubert hoping to surprise him into confession?

Tom thought, 'I should treat this more seriously. I could get myself killed.'

Yet he was light-hearted.

They took the road into the hills. Tom wasn't much concerned about the detail. They would find Alvírez's corpse or not. And if they did, he'd have some explaining to do. Meantime Joubert nursed his belly and seemed to smoke in his sleep. Tisserand watched the road and grunted instructions to the driver. They passed one of the trucks taking workers to the camp under construction somewhere.

At a spot on a bend where some trees had been cleared, they stopped.

'Are we here?' Tom asked.

Tisserand swung round in his seat, saying nothing.

Joubert stirred himself slowly. 'This is the place. Monsieur Rensselaer, is this the place?'

'Where we parked? It could be. I wasn't paying attention.'

'Tisserand?'

'I think so. Monsieur Tom?'

'You're probably right.'

Tom got out of the car, shook down his clothes, lit a cigarette and leaned against the coachwork.

'Isn't this a morning to be out and about?' he said.

'Are you ready, Monsieur Rensselaer?' Joubert asked.

'Oh, you want me to come with you?' Tom spun his cigarette onto the roadway.

'You will lead?'

'Lead where? No, I don't think so. This is your show.'

I asked Tom, 'Was it the right spot?'

He grinned. 'D'you want the truth, Pat? I didn't damn well *know*. It was just a bend in the road somewhere up in the hills. Oh, it had to be there or thereabouts – but the exact same spot? Tisserand seemed to think so, though he didn't sound too convinced.'

'I see.'

'No you don't. You weren't present. Tisserand started acting like a gun dog, pointing out trees and saying "Yes – yes – here – I recognise". Yet, as far as I knew he'd never been there – I mean not into the trees. Teresa and I hadn't seen him but his certainty became infectious. I started telling myself he *knows* what he's doing. This *is* the place!'

I didn't know what, if anything, had been found in the hills. The police dropped Tom at the gendarmerie and he came to the Hôtel de la Gare where I was spending the morning writing at one of the tables as a break from my cottage. I stopped and we took a drink under the lime trees.

Tom went on, 'Let's suppose I killed Alvírez … '

'I can't think of a reason why you would.'

'I'm taking things from Joubert's point of view. I'd still be dumb to bury the body. It'd be easy to fake an accident.'

'Not if you shot him.'

'I don't have a gun.'

'Or stabbed him.'

'Okay, that would be a different case. But let's assume ... I don't know ... I punched him on the jaw or hit him over the head with ... say a lamp? The smart thing would be to throw him down a ravine where it'd look as if he'd fallen and broken his head or whatever on the rocks. What d'you think?'

'Were the police searching a ravine?'

'No, a spot on the hill where the trees thin out.'

'They might still be able to tell from the injuries that he'd been murdered.'

'So what? At least there'd be a *chance* of passing the business off as an accident. But not if he was buried.'

'I can see that,' I agreed.

It didn't occur to me that Tom was figuring how he might have done things better.

I asked. 'Is that how Alvírez died – broke his neck or was hit or something?'

'I've no idea what's happened to him,' said Tom.

Joubert puffed his way between the hornbeams, snagging his feet on roots and vines. Tom moved lightly and easily. He laughed inwardly at his amateurishness in the matter of getting rid of corpses. Next time ... But of course there wouldn't be a next time.

From ahead came a call from someone who thought he was on to something and Tom almost wished he was.

It was a cairn of fieldstone, the length of a man, with signs of burning on some of the stones.

'Do you recognise this?' Joubert asked

'I can't say I do,' said Tom.

'What do you think it is?'

'Do people camp in these hills? Shepherds? Charcoal burners?'

'Clear it,' Joubert instructed his men.

Tom stood back, lit another cigarette and examined the sky. He was half-minded to confess. 'Yes, I killed Alvírez. He was a louse and no one will miss him.' Surely, if he were to confess, then others would accept he'd done the right thing?

Of course he didn't confess.

'Nothing,' murmured Joubert.

'Really?' said Tom. He was genuinely surprised though he could see now that stones had been thrown together for shelter and fire, most likely a long time ago.

Joubert gathered his men, spoke to them, and they pushed on higher into the hills until it was noon and everyone grew tired.

Tom thought he was free. But he'd forgotten about Maillot.

CHAPTER THIRTY-ONE

Dr Maillot was in the same stifling hole at the *gendarmerie*. The old man kept up his raffish style, wearing a jacket and tie for my benefit, but he smiled at me weakly as he held out a hand.

When I arrived Joubert was prowling in the outer office. Tisserand tipped me that the Doctor was no longer an interesting prisoner, just a piece of untidiness. Instead, all attention was focused on Alvírez, who they firmly believed was murdered, and on Tom, who they were sure had done it.

I said, 'I thought you searched the hills – twice wasn't it?'

'Also with Madame Malipiero.'

'Didn't you pick the last spot personally?'

'It was the wrong place,' said Tisserand as if Tom had forced it on him in a three-card trick.

Tisserand always used my surname. But Tom was "Monsieur Tom" and the two had been on good terms; in fact I think Tom bought a present for Tisserand's wife when she had a baby.

With that in mind, you'd think he'd find the notion of Tom's guilt too out-of-character to be credible. But, as I understood later, when I had to make something out of the rumour that Tom had murdered his wife, it isn't so simple. I mean that we get most of our ideas about people after the event, and things that now seem "in character" were once uncertain because we hadn't seen how someone would actually behave.

I'm digressing. Maillot was waiting on his cot in an eager tremble.

'Patrick, Patrick, you are like a son to me.'

'I don't know about that, but I'm your friend. Are you all right? Viremont said you wanted to see me.'

'To talk, that is all. I am old and lonely, Patrick. So pathetic that I make myself want to laugh, *moi même*. If I was truly *philosophique* I should meditate on my sins. But I will tell you a secret: I am no wiser with age. I suspect that wisdom is no more than folly mixed with tiredness; hence it comes with the years. What do you think?'

'You could be right.'

'Come, sit next to me.' He patted the thin mattress.

I offered a cigarette.

'Thank you. I shall keep it to relieve my boredom when you are gone.'

'Take the packet, I don't mind.'

'Thank you.' A tear crept into his eye. He wiped it. 'Disgusting, *n'est-ce pas?* I was not always so emotional.'

'*C'est la vie*,' I said.

'Now you are making fun of me. May I have fire? Ah! Now – ' he glanced at me slyly. ' – tell me: did you advance my little business?'

'You mean with the girl's mother?'

'Yes.'

'I spoke to Tom and Ben.'

'And?'

'I think Ben might be prepared to produce the money, but he takes his cue from Tom, and Tom won't hear of it.'

'Why not?'

'He thinks what you do is wrong.'

'Ah – he is a prig, that one.'

I said, 'I don't think so. No one likes a prig, but everyone loves Tom. You've met him?'

'Once, in the hills and another time, too.'

'You didn't like him?'

'No. He was too … perfect. And I disagree with you. I don't believe he is loved.'

I laughed. 'Away with you!.'

He'd spoken indifferently as though the matter were self-evident. When I persisted in my opinion, he said, 'Your Mr Rensselaer is *not* loved, I tell you. He is admired. It is not the same. Admiration does not last.'

'No?'

'Consider Joshua ben Joseph – your Jesus Christ. One moment he is the idol of the crowd, who spread palms at his feet, and next he is reviled by that same crowd. Why? Because they did not love him. They admired him and were jealous of him, and, when he was weak, they despised themselves for their admiration.'

'I don't think the two are exactly comparable.'

'No. Mr Rensselaer is an intelligent American. Jesus was an ignorant, fanatical Jew. Ah, what does it matter? Perhaps you are right. But I think I see clearly because I do not admire Mr Rensselaer.'

'That's pretty obvious.'

I suppose I resented what the old man said. Now I think about it, I disliked him rather as I disliked my Uncle Gerald despite his winning ways. I've listened too much in public houses. They're more stuffed with pretended wisdom than the Bible.

After a moment Maillot asked, 'Is it true that Monsieur Rensselaer intends to marry the little Malipiero?'

'You've heard.'

'Yes, even here. The town talks of nothing else: that and the disappearance of Monsieur Alvírez which everyone considers to be murder.'

'Really? And who's the criminal?'

'Madame Malipiero, naturally. She is alone and beautiful and so Monsieur Alvírez must be her lover – if he is not her husband.'

'Of course.'

'But, seriously, Mr Rensselaer intends to marry the girl?'

'Yes.'

Incroyable. There is madness in the air. What does he know of the family?'

'I can't speak for Tom. I don't know much, but he sees them at La Pinède most days. I suppose he's found out everything he needs.'

'The relations between *madame mère* and Alvírez for example?'

I shrugged. 'Did you ever speak to Alvírez again?'

Maillot answered cagily. 'I saw him about the town. Now, here is something interesting. Once, perhaps twice, he was with André Houblon.'

'I'm sorry?'

'One of the infamous Houblons of the Rue des Oliviers.'

'Isn't that where the girl lived, the one who died?'

'There is no connection,' Maillot said. 'A cousin perhaps – it is too much to understand, this town where fathers sleep with daughters. André Houblon is the child who was *not* killed in the accident on the cliff of La Pinède.'

I didn't recognise the name but remembered a stocky, vigorous boy. 'He's only twelve or thirteen. Why should he have anything to do with Alvírez?'

'*Qui sait?* I saw Alvírez dispatch him to buy a newspaper – and then watch as he ate an ice cream.'

I shuddered at the thought of Alvírez, in his grossness, studying the boy.

The Doctor remarked with casual insincerity, 'I don't propose anything improper. Even so, it is suggestive, *n'est-ce pas*? The circumstances – the pattern of relationships between the two boys, one dead and one alive, the disappeared Monsieur Alvírez, your Mr Rensselaer and – always – the Malipiero women? It is like … ' he sought inspiration ' … the figures of a dance.'

I said, 'You wouldn't make such implications if you knew Tom Rensselaer as I do.'

'I imply nothing,' said Maillot.

'Yes you do. You're hinting that there's something nasty in the affair. I don't know why or how it concerns you, but you couldn't be further from the truth. You said Tom's a prig. Well, I don't agree with the term, but you're right that he has a delicate moral sense. Too delicate maybe.'

I repeated the story of Tom's reaction to the accident on the rocks; his horror that André Houblon, the survivor, had diverted it onto the other boy.

'Tom thought it was wrong – that the wrong boy died.'

Maillot was puzzled as I'd been. 'But why? How does it matter which boy was killed?'

I'd given thought to the subject and explained as best I could; though not well since it was something I understood with the head, not the heart. Underlying Tom's attitude – maybe rooted in recognition of his own undeserved privilege – was an awareness of a vast cruelty and injustice in the very fabric of Creation. It was this force, impersonally and without reason or malice, that had tumbled a rock from the height of La Pinède to strike whomever it would.

Tom had said to me, 'It isn't evil, this Thing, no more than death or entropy are evil. It has no intelligence, no lightness or spark of life, no sense of order. It's inert, heavy, opaque – chaotic out of no more than sheer stupefying dullness.'

I couldn't relate this to the boy, André Houblon.

Tom said, 'I don't want to be hard on the kid, believe me, Pat.

I don't say I would have acted any differently. But when he pushed the rock aside, he gave in to the wrongness at the heart of things and began to work with it instead of against it. He conspired with death instead of defying it.'

I asked, 'What should he have done? Let himself be killed? That's what it amounts to.'

Tom didn't have an answer. He wasn't trying to convince me.

All of which I explained to Dr Maillot. He grunted, sniffed, mopped sweat from his brow and snatched at flies. But he understood well enough because he let me ramble to the end without interruption; and, when I was finished, didn't call me an idiot or contradict Tom, but only scratched and complained of heat rash.

We spoke a little longer. I offered to get his linen washed and bring a bottle of cognac. Maillot's cell gave the smallest of views onto the Promenade des Russes and, to distract myself from his misery and my own disgust, I looked out onto a waving palm tree and a violet sky with a single star.

Behind me Maillot murmured with bottomless regret, 'You will talk to Mr Rensselaer again, eh, my friend?'

'About what?' I asked.

'He will know.'

'The business of the girl's mother? I don't see why he should help you.'

'He ought to.'

This was the last thing said, other than the usual farewells.

Maillot frightened me. But I didn't know why because I knew nothing of the events of the fateful Tuesday when Tom got rid of the body. Yet I was sure that Tuesday was somehow important and I understood Maillot claimed to have seen Alvírez that day. I suspected, too, there was something sinister in the relations between Teresa Malipero and Alvírez, and now it seemed there was a connection between the dead man and the Houblon boy who'd escaped the rock fall.

It was a terrible realisation because I saw that, even if Maillot had the capacity to destroy him, when faced with a choice between that and doing what he thought to be wrong, Tom would simply let the evil fall on him.

CHAPTER THIRTY-TWO

I used to drink with W. H. Auden in a pub called *The London Pride*. This was in my Hollywood period after the War; and, though my friend gave me his name, I don't suppose it was genuine. Most likely he was an out of work character actor with a new line in cadging drinks. Still, it was a good line and he knew some poetry.

One of Auden's poems – both the real Auden and the fellow I knew, assuming they weren't the same – was the *Musée des Beaux Arts*, the one about Icarus, who falls from the sky while the World goes about its business and no one pays attention. I knew the subject because Tom had mentioned the painting: the same that Auden had in his poem. It was by Breughel, but I've never seen it and I doubt that I ever shall. It would be too poignant.

Like the boy from the bluff of La Pinède or Icarus from the sky, Tom Rensellaer fell. But in Tom's case he fell for more than forty years. From time to time I've glanced up in amazement, but mostly I've attended to my own affairs: loving my wife and raising my children.

Forty years is a long fall. And for all I know he's falling still.

The story that Tom murdered his wife came during an interlude when it seemed his life had taken an upturn: the time when he was involving himself in the civil rights movement, before drink and the South revenged themselves. That fact and the implausibility of the accusation meant that, after the initial shock, I put it out of mind, though sometimes I'd revisit the idea as a curiosity.

On such occasions I'd find my thoughts were detached, something that happens with notions we don't fully accept. So, instead of thinking about how crazy the theory was, that Tom was a murderer, I'd turn to the detail, wondering, for example, *which* wife he was supposed to have killed? After all, this was America, and who was to say that over the years Tom hadn't had several wives? And killed them, for that matter?

I was, of course. Because I knew him.

I remember nineteen sixty-eight because of the Paris riots. That year I did another American book tour.

I'd had no contact with Ben since that day, five years before, when he told me as nicely as he could that he didn't want to see me again. Even now I wouldn't have contacted him except that his name was linked to Tom's in the story about the murder. I couldn't think of any other way of getting to the truth.

I decided not to telephone. I'd have to give a reason and the subject needed a face-to-face discussion. So I wrote a letter once I knew I'd be in New York for a few days.

The reply was surprisingly warm. Ben didn't mention our last meeting. He said he'd wondered how I was getting along and that old friends shouldn't be let go and more of the same kind. If it was true and I was going to be in the neighbourhood, I should drop in on him and we could chew over old times.

I told this to my wife and we quarrelled. She said I should let the past go.

Phil Alpert had had a heart attack. I stayed at Ira's place in Richmond Hill. Ira told me he was doing all right in the ghost-writing game and we joked about his dead days as a Jewish radical. We cracked a bottle of Wild Turkey. We swore undying love. I think he died about seven years ago.

Ben had an office in the Benedict Building in Sixth Avenue. He was a beefy man in his fifties in an expanse of blond wood trimmed in ebony. He said, 'What d'you think? The Art Deco stuff is original to the building, but the Biedermayer furniture was an interior decorator's idea – said it would complement the thirties' look with a touch of class. Damn it but it's good to see you, Pat!'

Ben came from behind the desk. He gave me one of the meaty Mediterranean hugs America owes to the Mafia. He looked well, but had a glow of inspiration as though he'd got religion or fallen in love. It was strange and touching.

I said something about it was good to see him too. He moved to order coffee from his secretary and said, 'After all these years, Pat, I still hear the lilt of Oirish in your voice.'

'I'm working on it.'

'Ha ha! And life? It's treating you well? Business? Still writing?'

'I get by.'

We talked a little of my wife and family. Ben confirmed he'd never remarried after his divorce from Maisie. But it struck me that he didn't act like most divorced men. He wasn't resentful about the past or wistful about the present. He spoke about Maisie as if she was someone he'd known at college years before, hung around with and then dropped for no reason except that you couldn't keep these things up for ever.

He looked at my cup. 'Can I offer you something stronger? I've got bourbon and scotch.'

'Too early,' I said.

'It never used to be,' he said. 'Remember that summer in France? I swear we were loaded from dawn till dusk.'

'I was younger.'

'You've stopped?'

'Eased up, that's all. You have one if you want.'

'I don't,' Ben said, 'I'm in recovery.'

'What's that?'

'The whole megillah – the twelve step programme and all.

"Hullo. My name's Ben and I'm an alcoholic. Drink so screwed up my life that I became a multi-millionaire".'

'That's quite a testimony. I suppose there must be AA groups where it would make sense.'

'You mean the country-club set? No. I went to their meetings coupla times but they reminded me of why I drank, not why I stopped. These days I hang around the cellars of Lutheran churches with bums and journalists. It's a good way to see the city.'

'I bet.'

'It's true. You get to discover things. Did you know that these days the Benedict Foundation spends more on good works than it saves in taxes?"

I was glad for Ben though not sure I liked the new version. But Jehovah's Witnesses and reformed alcoholics learn strategies to handle the discomfort they cause in normal people, and Ben smiled.

'I suppose you're wondering why I'm happy to see you after what happened last time. It's part of the Programme. I have to confront the past, undo the things I did wrong, apologise to the people I offended. A drag, huh? You never did me any harm, Pat, yet I dragged you into my booze problem.'

'And Tom? Do you have any apologies to make to him?'

'You have some suggestions?'

I didn't know. The thought had just popped into my head. And with it came the realisation that none of this – my being here – made sense without Tom, and it was he who bound us together, just as he'd done in France. Tom and his Argentinian Virgin.

Ben went blank. He asked, 'What d'you know of Tom? You have any contact?'

'No. I haven't seen him since we left S. Symphorien. I think we last wrote in nineteen fifty. Two or three years ago he was on TV.'

'The Negro rights stuff – I know about it. Anything since?'

'I heard he was disbarred. Someone said he was drinking.'

'Don't tell me. Poor bastard.'

'The drinking – it's not like Tom. He was always careful.'

'You mean because he saw what the booze was doing to me.'

'If you like. I thought you might have an idea. You never did say what the problem was between you two. There was a problem, wasn't there? I'm wondering if the Programme means you've made your peace with him as you have with me.'

'In a way.' Ben smiled wanly. He murmured, 'My name is Ben and I'm an alcoholic ... So you want to know about Tom? He's living in St. Louis. He's a bail bondsman.'

'Christ.'

'He's a lousy bail bondsman – a soft touch in a hard business. He has a storefront office in a bad neighbourhood and flops down in the room upstairs when he's ever there – which isn't often since most of the time he's at the tavern across the way, where he recites poetry and talks about painting to the blue collar guys who work the river. Once in a while he attends a small church: The Gnostic Gospel of the Divine Sophia. It seems to be mostly a women's group, but they tolerate Tom, drunk or sober, as a kind of saint. I don't suppose that surprises you.'

'You've seen him?'

Ben shook his head. 'No. I don't want to. It would break my heart. I set an investigator to find him twelve months ago. He still sends me reports once a quarter.'

'How does Tom get by? I mean if business is lousy.'

'I transfer money to his bank account – bits and pieces, never enough in one slug so he'd notice.'

'That's good of you.'

'Praise be to the Programme.'

This was a lot to take on board. Some facts, like the sudden death of a child, are beyond us and we can respond only in ways that are stupid or conventional. I put the obvious question, 'Is he alone?'

Ben answered, 'I wouldn't say he was lonely.'

'Maisie once told me he was the loneliest person in the world..'

'Did she? Hmmm – well there's something to that. What I meant is that Tom isn't lonely as you and I might be lonely.'

'No? How so?'

'I'm not sure. Maybe he communes with God or something. Maybe that's what the women in the church-of-whatever see in him. You know the damned odd thing, Pat? Though everyone always agreed that Tom was a good man, he never did a thing that was especially good – not something you could put your finger on. I've given millions away, yet no one in their senses says Ben Benedict is a good man. But Tom … You follow me?'

I nodded. Ben nodded too. It made no difference. Tom was a good man and that was all there was to it.

Ben looked at me and said, 'You didn't come to see me for old times' sake. Spit it out. There's something you want to know.'

'I overheard a couple of men in a bar. They were talking of you and Tom. They said you helped Tom murder his wife.'

'I did?'

'That's what people say.'

Ben sighed. 'Jeez, it's been years since I first heard that rumour – it has to be twenty or more. Let me ask you: do you think Tom murdered his wife?'

'When he wrote to me in forty-five he was already on his own.'

'You haven't answered.'

'No, I don't believe Tom's a murderer.'

'But I might be? Thanks for the compliment. Don't bother to apologise. You may be right. I *could* murder someone – though I don't say I ever did.'

Against the wall was a credenza and on it a tortoiseshell box. Ben opened it.

'Smoke? Since I gave up booze I find I'm smoking more. What about you since you cut the sauce? The same? You know,

Pat, it's funny to be accused of murder – and of Tom's wife for Chrissake! D'you remember how it was that summer, after Katerina agreed to marry him? Did you ever see anyone so much in love as Tom with his Argentinian Virgin?'

'No.'

'No. Yet what was she, once you'd got over her youth and her beauty? Just a kid with nothing much to say for herself. We all of us knew that, but we went along with the affair like it was the Great Romance such as the world has never seen.'

'We were – ' I looked for the word ' – entranced.'

'Entranced … ? Yes, we were entranced like you say. What d'you suppose was the cause? The heat? The sun? The liquor we put away? Was it youth, huh? The Riviera? Palm trees? The War? The whole world was in torment and things between Maisie and me were all gone to hell, but there was Lucky Tom Rensselaer and his beautiful girl with the light of God shining down on them!'

'And?' I asked.

I noticed a tremor in Ben's voice, a pulse beating in his beck, a tired fold of flesh at his jowls. He looked used up and ugly, and I probably looked the same.

He said, 'Sometimes Tom made me sick to my stomach.'

CHAPTER THIRTY-THREE

Did Tom and Katerina love each other?

That morning, when he announced his engagement, Tom explained, 'You have to *will* yourself to love. I'm talking about the long haul, not the sexual infatuation that passes for love in the movies. If I had a liking or a sympathy for her, I think I could love any woman.'

'Even the ugly ones?'

Tom laughed. 'You got me there. The ugly ones don't seem to come my way. But I don't see why the principle shouldn't hold good.'

'You must see things I can't.'

'D'you think so?' he asked. 'Hmm. Well, you're younger than I am and I guess that makes a difference.' Then, 'God, I don't know how you can miss it! Every time I look at a woman – even one I don't care for – I see the glory in her!'

'The glory?' I said. I was shocked as if he'd said something indecent. I thought "glory" was a word chosen by a man who studied women too intensely, and that they wouldn't like him for it if they knew.

'I can't think of another word,' Tom said. 'I'm thinking of the quiet glory I see in them, when they go about in the ordinary way, just being women doing what they do.'

We fell to talking about the wedding. There would be a simple civil ceremony at the *mairie*, but afterwards Tom planned a big party at the Czar Aléxandre.

The American consul came to sort out some paperwork. Complicated arrangements were made for the couple and Teresa to return to the United States via Portugal and a steamer to Brazil.

Meanwhile the summer dragged on and, on the hills where the forest had been felled, the maquis was burning.

I was still worried about Maillot. I liked him, but I knew he was capable of a desperate evil. I didn't know what he knew or what he'd had seen, but it affected Tom and I tried to warn him. He wouldn't listen.

Then, with days to go, I caught Tom alone. We were all out riding and he pushed off on his own into the trees, where I followed him. I found him in a clearing, sitting on a rock, dreaming over a cigarette.

'Oh, hi there,' he said. 'You left the others?'

'I'd like a word.'

'Well, you've got me. Say, you don't want to talk over all that fatherly stuff like you're supposed to before a wedding, do you?'

'We don't do that in Ireland.'

'My uncle tried it once – took me aside in his study – made women sound like an unreliable investment. Why don't you come and sit down here?' He moved to make space on the rock. 'Isn't this a gorgeous day?'

I didn't answer.

Tom sighed.

'Well, you've obviously taken some trouble to get me aside. Why don't you tell me what this is about?'

'Maillot – I'm certain he knows something. I think seriously that you should speak to Ben, see whether money could get the old fellow out of jail.'

'I can't do that.'

'Then maybe you can tell me what it is that Maillot knows.'

'I've no idea.'

'Won't you help even to save yourself?'

Tom looked away, seeing something over the far ocean. 'That least of all,' he said.

I was angry and lit another cigarette. Tom was quiet.

I asked, 'Is it because the old man's an abortionist?'

'Yes.'

Frustrated I snapped, 'Maillot was right to call you a prig!'

Which amused Tom, as if the insult made him more sympathetic to Doctor's plight.

'Did he really? That's a good one. I don't know I'd have said "prig" exactly, but I know what he means. Ha ha. Look, I don't know how to explain this. I've got nothing personal against Maillot. I try not to judge. He may be a fine fellow. He may have very good reasons for what he does. All the same, I can't help him.'

'Why not?'

Tom didn't answer directly. He said, ' Did Maisie ever tell you she had an abortion?'

That took me aback.

'I don't swear it's true. I rather think it isn't.'

'I don't know what you mean.'

'I mean Maisie isn't … quite right. None of the Bryan girls are. Their mother, Consuela, is in a madhouse and the girls have been causing a riot for years – you'd know that if you lived in New York. Maisie has been in one scrape after another since she was sixteen.'

'Good God.'

Tom got up. He went to the horses. He poured some water from a bottle into his palm and let them lap it.

'Well, now you know. The abortion story comes from Maisie to explain what she was doing in Switzerland. Back home they tell it different. She had a thing going with Chester Miller. When he threw her over for the Weinfeld girl, they say Maisie tried to break his head open with an oar – the Miller place was where we used to go boating in summer, though our paths never crossed before Paris. There were other rumours about something she did to Hermione Lodge, who got engaged to Ward Beecham, whom no one thought Maisie was even interested in. Are you following this? The short of it is it was all getting out of hand, so her father packed her off to Switzerland where she was more or less kept under restraint for a year. Once she was well, she cut loose from her aunt and came to France, which is when the abortion story got spread around. I don't know why, and I can't definitely say it isn't true. My own opinion, for what it's worth, is that she didn't want people thinking she was nuts, but she wanted a bit of drama in her life.'

'She says … '

'That she and I had an affair?' Tom looked at me with infinite weariness. 'It's what she tells everyone and I don't bother to deny it as a rule. But it isn't so. You know me, Pat,' he said. 'Do you really think I'd take advantage of a girl as damaged as Maisie?'

'But why do you let her stories go unchallenged?'

'I'm awfully fond of her, I guess. She reminds me of so many other girls I know; the difference is only one of degree.'

Before I could say anything, he surprised me by asking, 'Are all girls like Maisie?'

'I don't think so. Surely you know?'

'I can't say I do. The ones who fall for me seem to be in a mess one way or another. That can't be right, can it? There've got to be some who are just plain uncomplicated happy, haven't there?'

'Hetty?' I suggested.

'She's happier than most. But when you dig beneath the surface.'

'Maybe the unhappiness of women doesn't interest most men and so they don't see it.'

'Well *I* see it, God damn it!'

He gave more water to the horses. His raised voice had made them nervous.

He said, 'I let Maisie say what she likes because it doesn't hurt me any and it seems to give her some comfort. She wanted to have an affair, but I wouldn't, and that's all there is to it.'

'And Katerina?'

'Don't you think I ask myself what's going on, or if I understand my own motives?' There was agony in his eyes. 'I wonder sometimes if I'm not some kind of monster, who feeds on women's emotions. What d'you think of that? Wouldn't it be absolutely the worst thing to be? Just the thought of it terrifies me.'

He returned to the subject of Maisie, 'She left the sanatorium and came to Paris.'

'She was on her own?'

'Yes and no. There was another girl – Wilma Hershey, who had consumption – but they weren't close. Then there was a bunch of characters who'd got a whiff of the Bryan money and wanted some. The particular night she was on her own at the George Cinq – stood up by some fellow – and Ben and I were there with a couple of girls, just dancing before pushing on to a *bal musette* we'd heard of.'

'You mean Maisie was stood up?' I found that hard to believe.

'She may have lied about that, too – ' Tom acknowledged ' – not wanted to admit she was a lonely girl trying to pick up a date. Anyway, she came over to our table, brash and beautiful, and asked me to dance. She was so confident that I supposed she was with someone and had maybe asked me for a bet. I had no idea … I guess it doesn't matter. The outcome was she became part of our crowd.'

'Then Ben married her. Did he know about the supposed affair and the abortion?'

'I tried to warn him Maisie was unstable. Not that a warning was needed since he knew about the Bryan girls and the scandals back home.'

'I suppose he fell head over heels.'

'No,' Tom said. 'That isn't Ben's style. His family sent him abroad because of his drinking. They kept pressing him to get married to some nice girl and settle down. Ben married Maisie because he thought she'd do. She came from a good family and was fun when she wasn't brooding. He didn't believe she and I had had a fling – not that it would have made a difference – and he didn't care about the abortion. For that matter he didn't care that Maisie had been locked up in a sanatorium; in fact quite the opposite since the same thing had nearly happened to him.'

'So he married her and now they're both unhappy,' I said.

'You could put it that way,' Tom agreed. 'I guess I could have put things more strongly when I tried to pull Ben back. But – ' his blue eyes fixed on mine ' – I don't like to push my opinions down other people's throats. I mean: who was I that I had to be right about Maisie? What affair of mine was it to spoil the poor kid's chance of things working out between her and Ben? I don't like to judge people, Pat.'

'You've judged Maillot,' I said.

'No I haven't,' Tom reminded me. 'I told you I don't hold any views about Maillot as a man. I just won't have anything to do with this abortion business.'

'But not because of Maisie. Why then?'

'My sister Alice.'

'Who killed herself?'

Tom nodded; and for once I thought he might cry. It was odd to see him like this, in plain day on a lovely hillside. I looked away and Tom pulled himself together.

He said, 'She fell in love with a musician. My uncle put a stop to it, but not before she was expecting a child. He paid for a clinic somewhere; and that was it so far as the family was concerned.'

'But not for her.'

Tom sighed in the crisp way people do when remembering old tragedies. 'She killed herself. She didn't explain, didn't blame anyone. She was a quiet girl and didn't want to cause trouble. Still, she had an abortion and died of it, and that's why I won't help Maillot.'

That was his answer and I had to accept it. What I didn't appreciate at the time was Tom's courage in taking his stand. You see, he believed Maillot had been walking in the hills the day he buried Alvírez. He remembered the noise that had frightened Teresa and understood what it meant. Maillot had seen him and had the power to send him to the guillotine.

CHAPTER THIRTY-FOUR

At the time I didn't ask how Tom paid for the wedding. Thinking about it now, I guess Ben paid like he paid for everything else.

The idea was a modest ceremony. Not because of money but because Tom didn't want to insult people who were struggling to make ends meet, with the War and everything. Katerina and her mother would buy smart but serviceable dresses and hats, and the men would wear lounge suits. And afterwards we'd all of us walk through the town to the Czar Alexandre with sunshine and joy around us, and it would all be just perfect.

Poor Beauclerc was beside himself. Tom had laid hand on every luxury the hotel could get and Ben had been working his contacts. One night a truck arrived from Marseilles with Ben in the passenger seat, and the driver was a swarthy type who carried a gun. Next day Beauclerc said he'd come by some hams, foie gras, truffles, and enough wine to sink a ship. In short it was a time of miracles.

Beauclerc told me, 'Monsieur Rensselaer – he is incredible, that one! He has the manners of a true aristocrat. It is like the old days!'

Except the Czar Alexandre had never attracted aristocrats except a few shady Russians in the twenties. Though accuracy didn't exactly matter. In some fashion the hotel had been created for Tom. The baroque excess, its tawdry grandeur which was more than the respectable bourgeois clientele could ever enjoy in their humdrum lives: all of it implied the existence or at least the hope of someone – prince or prophet – who would reveal its true purpose.

Tom would do this. His wedding wouldn't be an ordinary day but a defining moment. Like the balmy summers before the horror of the Great War it would fix an image so powerful it would be impossible ever after to talk of this time and place except in its terms. The Hôtel Czar Alexandre might sleep for a century and rot for another one, but the framed photographs in the lobby, the names in the visitors' book, and all the ephemera of menu cards and guest lists would hold this moment.

And afterwards?

Oh, tourists would come for nostalgia's sake and writers seeking a setting for a bad novel. They'd come because that's what people do who want to live intensely but don't know how. They'd come with their ignorance and their longings, and they would feel the wonder. I mean that they would see the image of one shining day, blessed and perfect – a day that would have to stand for a host of invisible years. And they would cry inside because they hadn't been there on that day when Tom Rensselaer married his Argentinian Virgin.

The dustsheets were taken off and the dining room was opened to its full splendour. It was a sunlit palace and we crept in it like children.

Though not Tom, of course. While the rest of us sat under the painted ceiling in the glitter and gleam of glass and cutlery, he took himself off to the kitchen to praise the cooks. That's how kings and princes act.

When he came back, he asked, 'What d'you think? Will it do?'

Oh, it would do right enough.

'You'd tell me if I've got it wrong, wouldn't you? I don't want a vulgar show.'

'Weddings are always vulgar,' said Maisie. 'That's the source of their charm – and their embarrassment. Do stop worrying. It'll be okay.'

'Philippe says he can do me an ice sculpture. They used to be the rage in New York.'

'No ice sculpture,' Maisie said firmly. 'It's flashy and won't last two minutes in this heat. Then the basin will be used for corks and cigarette butts. The important thing is the flowers. Get those right and the rest'll fall into place.'

'You're a treasure,' Tom said.

Maisie coloured. I thought of the sad girl of the George Cinq who'd wanted Tom Rensselaer to fall in love with her. And the one who was prone to fits of murderous violence so that her family had locked her away.

'Are the swallows gathering to fly south?' Tom asked as we strolled to La Chênaie. 'No, I guess it's too early. It's funny to think that this year I'll see Fall in New England. I've talked to Katerina about taking a cabin for a spell before getting down to work in the winter.'

'Painting?'

'No – law or bill broking. You're forgetting I'll be a family man with a wife to support.' When he glanced at me I saw something desperate. 'No more Lucky Tom Rensselaer,' he said and tried a grin. 'Just plain Tom with all the other Toms travelling in from the suburbs to make a living. In some ways it'll be a relief. I'm tired of being what other people want.'

'You once told me you were the last of your generation.'

'Did I really say that? I suppose I did. And in a sense it's true, though don't write it down for God's sake, Pat. It sounds pretentious.'

'How is it true?'

'Oh – in that part of me will die here. The young part, the idealistic part. It isn't so bad. I'm thirty-one years old and I think there are different satisfactions ahead of me. It's just I'd hoped to do a little more while I was young and God was smiling on me – more than paint a few pictures. If you don't mind, I'd rather not talk about this. I don't have anything original to say.'

It began to rain. A storm was blowing in from the west. The rain turned the shoulders of Tom's linen suit brown. He held his face up and whooped and hollered for pleasure.

The black police Citroën was parked in the lane outside the house. Joubert had wound down the window so he could smoke. Tom went bounding over to him. He shouted, 'Hi there! Looking for me? Come to arrest me?' as if it was a joke between old friends. And maybe it was, because Joubert looked as though arresting Tom was the last thing he wanted. He held out a hand to be shaken.

I noticed a boy in a red beret sitting in the back of the car. Tom saw him too and said in French, 'Hullo there, son.'

Joubert said, 'This is the boy who survived the accident. His name is André Houblon.'

I remembered Tom had peculiar views about the accident, as if it were a cosmic event and not simply the kind of thing that happens to boys who play at climbing. As I recalled, he seemed to think this one was somehow to blame because he'd deflected the falling rock onto the other boy. I thought the idea might make Tom cool towards André Houblon, but he said, 'I'm sorry about your friend,' as sincerely as he ever said anything.

I don't know what the boy answered. He mumbled something in a thick patois.

Tom got into the car.

I was left to explain everything to the others, but it was difficult to say exactly what had happened. Had Tom been arrested or not? Would we see him again? There was some talk of calling the American consul, but Ben said we'd look like dopes if we did and we should give it some time. Then, an hour later, Tom came striding jauntily down the path with a smile on his face and his jacket slung over one shoulder. The storm had passed and the sky was filled with brilliant grains of rain and a rainbow.

He said, 'I think I deserve a cognac, what do you say?'

Ben was sullen. He said, 'You sound like you've been having fun.'

'No, not fun. But I don't mind helping Joubert with his investigations. He's a decent fellow, even if he is trying to tie a murder on me.'

'Is that what he's doing?'

'Sure. Oh, don't worry. He won't make it stick. But you have to admire him. He's come up with quite an elegant theory. It seems a shame that it doesn't work. Now, no more questions until I get that brandy inside me. Then I'll tell you all you want.'

He'd tell us all we wanted except for certain little secrets

Tom intended to keep to himself. But he did explain Joubert's theory, and, to give him credit, it was a good one and came within measurable distance of the truth.

We poured ourselves shots of brandy and sat around with the treetops rocking and a mistle thrush singing in the sad way they do. I said I assumed he'd been taken to La Pinède, thinking the police might want to confront him with the women and tear at any inconsistencies in their stories. I asked what the business was with the Houblon boy.

'Oh, it's to do with Joubert's theory,' Tom said.

'It involves the boy?'

'Yes.'

'Well?'

'Oh, you know the way it is with theories. Sometimes someone'll put one forward and it makes you see things a whole new way – makes you question yourself, as if you'd never understood the world. I mean Joubert surprised me. I'd never supposed any connection with the boy.'

'And what is it, this theory?' I asked.

Tom said in a lazy drawl, 'Oh, it involves Alvírez and the boy and something about a stolen diamond necklace.'

CHAPTER THIRTY-FIVE

Tom looked at the boy and knew he was there to tell lies. It was stamped on his mean face and Tom felt sorry for him.

On the other hand Tom was prepared to tell lies on his own account for the sake of the women, and that made him mildly ashamed to see Joubert. After the storm the garden of La Pinède was filled with the scent of flowers and damp earth. It called up vague memories of his mother and his sister Alice and a large house that belonged to an elderly cousin from a branch of the family that had become extinct. And in a general way the house resembled La Pinède.

Tisserand was waiting with the two women. Joubert was smoking one of his pungent cigarettes and explaining something Tom couldn't catch. Teresa offered a *tisane*. She stared into Tom's eyes and dared him to match her courage

'Are you going to tell us what the point of this is?' Tom asked. He took a seat and lit one of his own Virginia cigarettes.

Joubert said, 'I wish you to listen to some things this child has to say.'

He began to take the boy through his paces, translating when the accent was too thick or he used too many dialect words. And, contrary to his first impression, what the Houblon boy had to say struck Tom as true.

Joubert explained, 'This boy comes from a bad family. His father is dead. He is raised by his mother and an "uncle" who is also her lover. He does not go to school if he can avoid it, and wastes time about the town and on the beaches.'

It sounded as though he was asking for advice.

Tom said, 'How come he knows Alvírez? I take it he does know Alvírez?'

'Monsieur Alvírez was in the habit of drinking coffee of a morning at the Café la Belle Étoile, which is in the Promenade des Russes. He saw the boy. He invited him to an ice cream.'

'You mean … ?'

'I mean only so much as is necessary. Monsieur Alvírez told the boy a story – that there was a great treasure at the Villa la Pinède, a diamond necklace worth many millions of francs. It is a story I believe because Monsieur Alvírez could be indiscreet and repeated the same to others, *and* he was in a position to know from his acquaintance with Madame Malipiero. So the necklace, we may accept, exists.'

As he watched the lad, Tom wondered if Alvírez had begun his career like the Houblon boy. It might explain his greed and insecurity with strangers. 'A plan was developed,' Joubert went on. 'The boy agreed to become a spy – possibly a thief. One can understand the excitement, yes? And theft is no great matter for boys of any kind. It was arranged that he would enter the Villa la Pinède and find the valuable necklace – and steal it, perhaps.'

He looked at Teresa Malipiero. 'You had no suspicions?'

She shook her head. A little too firmly, Tom thought. He covered by asking, 'Did he succeed?'

'On several occasions he penetrated the house but was unable to discover the necklace. I enquire of Madame Malipiero her suspicions because the boy says he was disturbed – almost caught – most certainly seen.'

'That isn't true!' Teresa exclaimed.

Tom said, 'Boys and thieves both suffer from nerves and imagination.' Then the chilling drift of the conversation struck him. 'Are you saying there's some connection with the accident. The boy was trying to break into the house? Come off it. It was broad daylight. And in any case, why scale the rocks when he could sneak over the wall from the path?'

'Who knows?' said Joubert. 'A sense of adventure perhaps? Were you in the garden that day, Madame?'

'Hold it there!' Tom said. 'Don't answer the question, Teresa. This enquiry concerns the disappearance of Alvírez, not the death of the child. No one has suggested that was anything except an accident. It's guesswork that a piece of the wall struck the boy – most likely it was a loose rock from the bluff. In any case the wall is ruined and bits of it could fall away at any time. So why don't we stick to the point?'

Joubert nodded. 'If you like. I note your concern for Madame Malipiero. It is very creditable.'

For a moment there, Tom had been shaken. Now he was sure Joubert was only speculating – intelligently, maybe – but only speculating. Tom had enough legal knowledge to tell that the Inspector had no evidence.

'You are smiling,' Joubert said.

'Am I? Pardon me – you're right – I'm sorry. Being suspected of murder has its funny side. No? Well, you'll just have to believe me about that. I think you were about to tell us something. A theory? You must have a theory. Okay, sock it to me.'

When Tom repeated this to me, I couldn't help feeling sympathy for the police. The French system bore down on suspects with little room for manoeuvre. Joubert couldn't understand Tom's confidence born of privilege and the power of a great empire that every American took for granted.

Still he came on bravely.

'Let me begin,' he said, 'by telling you that I do not believe you saw Monsieur Alvírez in the hills the day after the funeral.'

'I've always admitted I could be wrong on that point,' Tom reminded him.

'Please do not interrupt. As I say, I do not believe you. I think you are lying.'

'Just a moment ... No, I'm sorry, go on.'

'Monsieur Alvírez is very distinctive – his appearance, his clothes, his manner. He is not a man one could easily mistake. So, if not him, whom did you see? No one else has come forward who claims to have been in the hills that day. Yet it could *not* have been Monsieur Alvírez because I have the testimony of Monsieur Beauclerc and the hotel maid that he did not sleep in his room on the night of the funeral and it is therefore clear that he disappeared on *that* day and not the following. Therefore, you did not see him in the hills. You saw *no one*.

'So, Monsieur Rensselaer, I ask myself why you are telling this lie? It seems to me to indicate that you are implicated in Monsieur Alvírez's disappearance and have cause to distract me from the time and also the place where he was last seen, an occasion which cannot have been innocent. From that I infer that Monsieur Alvírez is dead.'

'Well that's plain,' Tom said. He asked, 'Would you like to

smoke? I know you would, and I'm sure none of us mind.'

'Thank you,' Joubert said. He smiled at Tom without animosity. He pulled out a soft paper pack. The cigarettes were loosely wrapped so they had to be gripped tightly in the lips or fall apart. Watching him, Tom thought he'd like to make a drawing. He wasn't really as calm as he appeared, and he glanced at the women.

And in that moment he didn't know who they were.

'Shall we go on?' he said to Joubert.

He didn't know who they were. That was the one truth Tom wanted to suppress even in his own mind. He told himself that no man ever knows the woman he's going to marry; yet for most men things work out pretty well. And, too, he had the assurance of his own good faith, and wasn't it true that you get what you give?

The moment passed. Joubert was saying, 'The indications are that the murder was on the day of the funeral. Madame Malipiero, you went to the cemetery, as did you, Monsieur Rensselaer.'

'That's right.'

'Thus the Villa La Pinède was empty and open for Monsieur Alvírez to enter in an attempt to steal the diamonds, which is what I believe he tried to do. But he was mistaken in his timing. You, Monsieur Rensselaer, I understand, returned to your cottage with your friends?'

'Correct.'

'Ah,' Joubert sighed and looked at Teresa. 'So I am left to suppose that Madame Malipiero returned to La Pinède and disturbed Monsieur Alvírez in the affair of the theft. There was a struggle? Yes. Monsieur Alvírez was killed – in the manner of an accident or self defence?' He turned to Tom and, with a fall in his voice as if the matter were settled, concluded, 'Your part, with the aid of your automobile, was to assist the next day in the disposal of a corpse – somewhere in the hills alongside the road to Grasse, where, I assure you, we shall find it.'

Tom had to give it to him. Except in the matter of Teresa's guilt, Joubert's theory squared with Tom's own. For a moment Tom found himself actually frightened. This untidy, quietly spoken policeman in his soiled suit was capable of getting to the truth of things or near enough to make a case against the women or Tom himself.

Tom looked at Teresa, wondering if she'd accept the excuse of a terrible accident. There was an element of generosity in Joubert's explanation of self-defence. If Teresa had deceived him on this point, he could forgive her.

'It isn't true,' she said, defying Tom as much as Joubert.

And Tom knew it couldn't be true.

'Well, that's fine,' he said. 'Tell me something: d'you have the diamond necklace? No, I don't suppose you do. Teresa, have you got it? Go make a search.'

Joubert snapped at Tisserand to accompany her. He asked, 'Is there some purpose to this?'

'I think so,' Tom answered. 'Your theory is that Alvírez was killed in the course of stealing the necklace. In that case it has to be here: Madame Malipiero has it. Or are you thinking that there was an accomplice who got away? No – I don't think that works. Alvírez's accomplice was the boy there, and, as I recall, he was at his friend's funeral and so couldn't have been here at La Pinède. So, unless you're going to invent a second accomplice of whose existence there's no evidence at all, the necklace has to be here. Well, we'll see. Another cigarette?'

They took a turn in the garden under the long shadows of the cypresses. It was late afternoon and, in the middle distance, the saffron-washed houses were turning a dun colour.

Joubert sucked greedily on his cigarette. Several times he began to speak, but each time he gave up. Instead his slow heavy eyes caught Tom's and Tom was reminded of two silent drunks at opposite ends of a bar who will examine each other with the same intense meaninglessness.

Tisserand came out of the house. The women stood framed by the door.

'The necklace has gone,' he said.

Unsurprised, Joubert asked, 'When did this happen, Madame?'

Teresa shook her head. 'I don't know. I've had no reason to open the box for many weeks.'

'Monsieur Rensselaer, you knew this would be so?'

'Only because I believe in Teresa's innocence. Look, I buy this much of your theory: I believe Alvírez is a thief. But the rest? Well, you don't really have anything, do you? No necklace. No corpse. In fact nothing at all. If I had to explain the facts, I'd say Alvírez got clean away with the jewels and that you'll find him and them in Spain.'

'And all of this because the stupid police have not found the necklace here in the house?'

Tom didn't answer.

Joubert was thoughtful for a moment. Then he said, 'We may speak frankly, I think. Whether I can prove it or not, I know that Monsieur Alvírez was killed on the day of the funeral. Here – perhaps even in this room. You, Monsieur, helped dispose of the body.'

'If you say so.'

'Please, let me finish. I am sure that you are sincere. You believe Madame Malipiero and her daughter innocent. But what is the basis for that belief? It is nothing more – is it not? – than the fact that the necklace cannot be found? Monsieur Alvírez did not carry it away: your story that he is in Spain is nonsense, as you well know. Neither, as you say, did the boy. So it seems that we are left with the second accomplice, who, as you pointed out, is an absurdity. We both know he does not exist. Ah! But for you he *must* exist to provide you with an alternative murderer, if it is not to be Madame. And your evidence? Why, the "fact" that Madame does not have the necklace, of course!'

'And, I remind you, it *has* disappeared.'

Joubert shrugged. 'So it seems. Yet a necklace is a small thing that may very easily be hidden – even by Madame. In my opinion, it means nothing that we cannot find it. Only for you, does it mean *everything*. Its disappearance is the foundation of your faith in the innocence of Madame Malipiero.'

'So what? Nothing changes unless and until you can prove Teresa still has it.'

'It is very valuable. It will turn up, of that I am sure.'

Joubert lit another cigarette and signed to Tisserand that they were leaving. Tom walked them through the garden to the gate, where the Inspector halted.

He turned to Tom and said, 'I advise you to save yourself, my friend; for I assure you that the necklace will be found. And on that day your theory of a second accomplice will be destroyed. You will know then that Madame Malipiero is a murderess. And the knowledge will destroy you.'

CHAPTER THIRTY-SIX

That day in nineteen sixty-eight, when Ben decided he could face both sobriety and the memory of Tom, he asked me, 'How d'you feel about lunch. It's a little early but my diary's free. What d'you say?'

I said I was fine about lunch, and so we left Ben's den on top of the Benedict Building in Sixth Avenue and went to a restaurant.

Since giving up drink, Ben had put on weight. He had the rolling walk heavy men get and with it a certain elegance like a big ship under sail. The years had made me pinched and taut: I think of the flyweight boxers my Uncle Gerald used to back: small, angry men.

The place was round the corner – *L'Escargot Sans Foyer*. The maître d', in full rig, guided us to a table in a candle-lit grotto of red and gold. Ben lit a cigarette and smoked pretty much through the whole meal. I put away a couple of stiff martinis. I forget what we ate.

Perhaps there was something to the Programme, because Ben was mellow for a man who didn't touch alcohol. He squinted at me through the smoke and asked, 'Whatever happened to the Irish kid we used to know?'

'He grew up.'

'We all grow up.'

'Maybe. But I grew up the way you all made me?'

Ben seemed to understand. He asked, 'Is this how you thought things would turn out?'

'No.'

'That's what I guessed. We're all living a life that was made for some other guy.'

I nodded, though what he said sounded like an alcoholic's wisdom. We both sighed.

Ben looked at me. Then he wanted to know, 'D'you have any explanation how it is that Tom Rensselaer has led us by the nose for near thirty years?'

'I wouldn't put it like that.'

'No? How would you put it? You haven't seen him since the start of the war, nor heard from him since – when was it? – nineteen fifty? Yet you've buttoned me because someone dropped his name in a bar, and here we are still talking about him.'

'I meant you make it sound as though this is something Tom wants.'

Ben apologised. "Yeah, you're right. I'm sorry. But the facts speak, don't they?'

I acknowledged they did.

'So there is something to explain,' he insisted. 'Let me tell you something. At college I knew a dozen guys as good-looking as Tom and a damn sight richer. Just as talented too – except maybe in the painting department. So what is it? We all fell for him because the bastard could paint, for chrissake?"

'No, it wasn't that.'

'No, it wasn't,' Ben agreed. 'I know what it *wasn't*. I want to know what it *was*. You, for instance – I remember you always studying Tom. You … ' He bit his lip. 'I was going to say you followed him like a dog, but that wouldn't be fair. One thing about sobriety that pisses me is that half the time I'm not as nice as I used to be. So?'

'I'm a writer. I study people. It's what I do. And you? What's your interest?'

'Time was I would've told you. Leave it that I have my reasons.'

'Okay.'

Though I've forgotten the food, I remember Ben drank *Dr Pepper*. It was odd to see a beefy man in a well-cut suit drinking *Dr Pepper*.

He said, 'Lets quit that subject and move on. Who d'you think Tom was in love with, the daughter or the mother? Don't tell me it didn't cross your mind. If you don't like that one, tell me what you really thought of Katerina.'

'Why are you asking if he loved Teresa?'

'It always seemed more logical. When it came to sniffing poon, Tom was generally easier with older women. Something to do with his mother maybe? Then you only have to compare them. I liked Katerina – don't get me wrong – but there was really nothing to her. Oh, she was intelligent right enough, but unformed. A Pygmalion like that Shaw fellow wrote about. Now, Teresa – well, she was another proposition. A smart broad, as we used to say. Only I was never sure Tom could see the difference. I often wondered – and this probably sounds dirtier than I mean – if, in marrying the daughter, he didn't also marry the mother. D'you follow?'

I wasn't sure where this was leading. To a motive for murder, maybe? One with a whiff of Hitchcock and Freud.

'I don't have an opinion,' I said. I lit a cigarette and drew him back to the subject that interested me. 'Anyway, about the rumour … '

'That I helped Tom bump off Katerina?' Ben gave a dry laugh. 'Actually there was another. That I helped him kill Teresa. Are they the same or different rumours? Did we kill one, or both or neither? You see how it is with that kind of story?'

'You tell me.'

'Jesus! You know me and Tom!'

'I've been thinking about that: about what's in a person's character and what isn't. If you want the truth, I don't know. Without the evidence, I'd say Tom would never kill his wife. But give me the proof that he did, and I'll give you ten compelling reasons why that's exactly what he would do.'

'And me?'

'The same principle, but slightly the other way round. If Tom asked you to help murder his wife, I'd say you would do it. But if I learned you refused, I could think of reasons why you might. Am I explaining myself?'

'You mean you genuinely don't know?'

'That's it.'

Ben laughed. 'It's at times like this that I wish I hadn't given up the booze. We could get stinking and I'd tell you the truth, and you'd *believe* me – no "evidence" or any of that crap.' He looked at me, doubting I was ignorant of whatever there was to know. He said, 'I forget you were never really one of us. It was Tom first saw something in you – Hetty later and maybe Maisie too.'

'And you?'

'I got to like you well enough. If you wonder why I'm saying this, it's because I'm trying to figure why you're still in the dark. And – if you are – I'm not sure I shouldn't leave you there. For your sake, not mine.'

'Maybe I should go?'

Ben sighed. 'Hold on, I'll tell you what I can.'

He began with France, our leaving S. Symphorien. I went to Ireland, where I spent the rest of the war. The others returned to the States by a complicated route. In New York they parted.

'And never all of us together again. Kind of sad, huh?'

'Go on.'

'Tom took Katerina to the apartment in Park Avenue, the one that belonged to his Uncle Jonathan, who didn't use it. Teresa stayed with them. What d'you think of that?'

'Where else was she to go? Argentina?'

'Argentina? Why? Oh, I see where you're at. Well, forget it. Katerina and Teresa were never from Argentina.'

'Not Argentinian?'

Ben had said it so matter-of-factly that it was as if I hadn't heard. He went on, 'Trust me, you don't want to know more than that. Where was I?'

'Park Avenue,' I said, still trying to get my head around the notion that the Argentinian Virgin was from … wherever.

'That's right. They went to the apartment, unpacked and stayed the night. Just the one night.'

'Why?'

Ben gave me a meaningful stare, another of his old alcoholic's tricks. 'Because Tom discovered something and the following day Katerina and her mother *vanished*. Which, Paddy my boy, is where the story stops. If you go any further it's on your own head.'

I don't remember much of what happened next. I was stunned. I babbled questions while Ben folded his napkin and called for the bill. He left the booze tab open and I kept on hoisting martinis until I was poured into a cab.

I asked him: did he mean 'vanished' or 'murdered'? He said there was no murder.

Then what had been his part in the disaster between Tom and

the women? Nothing. He said he hadn't been involved until Tom came to him in a state and told him everything.

Hadn't Tom looked for Katerina?

'No,' said Ben. 'He didn't even try.'

I pleaded with him, 'Are you going to leave me like this? Half crazy with nothing except hints?'

He softened a little and called the maître d' for a pen and a sheet of paper. When it came, he wrote down a name, Dr Nathan Shapiro, and an address in Westchester County, folded it and pushed it across the table, overlaid with his hand.

'I'll give you this,' he said, 'but I don't recommend you take it. If you do, just put it aside a while. Go home. Think of what I've said. Talk to your wife. Only then should you make a decision. My advice – '

I was angry. 'Why should I listen to you, you superior bastard?'

He wasn't offended. Tired maybe. 'There's nothing you can do, and the truth will only hurt you, believe me.' Already he was asking for his coat and had put it on before he said anything else. And when it came, it was with sorrow and frustration.

He said, 'What I can't stand about Tom is that he let all of this happen to him. Sure, his marriage failed and he lost his ability to paint and couldn't make a go of writing movie scripts. But so what? Is that a reason to give up? Because that's what he did.'

Then, in a note of bathos, he said, ''It's so un-American it makes me want to puke. I used to wonder sometimes if he wasn't a communist. What with the Negroes and all.'

Those were the last words I heard from Ben. He stepped out of my life and recently I read he died in one of the ordinary ways people die. It occurs to me that only rarely do we spot these moments for what they are, and that most times friendships end and we wonder how it happened, almost as if we weren't there. And in a sense we weren't.

I didn't notice. I was wondering who the hell Dr Nathan Shapiro was?

CHAPTER THIRTY-SEVEN

We lost Tom in the prospect of his marriage to the Argentinian Virgin. With him went the zest of our stay at S. Symphorien. Ben and Maisie saw to arrangements for their return home. I distracted myself with writing. Hetty spent a lot of time on her own. She mooched about the beach, the town and the hills, trying to fix places in her memory.

She said, 'What makes me sad is that I'll never come to Europe again.' I tried to console her. 'Why not? Once you're home, you'll find a good man. You don't know who he is, but he's there all right, waiting for you. You'll marry and, who knows, maybe he'll bring you back.'

She held my hand as we walked across the sand but the rest of the detail is lost. Most likely it was a morning that was tender in its ordinariness.

She said, 'I guess you're right – at least as far as getting married. I hope he'll be a nice guy. I think I've learned enough to spot the schmucks. But ... well, I don't see us coming here: him on his blue-collar salary and me on what I earn from waitressing, and with kids and all.'

'I thought you were going to be a movie star?'

'Oh, sure. I'll give it my best shot, but I don't expect it'll come to anything. Good stuff like that happens – but it happens to other people, doesn't it?'

I didn't attempt an answer. She didn't press for one. Looking at her, I understood that here and now was her shining moment: the cusp of life after which it never got better. Once she left this sunlit beach it would be to step into the sea and be swept to a darker shore.

'I wish I could paint,' she went on. 'Photographs don't really capture anything, do they? I'd like to take home something with a scent: lavender or mimosa or that blossom from those funny oranges ... '

'Bigarades.'

' ... those *bigarades*. You know, I can never smell bleach without remembering my Ma who used to housekeep. You'd think it'd be horrible, but it makes me think of her and go all soft. Yes, I'd like to have some of those ... whatever it was you said ... to keep, but they don't let you take 'em home.'

I've never thought of stories as closed. I didn't then and I don't now. Not if they have any meaning. I saw Hetty drawing out a fine thread of memory through the rest of a lifetime; a thread so light it would be felt only as we feel a breeze that carries a faint fragrance of a place once visited.

I, too, was affected by the decaying summer. I kept to my cottage more, called at La Chênaie less, wrote and, to my astonishment, finished the book. I took to wandering down to the Promenade des Russes where there was a small café with two tables outside and a trellis hung with bougainvillaea.

That's where I saw Dr Maillot again.

The old man was coming out of the gendarmerie with Tisserand and Joubert. He looked cleaned up the way my Uncle Gerald did when he showed his seedy face to my mother after one of his unexplained absences. My uncle was used to waking up memoryless in strange beds and strange rooms, a habit he treated as one of God's lesser revelations. And that was how it was with Maillot.

For a moment I felt a flush of pleasure at the sight of my old friend. The dead girl's mother had relented or the police grown bored; either way he'd been released. Then I saw the furtiveness in his face and I knew it wasn't so and that he'd bought his freedom with whatever threat it was he held over Tom.

I might have collared him there and then. I might have taken him back to the hotel, parked him under the lime trees and filled him with drink until I got it out of him. But I didn't. The situation seemed too urgent. And, you see, I thought Tom knew what it was. The fact is Tom thought he *did* know.

Nine parts of tragedy lie in ignorance.

I hurried to La Chênaie. I found only Hetty reading a book. She was pale and tired, and she looked up and said without interest that she fancied Tom was out someplace in the hills – not far, she thought.

I found him on the slope where the hill rises to overlook the Czar Aléxandre. He was there, pacing up and down, smoking. When he saw me, he seemed glad and, before I could get a word out, he launched on a speech, one of those that start in some strange place because they're preceded by thoughts you don't know about.

He said, 'You know, Pat, the Chinese have a theory. They say that when a dynasty falls, it's because the emperors have lost the mandate of Heaven. Floods, earthquakes, famines – these are the signs. No, hear me out. Sometimes that's how it seems with my family: ever since old JP in his glory days. My dad wasn't the smartest of men, but that doesn't explain the smash. The forces behind it were larger than any man could handle: the European economy, the Depression, all those things. Ben's folks went through a bad patch, too, but they weathered it. D'you see what I'm getting at?'

'If you're thinking about your marriage, then I don't see what the Chinese have to do with it.'

He gave a low, dreary chuckle. 'No, I'm not sure I do either, except that I don't think they're trying to say that a dynasty *deserves* to fall. The point is rather that Heaven doesn't give a damn. It grants good fortune and then says to hell with you. There's an amoral cruelty to it all, just as there was with the death of the boy.'

I tried to lighten things. 'You're saying you're frightened of the Curse of the Rensselaers?'

He grinned. 'Pat, Pat, I knew I could rely on you, though that isn't exactly what I mean. You remember my nickname?'

'Lucky Tom Rensselaer.'

'That's it – Lucky Tom Rensselaer,' he repeated. 'I've had it since I don't know when – all my life. You appreciate the irony? Ever since I was a kid, my world has been falling about my ears. Yet always it's seemed as if I'm lucky.'

I quoted my mother. 'Ah well, as long as you've got your health.'

He liked that. 'I wish I knew her. She has a point. Whatever else happened, I was always fortunate when it counted. I could rely on luck. I never had to justify being who I was.'

'And now what? You've got nerves about marrying, that's all.'

'Call it what you like, but I can feel my luck going. Don't get me wrong. In principle I don't mind; I never deserved it and I can't complain when I lose it. But all I'm left with is my own courage and I don't know if that's enough or even what it's for. Courage to retrieve the situation and fight back? Or courage to take my knocks? What d'you think?'

'I don't know,' I said. 'It's all Chinese to me.'

Tom was finished. I can't say what he meant or if there was any sense in it.

I came round to the subject that was vexing me. I explained about Maillot and asked what it was all about and what he proposed to do.

He took it calmly. He said, 'There's something I've got to tell you, Pat. Alvírez is dead.'

'I thought he might be. How did he die?'

'I don't know exactly. Teresa and Katerina found his body at La Pinède after the boy's funeral. Someone had bashed his head in with a lamp. I helped bury him – ' he waved vaguely ' – up there somewhere.'

He went on some more, wanting to hear it all said. I don't

know if this showed some special confidence in me. Whatever the explanation, it's how I learned the body had been found by the women around noon, but Tom hadn't been called on until late at night.

I pointed out the obvious. 'You realise that means one of the Malipieros could have killed him? They had the opportunity and, so far as I can see, are the only people who might have had a motive.'

He didn't get angry. He just said, 'You can put that idea out of your mind. I know how it looks, but it isn't so.'

'How do you explain things then?'

'We thought – Teresa and I – at first that Alvírez had called at the house with some news about Señor Malipiero, and that he disturbed a burglar. Now I figure it that Alvírez himself was the burglar, out to steal the necklace. I told you about Joubert's theory, and I think he's half way to being right. But he goes on to say that Teresa disturbed and killed Alvírez. I say that doesn't fit with the necklace disappearing. There had to be an accomplice.'

'The Houblon boy?'

Tom shook his head. 'Believe me, I've tried to make that idea work and it doesn't. The kid was at the funeral. Afterwards he went home with his people.'

'Are you sure about that?'

'By now Joubert will have confirmed it and he hasn't pulled the boy in again. In any case it doesn't matter what the boy did after the funeral. Teresa and Katerina went straight home and by then Alvírez was already dead.'

He tried to convince me. 'There has to be another accomplice. It's the only solution makes sense. I just don't know who it could be.'

And neither did I.

'What does Dr Maillot know?' It had taken me a while to get there, but now the question was out.

Contemplating this moment in advance, I'd wondered how Tom would react: whether he'd regret his high-mindedness.

He said, 'I suppose you think I was mistaken about that one?'

'I think you're a bloody idiot.'

'Really? Well, you're right, of course. But I'm not sorry, Pat, truly I'm not.'

'I'm glad I don't have your nice conscience.'

He laughed.

We kicked around a little among the pines. To the north the sky was tinged with smoke from the still-burning maquis and Tom remarked that we ought to be careful with our cigarettes. Then he went on, 'The day we buried Alvírez, Teresa said she heard a noise somewhere close by in the trees. I think I told her it was a squirrel – these pinewoods are full of red squirrels. That's what I believed.

'If I had to guess, I'd say the Doc was out on one of those walks of his and that he came across us while we were … doing what we did. Yes, I think so. I don't know what else there could be. What d'you think?'

'So he knows where the grave is?'

'Maybe.'

'Maybe?'

'Tisserand thought he knew, but, when it came down to it, he couldn't find the spot again. Who's to say Maillot will do any better? And – ' Tom added ' – they really do have to find the body. Maillot can't say he saw me bury Alvírez but he's no idea where.'

'Do you know where it is?'

'Uh huh – at least I think so. The odd thing is, Tisserand's confidence had me fooled. He picked a place and went charging ahead and I was calming myself down, telling myself he was wrong – knowing he was right, and preparing for the worst. Well, he *was* wrong. Yet the strange part is that his being mistaken made me think that I must be, too. As if Alvírez didn't die and Teresa and I were just overwrought and we never really buried anybody. Ain't that the damnedest?'

He sighed. 'My mistake was in burying him at all. I should've just thrown the body into a ravine and left it. Also I should never have said Teresa and I saw the guy on the Tuesday. I tell you, Pat, getting rid of corpses is a complicated business and you do the stupidest things.'

Meaning nothing in particular, I said, 'You're getting married tomorrow.'

Tom grimaced. 'To get married and be arrested for murder both on the same day – it'll certainly be memorable.'

'What'll you say if they find the body?'

'I guess I'll have to confess to killing him. I can't see there's any other real choice. I can't blame Katerina or her mother.' He added, 'I don't want you to think I'm being noble about this. I'm sick of people having the wrong idea about me. It's just that it's the only practical solution – always supposing I have the guts for it. Believe me, Pat, I'm not looking for martyrdom. I want to get a wife and raise children.'

'Then it all depends on the reliability of Maillot's memory.'

'That's about it – unless the body can be moved.'

'You've thought of that?'

'Haven't I just? But it isn't on. Joubert expects it. Tisserand and his men are keeping an eye on me. There's one of them here now – ' he flipped an indifferent hand ' – up the hill a ways. He's dressed as a hunter.'

I tried to follow the indication but saw no one through the dusty pines. Still, I believed Tom. I asked, 'Have you spoken to Ben about this?'

'Why put my problems on him? I've told you only because you won't leave me alone.'

I said, 'He might help you shift Alvírez if you ask him.'

To my surprise Tom looked pained. He said, 'One time maybe he would have.'

'There's something wrong?' I asked.

'Hard to say.' Tom patted his horse's muzzle. 'The fact is that Ben doesn't like me.'

'Oh?' I considered this. 'I can't say I've noticed.'

'No, I don't suppose so. I doubt Ben even knows it. But I've seen it before with friendships. They end and no one realises because there's no incident, no event on which to pin an explanation; and, without that, it seems shabby to lose someone for no apparent reason at all, and so we refuse to admit it.'

'I'm sorry.'

'You shouldn't be,' Tom said. Then, 'You know, at first they were so happy. You saw them. I blame myself for sticking around in Europe after they got married. I don't think they've had half a chance to make their marriage work and that's partly my fault for being here. The fool thing is, I'd have been happy to see them go home. There was nothing I wanted from Ben, nor Maisie either. I didn't need his money. I'd have got it from – ' he grinned ' – wherever the hell it is that money comes from.'

I laughed. I'm not sure why. Fear – nerves? Don't be mistaken: he really was prepared to let it all go and without a complaint. He was sorry for Ben and Maisie, not himself. As to his own fate he was blithe.

Certainly he never asked for my help, but I offered it anyway.

I said, 'I'll move Alvírez' body for you.'

CHAPTER THIRTY-EIGHT

I don't know why I agreed to move Alvírez's body except there are times when we affirm ourselves by actions that make no sense except as a protest against the meanness of life. I was twenty-four years old and things that now seem mad seemed then to be the way life was supposed to be lived

Tom objected. He said that it wasn't what he'd been driving at all – that the whole idea was crazy. I think he was speaking the truth but I ignored him. I was even pleased, because, in this act of affirmation, I'd prove myself his equal.

A similar thought came to me that evening before the wedding when I thought of Hetty. Armed with no more than her own bravery, she had to face her humiliation and it was this – her unbearable loneliness – that made me act.

I proposed we go night fishing.

My Uncle Gerald was a great night-fisherman. He had no time for the lawful, daylight stuff. He'd fish by lamplight from a small boat, while a spy on the bank kept watch and gave the world a drubbing with a blackthorn stick if it cared to poke its nose in.

I made a rod from cane and twine and took a lantern and candles, and Hetty and I waded out from the beach below La Pinéde and threw ourselves, breathless and giggling, onto the raft, where we lay a while, as nice as you please, with the stars above and the sea glistening on our bodies.

Hetty asked, 'D'you think we'll catch any fish?'

'I shouldn't think so, I said. 'My Uncle Gerald used explosive if he could come by any. But he was a poet and an old-fashioned man.'

'That doesn't sound very sporting.'

'No. I don't think sport ever came into it. It was a case of sitting peaceably and quietly sipping whiskey. Drinking isn't a sport, not that I heard of. A philosophy maybe?'

'Your uncle was a philosopher?'

'A poet, a philosopher, a politician. He belonged to a tradition that produced a few geniuses and a lot of men who were of no use except to keep the breweries in business.'

'Our neighbour, Mr Karpinski, was the same. At least, I think he was the same. He only spoke Polish so I can't be sure.'

'You don't speak the language?'

'Just kitchen Polish – names of things no one else eats: *bigos* and other stuff you do with cabbage; little snacks and special food for Easter. I know a song that my mother used to sing.'

She sang it now but only a few lines because she'd forgotten the rest. Her voice was surprisingly light. It took me a moment to realise she was imitating her mother, though quite unconsciously. 'It all goes,' she said, then noticed I was affected and nudged me playfully. 'Don't worry, Pat. My parents wanted me to become American and I did.'

The rest of our time on the raft was much as I've just described. At the end of two hours our candles ran out and we returned to our own cottages. We didn't catch any fish. Unlike me, my Uncle Gerald had been known to use a shotgun to take a salmon.

I don't know what I looked for from this encounter other than to comfort Hetty. I do know what I found. I fell in love with her courage, her intelligence and her realism and knew that above all other women, she was the one for me. Two years before, I'd have thought nothing of speaking, fine fellow that I was. Tonight I was tongue-tied. And what was the point? Hetty was in love with Tom. It was a condition from which no woman ever recovered, if Maisie was to be believed.

My plan seemed practical. Of all days, Tom's wedding was the one on which Joubert would least expect us to do anything. In any case he was watching Tom and the Malipieros, not me. I wouldn't take the car. I could do the distance on foot through the woods where it was unlikely I'd be seen, and if I was there'd be an end of it: we'd have to come up with another plan.

Tom agreed, but he was sombre. He said, 'Have you given any thought to the state the body is going to be in? It was beginning to stink when I buried him. God knows what it's like now. Forget the practicalities. Have you considered for a second the sheer horror of it?'

I said I had – though the truth was I'd no idea what I'd find –

and I went on to explain that it wasn't necessary to move the corpse far. However imperfect Maillot's memory might be, there was one point about which he'd be absolutely certain. He'd know which side of the highway he'd been on. If I could once get Alvírez' body across the road, it didn't matter where I left him because no one was ever going to search there.

'So you see,' I said, 'it isn't so difficult.'

I calculated two hours to locate Alvírez' body, an hour to move it and two for the return. Tom was getting married at eleven and I'd be back.

I stayed the night at my cottage and rose at four and walked into town, seeing no one except a girl pushing a mop around the bar of the Hôtel de la Gare. It was still cool and dark and, as I looked east, La Pinède was visible only as an interruption in the dense field of stars. A faint scent trembled from the lime trees. A film of honeydew covered the pavement tables.

Behind the town the path rose slowly past villas and a scattering of farms with terraces of vines and olives. I couldn't see them but heard a chorus of dogs. There's nothing lonelier. Without the burden of tools, I made good time as far as the margin of the woods where I halted until the day came up and I could see my way.

The sun broke only intermittently through the canopy. In any case it was an unreliable compass. Though the ground rose generally towards the north, the easiest route took me west or east according to the lie. In parts I had to climb round tangles of juniper, buckthorn and brambles. As the morning wore on, the heat increased. And I was wrong about time.

I took a break at nine after scaling an earth slide to a level patch of oaks and broom. Below me S. Symphorien floated like a haze on the sea and a little to the east a grey-green mountain rose on the far side of a valley to a sun baked peak. The road to Grasse lay somewhere in the valley, and I drank a mouthful of water and trudged in that direction.

That, briefly, was my journey through a silent countryside left to lizards and snakes. Now and then I scared a flock of chaffinches feeding in the scrub. Once or twice I found the droppings of *moufflons* and goats. For the rest, I sang a little to lift my spirits and thought of the others preparing for the wedding.

After an hour I reached the road. It curved in each direction to follow a spur of the hills and the views disappeared in heat shimmer. Whether I'd come too far or not far enough, it was impossible to say.

I decided to go on towards Grasse, thinking that, if I'd made a mistake, there was still a chance of finding the grave on the way back. Tom's instructions had seemed so precise, but, faced with reality, they no longer meant very much

I held to two pointers. On my left I ought find a thinning of the trees, enough to park a car. And on my right I should see a *mas* on the further side of a ravine and midway up the opposite hillside. Only once did they turn up together, and when that happened, I guessed I'd arrived at my goal. Yet it remained only a quiet spot on a country road, a place without resonance.

In the meantime Tom wed his Argentinian Virgin and I wasn't there.

In their moment of happiness Tom and Katerina were condemned to a slow death of which I'm the last mourner. But there are no laments for those who aren't loved, and Alvírez remains sordid to the end. In his case I hear no music.

I stood in sunlight on a silent road. I was exhausted and hurting from my accident, which may explain why it didn't seem important that I had a corpse to move. I pushed into the trees looking for the mound of stones Tom had left as a covering and a marker.

My water bottle was empty. The heat draped me in warm cobwebs. I lost my bearings among the land slips, the rock falls and storm water run offs and found myself at the base of a slope where spoil and stones had heaped up a tumulus. There was plenty of soft earth and it looked like a place someone in the body-burying business might choose.

I didn't think it was where Alvírez lay, though a squint-eyed look could see a cairn in the scattering of white rocks. What caused me to dig was that, if I didn't, I could hear Tom saying, 'You mean you didn't check *anywhere?*' and his disappointment would be worse than a reproach.

So I searched round and found a broken branch which I used to lever out one or two boulders, which in turn loosened the soil and let me scrape it aside. After half an hour I'd scooped out a broad pit. It was shallow but deeper than Tom said he'd dug and I might have stopped. But I didn't. The useless hole would be a testimony of my sincerity. I could stare Tom down and say, 'I worked my heart out for you, so don't complain. Whatever happens to you, *it's not my fault.*'

The last thing I expected to find was a bone.

It was small and it wasn't alone. In a minute I turned over a few more. I didn't know much about foxes but guessed one of them might have killed a goat and buried the remains like a dog does, or even left them on the surface where they'd be covered by the routine crumbling of the slope. Or – and this was reason to laugh – I might have found Alvírez.

The bones were a disjointed hand. The forearm followed. Then I saw other bones in the dump of earth at the side of my pit. I'd been turning them up and not noticing because they weren't supposed to be there. How many damn bones did a body have? And why were they so widely scattered?

Next I pulled on what seemed to be a bag of coarse denim. It was a blouson, I guess, like labourers wore – at least it came away with a mass of bone that looked like a rib cage, and with it a bundle of soft tissues not exactly flesh but more as if the earth were growing fat.

My head was spinning with heat as I began to pile up the charnel: more limbs, more rags – more than I could account for, though accounting for them wasn't on my mind only the grisly obsession of uncovering whatever I'd stumbled across.

There were six bodies – I mean six for certain though there may have been more. My count is based on the skulls. They were workingmen, to judge by the clothes. Who they were, I'd no idea. Each one had been shot in the back of the head. If I'm right, their hands had been tied.

After the war I read of the camps constructed by Vichy to hold Jews and undesirables, though I don't know that everything has been admitted. At the time we had an idea the trucks of labourers we saw go every day into the hills might have a sinister purpose, but no one asked and no one talked. As for these bodies, I suppose there's a connection, though I never learned what it was and in all the years since that time, I've seen no mention of them.

I try not to think too much about the horror I found in the hills.

Meantime Tom and the Argentinian Virgin were being destroyed in the very moment of their happiness. And they neither of them knew it.

CHAPTER THIRTY-NINE

It was mid-afternoon when I staggered down from the sun-drenched hills like a crazy prophet. I went to a bar and ordered a beer.

I sat there for half an hour, maybe more, piecing together meaningless images from the square. Empty beer and water glasses stood in front of me on the table. The lime trees shivered. A fly browsed jerkily on the white cloth.

Joubert's men hadn't been in the hills. I'd thought they would be. In fact I'd agreed to help Tom only because part of me had expected to find the police scouring for the Spaniard's grave and

I'd have the glory of trying and yet an excuse to give up. I couldn't understand it. The police *had* to have been there, if Tom was right and Maillot had seen him bury the body and betrayed him. What had happened?

I went back to my story. I'd told Tom that the old man had seen Alvírez on the Tuesday, which was the day after the funeral. The day on which Tom had got rid of the corpse. But what had Maillot really said? When I cast my mind back, he hadn't actually named the day beyond saying it was the day the Spaniard disappeared. I told Tom it was Tuesday; but that was only because Tom had fed me Tuesday as part of the lies to cover his tracks and distract everyone from the previous day, though at the time I didn't know. Yet, as Joubert had discovered, Alvírez had vanished on the Monday, which had to be the day Maillot was referring to. Which also meant that the latest time the Doctor could have seen him was in the morning before Alvírez went to La Pinède and got himself killed. Maillot knew absolutely nothing about the grave in the hills. If he had a secret, it was something else.

The waiter noticed me smiling and asked, 'You are amused?'

Perhaps I was. But it was the sort of amusement that brings you to tears: the awareness of human absurdity and the impossibility of knowing anything for certain. I thought of the bodies I'd discovered in the hills. They had nothing to do with Tom and would remain unexplained. Stories wander untidily into each other.

The waiter said his name was Louis. He wore a white shirt with detachable cuffs. His hair was oiled and combed over his bald scalp. I asked him to sit with me.

We studied the square, where the sunlight crumbled the yellow air. I asked Louis to tell me about himself. He told me the story of a decent man and his problems, and I gave him advice, which I don't suppose was worth much.

I asked him, 'Do you know Dr Maillot? He comes here sometimes.'

'*Bien sûr*, monsieur.'

'And Monsieur Alvírez?'

He nodded. I got the sense that he didn't like Alvírez. Then again, nobody did.

'Do you remember the boy who fell from La Pinède?'

'Marcel Goriot.'

'Did you see Dr Maillot or Monsieur Alvírez on the day of his funeral?'

Louis nodded. 'They took coffee and cognac together. Monsieur Alvírez had several cognacs.'

'Do you know what they talked about?'

This time Louis shook his head and we lost interest in each other. But he'd confirmed my suspicion that the two men had met and that Alvírez might have revealed a secret he would have kept if he was sober.

Meantime I had a wedding to go to.

I entered the salon of the Czar Aléxandre by the french window that looked over the terrace where Hetty once told me Tom had promised to marry her. The hired band was playing and a crooner was singing:

> Ça revient, la vie recommence
> Et l'espoire commence à renaître

The sadness of the song moved me with a kind of sentimental anger. I wanted to grab a girl and cruise across the dance floor, talk to her and not listen to anything she said, then go to the bar and pick a fight. But no one was dancing except a child who pirouetted, fell over, got up and pirouetted again. In the immense sunlit room only a dozen people sat. As I slouched in they gave me hostile stares.

There was no bride. There was no groom.

The air felt heavy with an intimation of disaster. I tried to remember whom Tom had invited. He claimed to be on friendly terms with half the town. 'To hell with it, invite 'em all,' Ben had grumbled. I saw tradesmen and people who enjoy funerals, malicious widows and little girls who'll dance at the drop of a hat. I saw gossips, fools and spectators with a nose for scandal and loot.

The German officers were there. Also Messrs Alphonse and Pierre. Monsieur Alphonse raised a lilac-suited arm and beckoned me.

'What horror!' he murmured gloomily. 'To see everything so spoilt.'

'What happened?' I asked.

'I do not know. There were inconveniences at the ceremony, but we were not there. We would not be here now except that this is where we live, and, *enfin*, one must have lunch.'

He spared me a bereaved look and I left him to speak to Captain Brenner.

The German said, 'We went to the *mairie*, but there was such a crowd, Herr Byrne, you would not believe it. We could not go inside. Then the police arrive. Five – ten minutes? Then everyone is shouting and rushing inside – the police, Herr Rensselaer, his lady, everyone.'

'Herr Rensselaer was arrested?'

Captain Brenner asked his friend.

'No – we think no one was arrested,' he said. 'But it is possible. You understand? The confusion.'

I was heat-struck and mad. I might have stayed and got drunk in the fine old Irish way, but the first glass sickened me. I could feel the scorn and pity of strangers.

I wandered into the lobby and saw Philippe Beauclerc through the office door. He had his head in his hands, the collar of his shirt had sprung from its studs, and there was a bottle in front of him. I gave him one of those see-you-soon waves that mean nothing.

Then I rushed to La Chênaie.

It was four thirty, maybe five. I was dying by degrees. The earth trembled under a mantle of hot air.

Our life at La Chênaie was breaking up and I was too ill from dehydration. I could only watch and whimper like a dog that knows it must stay while its masters go away.

Teresa was in the garden. At first I thought her dress was black, but it was ultramarine silk with sprigs of flowers. She was wearing the same hat with a demi-veil in which I'd first seen her.

She turned from looking over the sea and said, 'You don't look well, Patrick.'

Hetty came out of the house. She was wearing a vibrantly sunny peach-coloured frock. She put a hand to her breast and said, 'My God, Pat, you look absolutely awful!'

Teresa said, 'I've just told him he doesn't look well.'

Hetty ignored her. She bustled over to take my arm. 'You've been out in the sun too long. You're burned all over.'

'I've been walking in the hills,' I said.

'Let's get you in the house, my boy. You're weak as a kitten.' She smiled at me. 'Where on earth have you been – missing the wedding and all? Ha! There's a laugh! For God's sake hold my arm. Why weren't you there? Tom said you were doing something he asked – now *that's* mysterious for you!' She licked a handkerchief the way my mother used to do and wiped grime from my eyes. 'Better! Now you'll live. The wedding … I don't know … did you have any idea? Is that what … ? Now, don't you go fainting on me.'

She led me inside. The sunlight had made my eyes feel as if they were filled with cataracts. The room rotated. Yet part of me was detached. The still centre of things.

I heard Ben say, 'Hi, Pat. Jesus you look like shit. Honey, have you seen my suit – the grey?'

Tom told him, 'You loaned me the suit. Who's looking after Pat? Maisie, will you get him a drink of water?'

'Can't you see I'm packing?'

Katerina offered, 'I'll do it.'

'Will you, honey?'

They were packing. I heard drawers being opened and closed and cupboards banging.

Maisie said, 'Can you believe we've collected so much stuff? I mean – it's just *stuff*.'

Ben snapped, 'Leave it! Who gives a damn? It can all be replaced. Just make sure we take the photographs.'

Hetty asked quietly, 'Can I take my dresses? They're all I've got.'

Someone – Tom, I think – said, 'Where's that water?'

I felt a hand guide mine round the glass and the next voice was Katerina's.

'Here it is. Be careful, Patrick. Don't spill it.'

There was more, but in my blindness it was like a radio script.

Maisie said, 'Are we really going to Nice? What makes you think the Italians will let us through? My God, we don't even have an hotel!'

Ben said, 'I have two thousand in cash money. Tom, what do you got?'

'Five hundred.'

'Cash or cheques?'

'Cash.'

'I have another five grand in cheques.'

There was more but I don't remember it. Only Katerina saying tenderly:

'Patrick is very ill.'

I woke up. A blue bar of twilight glimmered through a shutter. A figure stood in the doorway against the light of an oil lamp. A record was playing *Je cherche un milliardaire*, and I heard a steamer trunk being dragged across a tiled floor.

Hetty said, 'He's awake. How are you feeling, darling?' She was sitting at my bedside, her hand resting on mine. 'You gave us all a shock,' she said. 'As if we haven't had enough shocks lately.'

Tom appeared in the doorway. His arm was laid across Katerina's shoulders and Teresa stood silently behind him. He asked, 'You okay, sport?' You had us all going there.'

'I'm fine,' I said. 'Too much sun, that's all.'

'Rest up a while.'

'I'll do that. And you?'

Oh,' he said, 'we're packing to go.'

He sounded as jolly as I ever heard him.

'Tonight?'

'That's the idea. I'll tell you about it. Meantime rest, d'you hear?'

'Sure.'

The door closed and I turned my head to the pillow. I began to cry.

I think some time passed.

Then Hetty said, 'You really are a mess, aren't you? She kissed my forehead. I clutched her hand.

Je cherche un milliardaire. This was Hetty's room. She'd shared it with Tom. It was her perfume on the pillow. And most likely she'd cried on it too.

Where had Tom been sleeping since he decided he loved his Argentinian Virgin? Perhaps, he and Hetty had continued to share a bed while Tom wondered and Hetty knew what the future would be.

I could see Hetty doing that. She was the best, the bravest, the most sincere of us. And in the end she was the strongest because she could bear the unendurable.

Ben opened the door. He asked, 'How's it going?' He closed the door.

Maisie stuck her nose in. She said, 'I've got more clothes than I know what to do with. D'you want, or I should throw?' She added suddenly, 'This has got to be the most exciting thing I ever did!'

Ben again: 'Two silk shirts and a jacket for you, Pat. I don't know about the collar size.'

Tom: 'I'd like to leave you with a souvenir. Any thoughts? I did an oil sketch of Hetty.'

'I'd like that,' I said.

'That's sweet of you,' said Hetty. And she meant it as she meant everything.

I must have dozed again. I came to and the night was hollow with echoes: the purring of a car engine, the barking of dogs. Tom came in, holding a candle in the dark.

He still had an air of feverish gaiety, as though he were a soldier going to war when war is fresh and joyful, yet ashamed in his heart.

'I feel like a heel, leaving you and all,' he said. He took a corner of the bed next to Hetty, who seemed to have been dozing too.

'You're going?' I asked in the face of the obvious. 'I thought you didn't plan to leave for a couple of days.'

'That was the general idea,' he said. Then, 'Look, Pat, I really appreciate what you tried to do for me.'

'I failed.'

'I guess so – but no harm done. Still, we've got to get out of here before Joubert figures out his next move. We're leaving for Nice now and, God knows, it'll be tough getting across the border by night with our papers stamped for the wrong date.'

'How will you manage it?'

'In the usual way – with Ben's money.'

'That'll work?'

Tom grinned. 'That and the fact I feel like Lucky Tom Rensselaer again.'

'Then all your problems are solved,' I said, and meant it. I thought of something. 'I shan't be coming.'

I wouldn't be going with them. It had never been planned that I would. In the end I was just the Irish kid who got lucky and wrote a book. As I said at the beginning of this story, I was with the Americans but never really a part of their group. And now I felt the starkness of my exclusion.

Tom said, 'I guess you could follow by train – I mean, if that's what you want. But we don't plan to hand around Italy long. At a stretch we can fit five of us in the convertible. Hetty has volunteered to stay behind too. She'll join us in a few days so we can all go home together. I don't expect the police to trouble you both. And you … ?'

'I'll go back to Ireland,' I said.

'Yes, that's probably the best thing,' he agreed. He'd fallen sad, but now he became jolly again. 'Still, it's been great, hasn't it? It's been … what's the word? C'mon, you're the writer – help me out, Pat – an *experience*?'

An experience? It was a pale word for what had happened to me, but it would have to do.

I remembered something. I said, 'Maillot doesn't know where Alvírez is.' I didn't care that Hetty could hear this. Neither did Tom. It seemed. 'What happened at the wedding?'

'Joubert turned up with Tisserand and the Doc. He tried to stop the ceremony. He said there were irregularities with Teresa's and Katerina's papers.'

'What sort of irregularities?'

'I don't know. I didn't give a damn,' Tom answered curtly, as if I were Joubert. 'In these situations you have to show who's in control. I told him the papers were history – that they didn't matter any more. He was too late. Katerina was married to an American citizen and she and Teresa had the protection of the Government of the United States. If he tried anything I'd cause the wrath of God to fall on him.'

'How did he take that?' I asked.

'He backed off,' said Tom. He laughed. 'What do you think of that?'

'Lucky Tom Rensselaer,' I said.

That seemed to please him. And I'm glad because I never saw him again.

He left the room, taking his tragedy with him.

CHAPTER FORTY

I can't say I wasn't warned. When Ben Benedict gave me the piece of paper with Shapiro's address, he cautioned me against using it; said I should think it over and talk to my wife. But in that case – if it was so dangerous – why did he give it me at all? For friendship's sake? Maybe friends do behave that way: leading each other into danger: off-loading some of the burdens and the pains. But the truth is I don't think Ben ever was my friend. And I don't think he could bear the fact that Tom was.

He was in love with Tom. The proof is in some papers and photographs he sent me before he died. Things from their time together in Paris. I know that even though I haven't studied them.

I ignored Ben's warning. I didn't know when I'd be in America again and I'd lived for too long with the ghost of the Argentinian Virgin.

The problem was I knew nothing about Dr Nathan Shapiro? Was he a doctor of philosophy or of medicine? What was his speciality? What did he have to do with our affairs?

My guess was he was a psychiatrist. Possibly Ben's before he put himself into the Programme.

The voice on the telephone said, 'This is the Shapiro residence. Rachel speaking.'

I said, 'May I speak to Dr Shapiro?'

'Dr Shapiro is at his office. This is his residence. May I ask who you are?'

'Tell me please, is Dr Shapiro is a psychiatrist?'

'I think you must have a wrong number. He's an oncologist.'

'That's a cancer specialist, isn't it? No, I don't think I have a wrong number.'

'He doesn't take patients at home.'

'Perhaps not, but I believe he'll see me. Would you tell him I'm a friend of Mr Benjamin Benedict? My name is Patrick Byrne.' I gave Ira's number.

In nineteen sixty-eight telephones had a habit of failing, and I thought nothing of it when the line went dead. That evening, as Ira and I were preparing a bachelor dinner, a return call came in. The caller said she was Margaret Shapiro, the Doctor's wife; the Rachel I'd spoken to was the nanny.

Margaret Shapiro was polite but cautious. I felt like a crank as I explained that I didn't exactly know why I was getting in touch except that Ben had said I could, and it all might make sense if she spoke to her husband. She said that wouldn't be necessary and I could come to the house the next day. She gave me directions.

It was a bland conversation. I wasn't frightened of what Shapiro might tell me, only vaguely uneasy in the way one gets when talking to a doctor about a relative. There's a foreboding that he'll say a loved one is about to die, but what frightens us is not the death but the discovery that we can let other people go: the shame of our own desire to survive.

I thought Dr Shapiro, the oncologist, was going to tell me Tom was dying, and I could feel a foretaste of relief that the events of that summer of forty-one would be brought to a close.

You see, a part of me needed Tom to die.

Shapiro was doing well. Ten acres of lawn and garden. A stream with a stand of hickories. A white colonial frame house built on a rise with the landscape rolling away like the softness of cloud tops.

I paid off my cab and shuffled to the door. I was wearing

tweeds and my Frank Sinatra hat because I liked the snappy band. The bell chimed distantly as only the doorbells of the rich do, and a Latino maid answered in a waft of lilies and beeswax while I burned on the step and wiped the sweat off my neck. Dr Shapiro was doing well in the patrician style that doesn't require bums to be thrown out but treats them decently and offers a glass of ice tea.

I followed the maid into a room with shades filtering the sunlight into faint blushes of parchment. I was posted on a sofa of bleached wood and left to admire a highboy in burr walnut and a collection of Mexican pottery. The maid brought lemonade in an iced glass. A bird in a wicker cage sang a couple of phrases and preened itself. A cloud passed over the sun and the pale walls swam briefly like moiré silk. Then Margaret Shapiro came in.

She was a petite, elegant woman of what the French call "a certain age", when they mean a very uncertain one, and she wore her hair in a short sculpted look that only chic women can carry off.

'I was playing tennis,' she said. 'I see you're got a glass of lemonade. I could drink a pitcher full. Then I've got to change for a ladies' lunch.' She reached for a little bell on a table and rang it.

'You were playing with your husband?' I asked.

'Oh, good God, no! Nate is a *doctor*. They never do *anything* that would be good for their health. No, he's in the city as usual.'

I noticed we skipped introductions. Margaret Shapiro never met people who didn't know her; nor would she embarrass anyone by seeming not to know them

'So, Pat, let me see if I've got this straight,' she said. 'You got in touch because Ben Benedict gave you Nate's name.'

'You know him?'

'Not especially. Nate thinks they have a club in common but doesn't claim to *know* anything. Benedict's friends are financiers – and gangsters, if the rumours are true, which they probably aren't.'

'And Tom Rensselaer?'

'I'm on a charity committee with Frances Rensselaer – that's with an 'e' not an 'i' – who's a great niece or something of J P Rensselaer, so there could be a connection there. Nate doesn't know any Rensselaers at all. But do go on. Why do you suppose the great Ben Benedict gave you our address?'

'I can't say. We were talking of old friends – whatever had become of them. There was a time – it was a long time ago – when we were young and spent a summer on the Riviera. Something happened. I can't say what. I mean I don't understand exactly what. I know only the way things looked, but I don't think that's the truth. I'm not explaining this very well, am I?'

It seemed, however, that I was, or – more likely – that Margaret Shapiro possessed some of Tom's confident sympathy.

The maid came with more lemonade and a plate of cookies. Margaret thanked her, poured a drink from the pitcher and said nicely, 'Take your time, Pat.' She glanced sideways at my Frank Sinatra hat and remarked, 'That's neat. I tell Nate he should wear a hat more often now that he's losing his hair.'

I grunted, took a cookie and sipped my drink. I was beginning to feel barely house-trained. I tried, 'You have a lovely home.'

'Yes, I do,' she said. 'Everyone is forever telling me how lucky I am. "You're so lucky, Margaret!" they say, which is true, and I don't claim to deserve any of it.'

Was she making fun of me?

I glanced at her eyes and read, behind the humour, a kindness and serenity. It was then that I glimpsed something of Tom in her. Her sublimeness.

And so, for an hour or more, I told her as much as I knew of the Argentinian Virgin.

'I'm fascinated!' Margaret said. 'Now, while I think of it, why don't we have a bite to eat?'

I said, 'Don't you have a ladies' lunch to go to?'

'Oh, *that*. They happen all the time. I shan't be missed.'

We moved to the garden. The lawn sloped to a line of golden trees. In the middle was a belvedere painted blue as the sky. I heard the voices of children but saw none.

'Do you have children?' Margaret asked.

'Two boys, pretty much grown up now. And you?'

'A boy and a girl.'

I studied her uncertain age. She blushed. I said, 'They must be young. You have a nanny.'

'What a gentleman you are, Pat! No, they're not so very young, but we like to keep Rachel on because they're attached to her.'

We took our places in the belvedere where the Latino maid laid a white cloth on a pierced metal table. I removed my jacket in the moist blue heat and sat in shirtsleeves and suspenders. I kept the Sinatra hat because of the imperfect shade, which left sunlight like loose pieces of a jigsaw scattered about the belvedere. Margaret asked the maid to take milk and cookies to the children, whom I'd still not seen. I realised then that the children of the rich live out of sight in a magic garden among the good fairies.

Margaret watched me.

'It is lovely, isn't it?' she said.

'I guess so. I mean it is. I'm not used to … '

'Go on with your story. You know, what strikes me is that Tom knew next to nothing about his Argentinian Virgin.'

'No one did – except Alvírez and maybe Dr Maillot.' I decided to voice an idea that had been troubling me. I said, 'I've always thought about this business in terms of Tom: what *he* knew or didn't know; the risks *he* took; the disaster that struck *him*.'

She was interested, 'And now?'

'I wonder … I wonder if I've got the whole thing wrong. It's a matter of perspective, isn't it? I could see things only from Tom's point of view because it was only him I knew well … that I knew at all. And that suddenly seems unfair.'

'To Katerina?'

'Yes.'

'But, surely, not just her? What about Teresa? Doesn't it occur to you that Tom might have solved the problem by marrying the mother rather than the daughter? Teresa was evidently in love with him and in many ways it would have been a more appropriate match. And what about Hetty? Do we forget her because she had the sense to let Tom go?'

Margaret added pointedly, 'Is "unfair" really the word to describe the way Tom behaved?'

'You want me to say his actions were *immoral*? I don't know I can say that. Tom always acted from the best of motives.'

'Did he?' Margaret asked sceptically. And I was shocked.

'If he didn't,' I said, 'I really am lost.'

We finished our lunch. Margaret told me something of herself. She was from a Chicago banking family but educated mainly at schools in the East. Her people had objected to Nathan Shapiro because he was poor.

'Before he got all this,' I said.

She laughed, showing her pretty teeth. 'Oh, dear! You really don't understand, do you? *This* is poor – at least so far as my family is concerned.' She sighed. 'It's all a matter of what you're used to, I guess.'

We strolled back to the house. The grass looked brittle in the sunshine. Margaret said, 'I was interested in your story of the Argentinian Virgin because I do work for a charity handling beaten and abused women, and it seems to me that that was Katerina's situation: that she was victimised by Alvírez, and then by Tom, though I'm prepared to allow that there are some extenuating circumstances in Tom's case.'

'You don't like him.'

'Tom? No, I don't see how anyone could. But I have the

advantage of distance. I'm free of the spell he seems to have cast over everyone. Fortunately he isn't my concern. Really I wanted to find out if I liked you.'

'And do you ... like me?'

She gave a slow, sly smile. 'Oh, you'll do well enough as a specimen of the half of humanity that doesn't have much good to be said about it. I was taken by the way you spoke about Hetty. It was tender. She sounds like a survivor.'

'She is.'

We entered by the french window into a boudoir of soft yellows and creams. Margaret invited me to take a seat, took one herself and faced me with a doubtful expression.

She said, 'Well, Pat, I guess you're wondering if you're any further forward – wondering why Ben Benedict suggested you call on us.'

'Do you know?'

She nodded. 'Of course. But I had to judge whether to help you or not.'

And will you?'

'Yes. Though whether what I know is of use, I can't say. The truth is I'm not certain what you want. Tom Rensselaer seems to be beyond anyone's help, and your Argentinian Virgin is no more than a fantasy who never existed outside the imagination of you and your friends. Didn't Ben tell you that Katerina and her mother didn't even come from Argentina?'

I nodded. I caught in Margaret's eye a glimpse of Tom's cosmic sympathies, and I was disconcerted again by the strange points of similarity in characters who were generally so different.

The maid came in. I don't know if Margaret summoned her. Things happen effortlessly in the mansions of the rich.

Margaret said something about the nanny, then spoke to me about tea: Earl Grey or Assam? Oh, Assam, I think, don't you? The tea arrived in a Shelley service with a millefiori pattern. Three cups? Yes, three.

'Rachel will take tea with us.'

And so Rachel came. She was quiet and undramatic, tapping on the door, pausing to be invited, glancing at Margaret and then at me, and saying hello in a gentle voice.

There was no *coup de théâtre*. No particular shock. I think I dimly expected what was to happen.

'Hullo, Patrick,' she said with the kindest of smiles.

'Hullo, Katerina,' I answered. I hesitated because her beauty still had the capacity to surprise. I said, 'It's been a long time, hasn't it?'

CHAPTER FORTY-ONE

I ought to call her Rachel because we were strangers. She wasn't the Katerina Malipiero I'd known in S. Symphorien. Rather, with the years, she'd grown to look like Teresa. She'd captured the same splendid, imperious beauty and held it firmly, though with an indifference her mother never had: the indifference of a woman whose awareness of her own sexuality has been suppressed. She had to be in her mid forties – not that it mattered.

Margaret opened the french window to let in the smell of new mown grass and the fluttering of the Japanese gardener among his roses.

Rachel said, 'I thought you were lunching with your girlfriends?' She smiled at me. 'Margaret has a social life you wouldn't believe.' Her voice and expressions had become pleasantly American.

Margaret returned the good-humour. 'I decided I'd give Pat the once-over to check he wasn't trouble. I kind of liked him, even with the goofy hat. But I do have things to do. D'you mind if I leave you two?'

Rachel said she didn't mind at all and Margaret, an elegant

nice lady to the last, spoke some farewells I like to think were sincere, and we were left alone.

But who was she? I've mentioned the beauty, which she didn't seem to think much of. Her hair, still black, was scraped back and tied with a green ribbon. Her dress was green, too: plain with a collar and buttons at the front, a little but not too much like an overall. Her legs were good and shapely as I remembered, and she wore tan pumps. She seemed comfortable with Rachel as she'd never been with Katerina.

We began with the usual stuff about weather and travel, where was I living now and was I married, what did I do and how long. She volunteered that she'd been with the Shapiros for ten years: good people, she wanted me to understand, who treated her as one of the family. No, she hadn't married after Tom. They hadn't divorced, not that she knew. And he was still alive, wasn't he? Ben had told her he was, but she knew no more than that, not what he was doing or anything; and she'd had no contact with Ben in a year.

That's how he came up: like "good-old-Tom-whatever-happened-to-him?" one of the characters in conversations between friends who haven't met in a while and have no idea what to talk about. I don't think there was any other way of doing it – not without going straight to the pain. But it was sad beyond words.

'How is your mother?' I asked.

'She died,' Rachel answered. She was calm in the face of an old grief. 'A long time ago. It was cancer. And your Uncle Gerald?'

I laughed. She smiled – she had a ready smile. 'Dear God, you remember him? He fell off a stool in a bar in Grafton Street and broke his neck. The bookies of Dublin were in mourning for a month.'

'You always made me laugh with your stories.'

'Did I? I'd forgotten.'

The truth was the old fellow died in agony of liver disease, repented and ended in the bosom of the Church. But he was a man of whom the truth always seemed beside the point: somehow deceitful.

The speed with which we passed over the subject of the two deaths astonishes me now. But you have to understand we were holding ourselves on a rein. The past, if you thought about it too closely, held only despair.

We talked a little more of this and that. Rachel was at her ease and I was reminded of conversations with Mormons and others whose serenity comes with a faint air of madness; though don't mistake me: her ease was genuine and any madness was mine.

I said, 'I don't know if I should apologise for not keeping in contact.'

She asked, 'Do you think you would have?'

'I … No, probably not. Only Ben seems to have kept tabs on everyone. Tell me – did he ever lose touch?'

She shook her head. 'No – at least only for the first few months after I left Tom. Once or twice I tried to disappear, but he was always able to find me.'

'He has an army of private investigators.'

'I ought to be grateful. Whenever I was in difficulties, he sent me money.'

I was surprised. 'Ben sent you money? Why should he do that?'

'I don't know. I had an idea that it might be guilt, but … well, that doesn't seem to make much sense, does it, Pat?'

'Not that I can think of,' I agreed.

The subject drifted to the Shapiros: their happy lives, their nice house. It was one we could unite behind: the eternal mystery of how other people achieve happiness. Rachel proposed we take a turn around the grounds, and why not? She offered me a hand.

'I'm glad you came, Pat,' she said.

We walked to the stand of hickories and stared into the stream. I hunted for flat pebbles and skimmed a few. Rachel stood on a rock that jutted in the water, her eyes closed, her face in the sunlight. I thought for a moment of the beach at S. Symphorien: of the Argentinian Virgin swimming in a lonely sea. Only now did I recognise how much all of us – except Tom of course – had hated the Virgin: her vacuous loveliness, her empty perfections. And yet I felt pity for the object of that hatred, who'd neither asked for nor deserved it, but only had it visited upon her like a curse.

Rachel skipped down from the rock. She'd kept not only the beauty but the taut, poised physicality of her youth. But it was all sexless and wasted. It was grotesque.

Looking at her, I wondered: why hadn't she divorced Tom and remarried? Was no one else good enough? Or was it that no other man would *dare?*

No, not that – there are men who will dare any woman, especially if they can't *see* her: men of raw self-assurance with the energy to make money and a fine eye for a car or a good set of cufflinks. Not that. And if not that, it could only be that we'd spoiled her, scarred her, twisted the spirit in her. We had done evil.

She came skipping from the rock with the day in her smile. She saw me and faltered.

Bemused, she asked. 'Are you crying, Pat?'

I put a hand to my cheek.

'Damn,' I said, making light of it. 'I think I am. Sure, isn't it a sentimental thing I am in me ould age, bedad?'

'Tom cried,' she said.

'Did he now? And why would that be?' I asked.

It was then that she told me, doing so quite calmly – prosaically even – and, as a writer, I am sorry for this, the plainness of it, but it has the merit of human honesty. She was, after all, not that fantastical creature, the Argentinian Virgin, but a woman composed of the same subtle essences as other ordinary women, the same transient joys and agonies, the perpetual struggle to be fully real in an all too solid unreality. If I hated the Argentinian Virgin, I loved Rachel Blumenthal in much the same way I've loved other women: that's to say without difficulty, sincerely, but never well enough. A conclusion which brings me back to Tom, who said he saw the 'glory' in women – a dazzling thought. But it led him to create a monster, the poor devil.

> I did not come from Argentina [Rachel wrote to me afterwards when she feared, with good reason, that no man would ever understand her: fearing that she would again be denied any authentic voice]. Neither did my mother or my father. We were German Jews who owned the famous Blumenthal department store in the Leipzigerstrasse in Berlin. We also had an apartment in the Ku'damm and a villa in Grunewald. We were rich and happy and we wished to escape the Nazis, which was our tragedy.
>
> My father was liberal and artistic. He collected paintings. I studied ballet and violin. He was a kind man who trusted the goodness of his neighbours and did not believe that the Hitler business would be pushed to extremes. It was for these reasons that he left the matter of our flight from Germany too late and, when the war broke out, we were left to get abroad however we could and with the help of whatever villains would assist us for money.
>
> My mother was a strong woman – much stronger and more determined than my father. It was she who found Señor Alvírez who was a Spaniard or an American – I never knew which: no more than I knew the details of the scheme they devised. You must recall, Patrick, that I was only a girl.
>
> I believe that Katerina and Teresa Malipiero existed, but they died. Do you understand that I thank them – pray for them?
>
> Señor Alvírez obtained identity and travel papers by bribery and forgery, so we could go to Argentina, which was a neutral

country. Before we could leave, however, my father was arrested and sent to a concentration camp.

It was decided we would go first to France. Señor Alvírez said that for enough money he could obtain my father's release to join us. I now think this was a lie, but at the time we forced ourselves to believe him because we had no other choice. Our fortune consisted of jewellery belonging to my mother and other gems bought by my father after selling his paintings.

That is how we came to be in S. Symphorien at the Villa la Pinède. How we came to know of the young, beautiful, mysterious Americans who lived in the little cottage and danced and were happy. Oh yes, Patrick, you were as mysterious to us as we were to you!

I do not know when my father died. He was alive or dead as best suited Señor Alvírez in his efforts to get money out of us. Alvírez was a liar, a thief and a blackmailer; and my mother did not believe we would ever go to Argentina on the papers he provided. We would stay in France until we were betrayed.

Instead – God forgive us – we found Tom.

Did I love him? That question goes to the heart of the matter, doesn't it?

The answer is confused by the fact that my mother insisted on lying to him. How could I fall in love with someone I was deceiving? Yet he was so handsome, so good-natured, brave, talented! I was frightened of him because he was more intense than anyone else I had ever met. That is what I remember: the fear, not the love. The shame of it all.

The tragedy is that what happened was the result of a misunderstanding. The first time Tom came to La Pinède and met my mother, they talked. But I don't think Tom grasped my mother's seriousness – why should he? He was chatting lightly and amusingly while she listened intently for every nuance so she could decide whether he was a friend or an enemy. There was talk – of the movie industry, I think – and Tom said something about the Jews involved in it. I don't believe he meant anything, but my mother decided he hated us – the Jews.

No, that isn't so – I don't know exactly what she believed, because she grew very fond of Tom.

It made no difference.

Rachel's letter pretty well summarises what she told me so far as concerns the core of the thing, the central lie, the pitiful absurdity of it: as if, for a moment, anyone who knew him could believe Tom hated Jews.

The problem was that Teresa had steel and ice in her soul. *She would not take the risk* – not when it affected her daughter. When she tricked Tom into the marriage, her actions were wholly cynical – that's a fact you can't avoid. Yet she didn't do it for herself. She was simply determined to obtain American papers for Rachel. And, as far as it goes, she was right.

Teresa didn't hate Tom. She loved him in her fashion. But she saw no reason why he shouldn't bear the burden of the injustice that had fallen on her family. As she saw it, no moral principle was compromised. They were all of them equally innocent and so it didn't matter who it was that became the victim. The situation was unfortunate, regrettable – that was all.

When Rachel explained this, I said, 'So you deceived Tom because you thought he hated Jews?'

She nodded.

I think I laughed at the awfulness. It was a cosmic joke so hideous it almost persuaded me to believe in God for want of anything else foul enough to support an explanation.

Then it occurred to me: '*That* was what Dr Maillot knew! That was what Alvírez had revealed and which would have stopped the wedding if the Doctor and Joubert had only arrived earlier.'

I imagined the morning of the funeral. Alvírez, at the café, putting back brandy to screw up his courage so he could steal the diamond necklace. Maillot plying him with drink out of curiosity and malice until Alvírez, in his desperate quest to be liked, tried to bind the old man to him by disclosing his great secret.

I asked, 'Didn't Tom want to know what was wrong with your papers?'

Rachel flushed. A note of pride and admiration crept into her voice. She said, 'No. You see, Pat, he *trusted* us. It didn't matter to him because he knew he was doing the right thing.'

I said, 'Yes. I understand. He was simply being Tom Rensselaer, the most decent man who ever lived. Dear Christ, the pathetic bastard.'

We'd reached the belvedere. I noticed a magazine. I fingered it while the Japanese gardener came over to give Rachel a rose and ask what he should do next. The lawn stretched out as crisp as new dollar bills. I was tired and middle aged and the veins in my legs ached. I took a seat and waited, watching Rachel's small movements, the fascination of her. The gardener left and she turned to me.

She said, 'When Tom asked nothing – when he accepted us as we were – then I loved him.'

'Uh huh,' I said, annoyed and sceptical. 'But I bet you didn't tell him the truth.'

'My mother wouldn't let me. She trusted no one. Not then. She told me to wait until we were in America. Once we were safe, it would no longer matter what Tom thought.' She hesitated. 'Can't you forgive us, Pat?'

'It isn't for me,' I said. My legs were throbbing, my head was spinning and I wanted to get drunk and damn her and Tom and everyone. Yet I'd come this far and had to press on. I said brutally, 'I suppose he found out in the end and threw you out.'

She was shocked. 'No!'

'But you did tell him? Once you were in New York and safe in his uncle's apartment, you told him. How did he take it?'

Rachel's eyes sparkled. Her smile, which always flickered either side of radiance, transfigured her. 'He laughed!' She exclaimed. 'He kissed me! He said, "Oh, is *that* all? I thought it'd be *much* worse." Do you understand, Pat? *He didn't care*: not that we were Jews – not that we'd lied. All he wanted to know was that we'd told him everything and that I loved him. And I did!'

Rachel told him everything – except about Alvírez's death, which couldn't be explained.

Tom had always seen that the necklace was key to the mystery of Alvírez's death. It was missing and no one doubted the dead man had intended to steal it. Yet it hadn't been found with Alvírez's body.

As Joubert said, either the dead man had an accomplice who'd killed him and walked off with the spoils, or Teresa still had the necklace because she killed Alvírez before he could get away.

Tom decided there had to be an accomplice, but someone other than the Houblon boy, who was at the funeral while Alvírez was at the house. He meant some convenient shady type like a character from cheap fiction. Someone I've not mentioned. Someone who doesn't appear in this story.

Joubert was right. The theory of the second accomplice was ridiculous. So were Teresa and her daughter killers? How else could Alvírez have died?

Whatever explanation you signed up to, the jewels had to be accounted for. Their disappearance was the only proof that someone other than the Malipieros had been at La Pinède when Alvírez died. If you didn't believe in that other person then the two women had killed him – it was as simple as that

Still, for a moment it seemed Tom had won his Argentinian Virgin. His forgiving nature had been rewarded. His faith in the generosity of life – in the protective genius who watched over

Lucky Tom Rensselaer – had been justified. What could go wrong?

'He found the necklace,' Rachel told me. 'My mother and I had hidden it.'

He found the necklace and knew that Alvírez wasn't killed by an accomplice. Rachel and Teresa had murdered him after all.

And the whole business of the marriage was revealed as a cynical fraud, and nothing the women said or did could be believed.

CHAPTER FORTY-TWO

I wasn't finished in the East. Senator Walter Cabot Wagner had a place in the piedmont about an hour out of Charlottesville Virginia. It was a former plantation with acres of trees and paddock and a view of the Blue Ridge. The Senator was in Washington, but I spoke to his wife and arranged to call on her.

I was driving a budget car and wearing my hat and a suit that was tired because I hadn't brought a spare. I parked on the gravel before a white ante-bellum mansion and limped on my aching legs to the door where a black in a charcoal suit and starched shirt answered and said the lady of the house would be pleased to see me in the French parlour.

I was ushered into a room of yellow paper, old European furniture, paintings and white busts of people who have busts made of them. On a table lay an uncleared tray with a Limoges tea service and there was a scent of beeswax and cigarettes.

A woman came in and said as though we'd met yesterday and knew each other in a casual way, 'Oh, hi Pat. Jerome said it was you.'

'Hullo,' I answered and, when she offered a cheek, I kissed it.

It was a lot of years since I'd given any thought to Maisie. Of us all, she was the least stable yet the most tough-minded. Probably it was this contradiction that made it difficult for me to imagine how things had turned out for her. Had she, like Rachel, kept her beauty? It was possible because she had the looks that last: the fine bone structure and the Bronzino neck. But acid in the soul attacks the body and I didn't think it likely though I couldn't be certain. After Ben she'd married a baseball player and then an actor before finally settling on the Senator. I'd never heard of any children.

The woman before me was dressed in an ivory silk blouse and trousers a shade darker. Her feet were slipped into gold sandals and her nails were painted gold. When she moved, her glossy chestnut hair flashed. It was cut short – bobbed, I think the term is – and the whole effect was sharp and pert so that I thought of Dorothy Parker, the wit and spikiness.

I removed my Sinatra hat but kept it by me. I was becoming proud of that hat like blacks were becoming proud of their colour.

'You've had a long drive?' Maisie asked. She lit a cigarette and inserted it into an amber holder.

'From New York, but I stayed overnight in a motel.'

'Can I offer you something? Sit down, for God's sake. Something? I normally take a glass of chardonnay this time of day. You were a whiskey man as I recall.'

'Chardonnay will be fine. These days I don't drink much.'

'None of us do. The effect of age, I suppose. Ben's on the wagon – but I guess you know that.'

'Tom isn't.'

'No, he's a lush from what I hear. You do come to the point, don't you? Tom Rensselaer … ' she sighed with theatrical languor. 'You know, I can go whole *days* without thinking about him – one time a whole week, but that was when I fell love with Harry Moore, who was my second.'

She struck a pose on one of the gilt chairs, one leg crossed over the other and a foot tapping air. I stood a moment as though my bumpkin brain had never got the hang of sitting, but it was clear we were going to be a while and so I took a chair, too. Jerome came with chardonnay in an ice bucket. Then he went away to fetch a second wine glass and Maisie and I went over the preliminaries, the stuff about spouses, children and dogs.

Was she still beautiful? Yes, in the preserved way of the rich. Attractive, too. The rebarbative manner that had once been a symptom of youthful distress had mellowed to wry cynicism with a note of self-mockery. Her face was sculpted over those magnificent bones and not marred by lines around the eyes. Her neck had thinned around the throat and was creased by circlets but it remained sinuous and expressive. Also, studying her, I thought she was happy after a nervous fashion: I mean the frail American happiness that has to be recreated each day by an act of will and faith in the future.

The wine woke a flush of old affection. She said, 'You haven't told me how glad you are to see me: how good I'm looking.'

'You look lovely. I mean it.'

'I wish I could say the same of you, Paddy my boy. But the truth is you're getting old and cheesy.'

'I take after my Uncle Gerald.'

'Your *uncle?*'

'There was always a doubt about the matter. My mother was a careless woman.'

'Oh, don't tell me about families. These days I'm in therapy.'

'Ben is in AA.'

'He always had a sociable nature. My man is a Freudian. He tells me terrible things about my sexual desire for my father. I don't believe a word of it but it doesn't matter as long as there's someone to talk to. They tell me that, in extremity, a Catholic can make confession to a horse. I can see the point.'

This remark took us on another canter over the past few years since we last met.

'So,' said Maisie, 'you stayed the course as a writer. Is it much of a business?'

'I get by.'

She leaned forward and examined me with genuine curiosity. 'Forgive me for saying it, Pat, but it sounds as if you've had a disappointed life.'

'I had the life you all made for me.' I wasn't sure what I meant by this. Writers often say things for the sake of the words, leaving the meaning to follow if it can. Maisie seemed to understand me.

We turned to a more comfortable subject: houses. Maisie dabbled in interior decorating. She offered me the tour. I declined. She asked if I'd stay for dinner. I made an excuse about flights and returning the hire car.

'So this is just business,' she said and added gaily. 'Ah well, you always were one for ferreting out the facts. When Ben called me, he said he didn't think you'd show here. I knew you would.'

'You and Ben are on good terms?'

'Of course. We've been friends ever since we divorced.'

'Then why divorce?'

She laughed. 'You mean you don't know? Oh my! How shall I put it? In sexual matters Ben was always a little "left-handed" – not that he'd admit it. I blame the year he and Tom spent together in Paris – I think it confused the hell out of him.'

'You mean Tom … ?'

'Tom? Good God, no. Not at all.' She put a hand to her mouth. I noted her teeth were a little dingy. There was an appalled girliness in her giggle as if I'd made a joke that was off-colour. She caught herself, quietened, and said, 'Naturally I can see how some people might get that idea. The thing is that Tom was never a man's idea of a man. I think he made them uncomfortable as if they could imagine themselves falling in love with him and they were terrified. In fact most men couldn't stand him though they wouldn't dare say anything because he was quite capable of knocking their heads off.'

'Why do you say that?'

'Good question, because on the face of it Tom was everything another man might look up to. He got the girls and could do the boxing and the sport and all the other manly stuff. When he told Ben he ought to take up hunting or mountain climbing, he wasn't being ironic; he'd done both. Now I think of it, I guess that was a part of what sickened other men – the ones who thought manliness was everything. He was just so damned good at it. Still, they could sense there was something wrong, something that didn't ring true.'

'Which was?'

'He loved women – which, of course, most men don't. He had crazy ideas about them but dear God how he loved them.'

'And women?'

'They *adored* him. There wasn't one who wouldn't have married him within a week of meeting him. How could they fail to love a man who cared so deeply and would forgive *anything?*'

Maisie took another sip of her chardonnay and fell silent, the energy gone out of her. But she'd said something that didn't fit with a remark she once made. I asked, 'If women loved Tom so much, why did you tell me he was the loneliest man in the world?'

She looked at me dully, 'Did I say that?'

I nodded.

'Then I suppose it must be true.'

'Why? How?'

She shrugged. 'There's only so much adoration women can take. After that we feel like a fraud. No woman can live up to Tom's ideal.' She stared at me and added absurdly, 'My psychiatrist blames his mother. I've often wondered. Whatever, the fact remains we can't stand the burden of perfection – it would destroy us. So what are we to do? There's only one way to defend ourselves. Tom loves us so intensely that, in the end, we find we don't love him at all. Poor Tom,' she sighed.

I asked for a cigarette. Maisie lit two. The sun had shifted and the shadow of a tree moved over the room. Maisie put on the appearance of calmness. She said, 'I'm going to break my routine and have another drink.' She reached for the bottle. 'I wish you hadn't come, Pat. I live with myself by not thinking of Tom. At least Katerina – Rachel, or whatever her name is – doesn't know the whole truth; what became of him and all. You didn't tell her, did you?'

'No.'

'Good. She's a sad bitch, but she didn't deserve what happened. Neither did Tom. I think Ben's man has lost track of him. What d'you suppose that means? I guess he's sleeping in boxcars, living off trash and drinking Sterno. You could weep, couldn't you?' she said with dry, angry eyes. 'The rotten bastard, just giving up like that!'

I leant to grip her hand on the bottle. She recoiled with shock.

'Who killed Alvírez?' I asked coldly. 'I want to know. That's what smashed things between Tom and Rachel and everyone has been lying about it.'

Maisie came back strong. 'What did she tell you?'

'That Tom thought she and Teresa had done it. And I don't doubt he did. But so what? What did you say about him? That he could forgive *anything*. I believe you. Even murder. It was Rachel who couldn't forgive herself, not after she and her mother had told so many lies. She couldn't bear that Tom should think she was a murderess. So she and Teresa left him.'

Rachel had been adamant about their innocence – at least so far as the killing was concerned. Neither she nor Teresa could explain what had actually happened and it was in desperation that they'd hidden the diamonds to prove the theory of an accomplice, a second burglar.

I waited and watched a dozen thoughts and emotions sweep across Maisie's face. She lit another cigarette. Her fingernails tapped across the case. 'I warn you, Pat. You should leave this alone.'

'Why, Maisie? *Why?* It isn't true that they killed Alvírez.'

'How do you know!' she shouted.

'Because Ben has been taking care of Rachel all these years. Why would he do that? He didn't even like her. You've said how it was with him and Tom. Rachel came between them. Damn it, Ben had every reason to hate her!'

'So? *So!*'

'So he's guilty of something. Both of you are. You know what really happened.'

She knew right enough. I could see it in her eyes. But for the moment she was spared by Jerome who heard the raised voices and came in only to be dismissed.

Maisie's defence was to humiliate me.

She said, 'You know, Pat, I was never sure I liked you. We used to tolerate you as the *ingénu*, the kid from the bogs who understood absolutely nothing. It was pitiful! Ben and I used to laugh; ask ourselves what your interest was. I've talked it over with Dr Goldstein and he says it's plain as day that you're a bit *that* way inclined yourself. All that hanging on Tom's every word, it makes sense, huh? Except that Goldstein doesn't know you, and psychiatrists spout a load of hokum. It's taken me a while to figure out, but I got there in the end and the fact you're here proves it.

'I read your books, by the way. Surprised? I notice how you always put yourself into the story. Always the observer. You seem proud of that, the detached all-seeing eye. Well, "sadist" would be a better word,' she added slowly. 'You don't give a damn about anyone – the pain and the misery don't affect you except that you want to see them, get the vicarious thrill, record them in writing like a pornographer so you can go over and over them in your mind. Hah! You don't believe me? *You*, the cold-hearted son of a bitch who put his fiancée into a book? Oh, Pat – ' she cried and her tears were genuine ' – you rotten lousy swine! If I were to tell you the truth, you'd deserve it, every agonising moment – because, believe me, this is a truth that won't go away! You'll have to live with it for the rest of your life!'

'Anything is better than the lie,' I said, but Maisie wasn't listening.

She stared at me and I saw the malice, the defiance, the pity of her. I saw the age in her face and the old suicide scar on her wrist. She was right. I do see things.

I could have pulled back, but truth is sometimes so vertiginous that it invites an irresistible leap. And I took this one.

'Who killed Alvírez?' I repeated.

Maisie hesitated. She picked up the bottle again with a steady hand. When she next spoke, her voice was devil-may-care and to hell with Patrick Byrne.

She said, 'Think about it. There was only one person it could be. The one person who had reason to go to La Pinède and didn't attend the boy's funeral because she claimed to be sick.'

In the end, I think Maisie was sorry for me.

She said, almost tenderly, 'Patrick – it was Hetty.'

'Hetty?'

'Yes … it was your wife.'

CHAPTER FORTY-THREE

    Her lips burn with chillies and she smokes a cigar.
        Her breath is my narcotic.
    Her scent is of cloves, of night fevers and spent seed.
        What man could resist the Argentinian Virgin?
    What woman could bear her horror?

This is an elegy to love and murder. Tom loved his Rachel and, in the end, she loved him. And, although their love was flawed and disastrous, I think it was fine. Love comes as it comes and always has done.

I loved Hetty. I knew it when, one day in nineteen forty-six, I wandered into a diner in Malibu where she was waitressing and she said with an open smile, 'Hullo there, Pat. Would you believe I was just thinking about you?'

Because we'd been friends, it didn't occur to us right away to become lovers. We walked out a while and talked of this and that: my movie career, which was fragile; hers, which was non-existent; and also about Pittsburgh and Ireland. The only thing we didn't talk of was our time in France.

'Oh, that's all in the past,' she'd say.

Gone With The Wind was still in the popular consciousness.

'Tomorrow is another day,' she'd say.

Three months after our first meeting we married and she returned with me to Ireland. We had two children and were happy. Now, more than fifty years later, she brings me coffee as I write and I catch her looking at me nervously.

She knows I'm a man who put his fiancée into a book.

As to murder, you probably think I have Alvírez in mind, but that isn't so. I got the whole story out of Maisie and Ben and, apparently, it was a case of self-defence.

Hetty was head over heels in love with Tom, but Tom was obsessed with Katerina and Hetty was too generous to complain. Who knows exactly what she had in mind on the day of the boy's funeral when she said she was sick and went alone to La Pinède, thinking the Malipieros would be there? To lay her heart before the other women and appeal to them? It must have been something like that.

Instead she found Alvírez, drunk, angry and brutal: ransacking the place for the diamond necklace. There was a struggle and she killed him with a blow from an oil lamp. I believe all of this, and in any case I don't care.

She confessed to Ben and Maisie within a day or two. Not to me because she didn't feel she knew me well enough and I might tell Tom.

Always Tom.

Yet why didn't she tell him? Tom who was capable of forgiving anything?

She didn't tell Tom because, in the simplicity of her adoration, she didn't want him to think badly of her. That was all.

Yet this remains a murder story.

We murdered Tom Rensselaer. We killed him as surely as if we'd put a bullet through his heart. We knew the truth that would have restored faith between him and Rachel, but, as we watched the disaster break about their heads and through the long years afterwards, we did nothing.

Why did we kill the man whom everyone loved?

Because he was the loneliest man in the world.

Because from his looks, his talents, his charm and his virtues we fashioned an idol greater than the man and prayed it would fill us with light. And, when the idol failed, when it was less than our infinite needs, when it wanted a life of its own, we smashed it out of jealousy, hatred and meanness.

Because all along it was Tom not Rachel who was the Argentinian Virgin: Tom not Rachel whom we turned into the monster of our fantasies and longing: Tom, who could never love us enough and whom, in the end, we loved too much and not at all.

You may think Tom brought it on himself. That he gave up and made fatal a wound that might have been mended. Certainly Ben and Maisie thought so. It was their consolation. Tom should have recovered – damn it, he *owed* it to everyone to recover. He might have been a scarred, limping thing but – what the hell – aren't we all? In Ben's eyes Tom was damned not by our deceits but because he betrayed the American Dream: it was as plain as anything: the man took a knock and just lay down and died.

So far as that goes, Ben's right. I don't say Tom was perfect. Somewhere on his travels, or maybe it was a taint of his gracious family, he'd acquired a European sensibility, a glimmer of a morality too subtle for a crude world. Still, I don't accept that his surrender was that of a defeated spirit. It was a renunciation of evil, a defiance of the wrong done to him, a flight from the possibility of saving himself by doing wrong to others.

Or maybe he was just a poor, sad devil with a worm of despair in his heart: the last of a worn out class and generation: the rearguard of a beaten army. Who can ever know?

I offer a clue, if not to the truth, at least to the way Tom saw it. We were talking about the death of the boy. He just wouldn't let it go.

He said, 'I think that, at the core of every person's happiness, there's a cruel injustice done to others. I don't say it's done out of malice. In fact it may be something our grandfathers did, like slavery or building empires. But we perpetuate and grow fat on it out of thoughtlessness – a horrible acceptance of the way things work. Don't mistake me. There's no remedy for this injustice, no changing it any more than we can change gravity: because it's rooted in the fabric of the universe, in the pitilessness of matter and blind physical laws. We can defy it, that's all. We can live our lives so that the fate to which we're condemned is an unjust one. But – understand this, Pat – there'll be no reward for living rightly. No praise, no prizes, no gift of immortality. The universe is ignorant even of our existence. And only we shall know that we've raised our small fist against it and – if we're lucky – found love in a creation so indifferent it doesn't care even to hate us.'

I don't say this is profound. It isn't even original except in what Tom made of it. If it's true at all, it strikes me as one of those truths that are terrible yet useless to know. Because how could you know it thoroughly and not be destroyed by despair?

My own opinion is that the best route to happiness is to be born that way. I don't know any other method half so good.

Home from the States in sixty-eight I went through the door. Hetty turned from her baking with flour on her hands and gave me a look of fear in which I also read a belief drawn from my own paltry experience: a belief in the redemptive power of the love each of us had for the other.

She asked, 'How did it go, *querido?*'

I said, 'It was a waste of time. I saw Ben and Maisie but they didn't know anything. I'm going to let the subject drop.'

I pretended not to notice Hetty's expression: the hope, the tenderness, the goodness. I took her in my arms and kissed her closed eyelids.

I didn't see any guilt and I was glad.

I asked for my dinner.

As for happiness, I've stared into its bleak, deceitful heart and gone on with a happy life though I built it on the bones of Tom Rensselaer, and on the legacy of slaves and empires no doubt. It's the American Way. The Irish Way, too, now I think of it. Finally it's been enough for me that I found love in the mundane glory of a woman – the very thing Tom believed in – and I'm thankful.

For Tom and Rachel it was different, and perhaps they had the best of it: a love that was ardent and fearsome beyond any lasting. I think of it condensed to the compass of a few hours and of two people in an apartment in New York. Rachel confesses her history and Tom forgives her, and, at that moment before the terrible discovery of the diamonds, everything between them is clarified. Rachel sees through Tom's glamour to the heart of a generous, humble man. And Tom, free of any obsession, at last sees Rachel in her authentic magic.

Outside, along Park Avenue, the lights go on. A Tommy Dorsey concert is broadcast on the radio and the thoughts of those who hear it turn to dancing. Everywhere in the city the music blows through open windows into a soft autumn evening. I hear it, and, though the melody is faint, it's the same to which Hetty and I dance with hesitant steps.